REUNION IN PALM BEACH
AND OTHER FLORIDA STORIES
BY EDWARD BRUCE BEW

PRINTED IN THE UNITED STATES OF AMERICA

by

Instant Publishers
P.O. Box 985
Collierville, TN 38027

Special thanks to the members of the

MORNINGSIDE WRITERS GROUP
(Sunny Serafino, Coordinator)

and the

FT. PIERCE WRITERS GROUP
(Florence Prusmack, Coordinator)

Your insightful critique was invaluable in the
writing of the stories in this book.

TABLE OF CONTENTS

Reunion
in
Palm
Beach

PROLOGUE

"Free at last! Free at last!" With an exaggerated flourish of her arms, Cindy tossed her cap and gown on her bed, "Four years of pure, unadulterated torture ended."

Darlene smiled. "Oh, it wasn't all that bad, Cin. We did have each other's shoulders to cry on when things got rough."

Fran and Karen came through the door as she spoke. "Yeah," Fran sighed dreamily, "and we did have Byron North."

"Really, Fran," Darlene snorted, "don't you ever think of anything but sex?"

"Listen to Miss Goody-Two-Shoes! Darlene, you spent more time with Byron than any of us, except Cindy."

"Cut it out you two," Cindy broke in, "the four of us have had a wonderful friendship during these college years and I, for one, am sorry we'll be parting. But let's face it. After today we'll be scattering in all directions."

"I'm off to New York!" Karen's voice bubbled with enthusiasm. "One of the corporate recruiters who came here last month must have liked me 'cuz I received a job offer in today's mail. I'll be working for an insurance company. How about you, Cindy? Is that job you lined up in Palm Beach when you were home on spring break still on?"

"Sure is. By this time next week I'll be a business-suit-wearing, briefcase-toting nine-to-fiver with an investment brokerage office."

"Phooey on jobs," Fran brushed her long raven hair back over her shoulders, "I'm going anywhere some rich guy will take me."

"Oh, come on, Fran," Cindy rolled her eyes, "grow up. Being the campus butterfly is one thing, but this is the real world we're going into. You'd better get used to it fast. Darlene is facing reality. She's going home to Wisconsin to run the family farm."

Darlene looked down. "Well, I know that's all I've talked about recently, but there's been a change in my plans. I'll be taking any kind of job I can get while my husband goes to law school." She threw her arms around Cindy. "I hope this won't upset you too much, since you and Byron were so close, but he and I are getting married."

"Upset? No way! Byron and I are just good friends now and I'm really happy for both of you."

"Isn't anyone going to console me?" Fran pouted, "Byron and I had a fling too, you know."

"You had a fling with every guy in the school," Karen sniffed. "Now tell Darlene you're happy for her."

"Oh, all right, I'm happy for you."

Darlene hugged Karen warmly. "Thanks for the support. I know you and Byron were close for a while."

Karen's face suddenly became grave. "Byron and I have always been just good friends. No romantic involvement." She paused.

"Someday I may tell you what a good friend he really is." Just as quickly she brightened. "Hey, let's not get morbid. Let's promise that wherever we go from here we'll always keep in touch."

"That won't be hard for you and me," Darlene turned to Cindy, "Byron is going to the University of Miami Law School, so you and I won't be far apart."

"I've a great idea," Karen blurted out. "Let's make a solemn pact that no matter where we are ten years from now we'll hold a reunion. How about it?"

"We'll get together often, Karen," Cindy smiled. "We don't have to wait ten years."

"But if we do drift apart," Karen persisted, "let's make a vow that ten years from now we'll all get together."

"Oh, all right, if it'll make you happy, I'm in," Fran shrugged. "Now let's go get a pizza. I'm starved."

CHAPTER ONE

Could ten years really have passed so quickly? Cindy thought as she dressed for one of the lavish parties Colin Jamison frequently threw for their friends and his business associates. But it was true. She and Colin had been married for five years, and she had served as his secretary for five years before that – the only job she ever held. The reunion agreement so spontaneously agreed to on college graduation day was almost forgotten until the arrival of Karen Knowles brief note.

Dear Cindy,

I'll be in Palm Beach soon and hope we can get together and talk about old times. Do you remember our 'reunion pact'? Ten years have passed, you know. We did somehow drift apart.

Love,

Karen

Same enigmatic Karen, Cindy thought. She attended my wedding but left immediately after the ceremony. Since then only a formal greeting card at Christmas.

There would be 150 to 200 guests here tonight, many of whom Cindy did not know. But that was part of being married to a wealthy older man. When Colin, twenty-five years her senior, proposed he was quite blunt.

"Cindy, I've worked hard as hell all my life. Maybe I spent too much time at work, but despite that Marion and I had a good marriage. Since she died, I've been a lonely man. I've made money – lots of money. I want you to share it with me. I can't promise you a fairytale romance, but I can promise I'll be good to you, I'll be generous to you, I'll be faithful to you. And when I die you'll be a very rich young woman."

Sex had never been important in Cindy's life. Even that first year in college when she and Byron North lived together she often wondered if there were something wrong with her. She could not blame Byron. In the awkward manner of his inexperienced youth he did try to please her. But something vague, some elusive thing her innermost feelings refused to identify, was missing.

During her years as Colin's private secretary she had come to know his temperament well. He could be gentle and compassionate in personal relationships but often ruthless where business was concerned. But what endured her most to him was his tender devotion to his first wife during the agonizing years of her terminal illness. Six months

7

after his wife's passing Colin proposed. Cindy accepted.

Life with an older man, especially a wealthy older man, she found to be quite pleasant. Tall and straight, with a trim muscular frame, Colin dominated the scene wherever he went. Straw-colored hair, with just enough gray at the temples to give a touch of distinction to his sculpture face, belied his age. His eyes, steel blue and piercing when he was angry, changed to reflections of a summer sky when his keen sense of humor surfaced, which it often did.

To her surprise, Cindy discovered she really enjoyed their intimate moments together. True, there were no clanging bells, or bombs bursting in air. Their lovemaking was more like the warmth of embers glowing on an open hearth, occasionally erupting in a cascade of sparks.

Cindy finished dressing and made a final inspection of herself in a full-length mirror. Not bad for a thirty-two-year-old, she thought with a smug mental smile. The image in the mirror revealed a slim athletic figure, a smooth complexion, and hair like golden silk. Being able to afford the best health clubs, the most talented hairdressers, and the finest cosmetics made a definite difference, she admitted to herself.

In regal splendor, Cindy descended the wide spiral staircase and joined Colin in greeting early-arriving guests. She acknowledged with broad smiles introductions to those she did not know, and warmly hugged old friends, serenely playing the part of the perfect hostess.

As the evening grew long, wearied of the endless talk of business and finance, she slipped away from the guests and stepped out onto a patio overlooking the ocean. The night was typically Floridian. A full moon sent a pale river of light across the water, and the delicate fragrance of jasmine filled the air. Only the splash of wavelets breaking against the shore, the soft rustle of palm fronds, and the faint murmur of voices from inside broke the enchanting stillness. She stood with hands on a railing, closed her eyes, and let the evening breeze caress her face and gently ripple her hair. She was unaware anyone had joined her until she heard a sensuous voice behind her whisper "Marry me and let me take you away from all this."

She spun around. Standing there, an impish grin on his face, was the handsome stranger she had observed arriving late. When their gaze met for a brief instant across the crowded room, she had the eerie feeling she had met him somewhere before. He had started toward her, but one of the guests grabbed his arm and led him into the game room where a high-stakes pool match was in progress.

"You startled me," she gasped. "I didn't hear you come out."

He smiled. "Startling you is the last thing I would want to do, Cindy Sebrell."

Cindy's heart raced. *Cindy Sebrell, my maiden name. This blond Adonis and I have met somewhere in the past. Where? When?*

"If you say you don't remember me, Cindy, my male ego will be irreparably shattered. I'm Dexter Matthews. We went to high school together."

9

"Dexter Matthews! Well, I'll be dammed. I saw you come in and thought you looked familiar, but I couldn't place you. You really have changed."

"Well, you haven't changed, Cindy. You're the same gorgeous dream I remember from high school. Come on, let's ditch whoever you came with and go some place we can make up for lost time."

How impertinent of him to think I might not be married, and how impudent to think I would leave the party with him.

She gave a merry laugh. "You don't really know who I am do you? I mean–now?

The patio door opened and Colin Jamison came out. "Oh, there you are, Matthews. Glad you could make it. I see you have met my wife."

CHAPTER TWO

In the weeks following the encounter on the patio, Cindy saw no more of the brash semi-stranger, but to her dismay she found the memory of his nearness arousing dormant shivers of ecstasy deep within her. Just normal, healthy fantasies, she told herself with a mental shrug. Though it was just late summer, and the Palm Beach "high season" not yet started, a constant whirl of parties, teas and charity events, as the lesser lights on the social scale tried to get in their licks before the top echelon of the Palm Beach hierarchy arrived for the winter, occupied her time. If Dexter Matthews was still in town, she thought, he certainly is keeping a low profile. Now that he knows I'm not available he's probably set his sights on more promising game.

Home from an afternoon lawn tea, wilted from the heat and the tension of trying to appear delighted to be there while fervently wishing to be anywhere else, Cindy slipped out of her limp skirt and blouse and into a filmy robe that clung to her shapely body. How good that cool shower will feel, she told herself. Noticing the red light on the answering machine on her private telephone line blinking a demand that she listen to a message, she touched the "answer" button. Darlene North's voice came through the speaker.

"Hi, Cindy. I've been pressured into serving as a hostess at a charity polo match Saturday. How about going with me? Call me back. Bye."

Cindy picked up the telephone and started to tap Darlene's button on the automatic dialer, but stopped. Later, she decided. Right now I need that sanity-saving shower.

Refreshed, Cindy stepped from the shower, patted herself dry, stretched out on a chaise lounge and called Darlene. "Hi, kiddo, I got your message, but it's too dammed hot to even think of going to a polo match. Right now I'm reclining on my lounge, naked as the proverbial jaybird, and the very thought of going out in the sun is intolerable."

"Oh, come on," Darlene giggled, "it can't be that bad. It might even be fun. Hey, you might get to meet the Prince of Wales. He'll be playing for the visiting team."

"Fun? Watching a bunch of sweaty men on sweaty horses chase a little ball around a field is not my idea of fun. Misery loves company and you just want someone to share your misery. Count me

12

out."

"Aw, be a sport," Darlene pleaded. "I can't get out of this and I don't want to go alone. Please, please, pretty please."

"Oh, all right," Cindy surrendered, "but you'll owe me."

The sun, a brassy ball hanging in a cloudless sky, scorched everything beneath it as Cindy and Darlene arrived at the polo grounds. "You'll pay for this, Darlene," Cindy grumbled. "I'm going to rope you in on the most boring, most unenjoyable, most nauseating social event I'm obliged to attend."

Darlene chuckled. "Don't be such a grouch, Cin. You might even have a good time."

They pulled into a parking lot reserved for event-staff members and got out of the car. Darlene walked over to the V.I.P. pavilion and returned with two armbands. "Here, put this on." She wrapped one around her own arm and pressed smooth the Velcro fastener. "You're one of us now."

The two mingled with spectators along the sidelines. Cindy, uncomfortable in the hostess role thrust upon her, let Darlene answer any questions asked. Suddenly a horde of player-mounted horses thundered past, and in a moment the voice of an announcer boomed from a loudspeaker "The point is scored by Dexter Matthews of the Palm Beach team."

Cindy looked up quickly, a hand involuntarily going to her face. At that moment Dexter spotted her. He cantered slowly over, smiled down and raised his mallet in salute. Then he turned and galloped back to join his teammates.

Darlene grabbed Cindy's arm excitedly. "Hey, friend, you've been holding out on me. Who's the gorgeous hunk?"

Cindy shrugged, trying to hide the wild beating of her heart. "Oh, I told you about him. He's the guy who came on to me at the party you and Byron missed while you were in Bermuda. We went to high school at the same time but I don't remember him very well. He was a senior when I was a sophomore."

"Well, you certainly made an impression on him. And speaking of impressions, he could make any kind of impression he wants to on me."

"Don't give me that bullshit! I know you too well. You wouldn't cheat on Byron."

"I probably wouldn't have a chance with him, anyway," Darlene sighed. "It's evident he prefers stately, blue-eyed blondes like you. Petite, green-eyed redheads like me could throw themselves at his feet and he would just shrug and walk away."

Cindy gave her a playful shove. "Don't be so melodramatic. If you ask me, Dexter Matthews will make a play for anything that wears pantyhose."

Summer passed and Cindy did not see Dexter again, but infuriating thoughts of him kept creeping into her mind. On the eve of a planned skiing vacation in Vail, Colin entered her room. "Darling, I won't be able to leave with you in the morning. I have an important business deal working and one of the principals won't be able to meet with me until late in the day. You go ahead

14

with Byron and Darlene. I'll take a red-eye flight tomorrow and join you the next morning."

"Must you work so hard, Colin?" A hint of irritation tinged Cindy's voice. "We really don't need the money."

He put his arm around her. "You must understand, darling, with me business is a game. I get the same rush from winning that another man might get from a sports victory or ..." a mischievous smile lit his face "...from successfully seducing an unobtainable woman." He released her shoulders and let both hands slide down to take hers into his. "It will be for only one day. I promise that after this new project is launched I will take it easier and spend more time with you."

The first afternoon on the slopes proved exhilarating but tiring. After a quiet dinner with Darlene and Byron, Cindy pleaded fatigue and went to her room. Showered and rejuvenated, she slipped into a fluffy robe and reclined before the fireplace. She looked up sharply when a knock sounded on the door. "Who is it?"

"Room Service. Management sent up a complimentary basket of fruit."

Clutching her robe close with one hand, and with the chain lock in place, Cindy cautiously opened the door a crack. Standing there, a devilish grin on his face, stood Dexter Matthews.

"What on earth are you doing here," she demanded.

"Following you." His manner was disarmingly flip. "Aren't you going to invite me in?"

"I most certainly am not."

15

"Well, you can at least have a drink in the lounge with a weary traveler who has come so far to see you." His eyes danced in mockery.

Cindy glanced at the clock on the wall. It was not yet nine o'clock "Oh, all right. One drink, that's all. Wait there while I get some clothes on." Her heart raced as she pulled on the pants and parka worn on the slopes. Catching a glimpse of herself in a mirror as she headed for the door she let out a silent oath. *Damn, I look like a frump!* Hurriedly she stripped off the offending duds. Her eye caught sight of the new snow bunny outfit purchased that day at the lodge's sportswear boutique. Well, Mister Matthews, she thought smugly, you're not going to get what you came for – but eat your heart out.

She joined Dexter in the hallway. This is outrageous, she thought. How dare this arrogant bastard follow me out here. But she felt her body tremble with excitement as he gently took her elbow and led her to the elevator. *What is that fragrance he's wearing? Polo! That's it. Ralph Lauren's Polo. Colin sometimes wore it.* With a twinge of conscience she wondered if Colin would approve of what she was doing.

"You are devastatingly lovely tonight," Dexter smiled.

"Oh, I bet you say that to all the girls." *What a lame thing to say. But I'm not thinking very rationally tonight. I shouldn't be going to the cocktail lounge with him anyway.*

Dexter selected a secluded booth in a corner of the dimly lit room and guided Cindy to it. A waitress materialized, took their order and glided away.

16

"Well, Dexter," Cindy broke the awkward silence. "What have you been doing since high school?"

"Nothing as spectacular as winning a Nobel prize." He flashed a disarming smile. "I went to Florida State and got a degree in finance. Took ROTC training there and spent two years in the army as a finance officer. But enough about me. Let's talk about you. How did you end up married to an old man?"

"Colin's not old!" Cindy snapped. "He's a charming, virile, mature man. But I don't have to defend him to you. He could teach you a few things about being a gentleman. He would never try to put the make on another man's wife."

"Touche, my dear! Touche." Dexter exploded in laughter. "I retreat. I retreat."

Their drinks arrived and the conversation turned to safer subjects. They recalled half-forgotten events from high school days, then progressed to anecdotes of college life. Cindy carefully refrained from any mention of her year as Byron North's roommate. She sipped her drink slowly, but Dexter downed his quickly and ordered another. The minutes flitted past.

Cindy glanced at her watch. "My God, Dexter, it's almost eleven. Colin will be here tomorrow and I want to be rested for a day of skiing."

"Does the old man ski?" Dexter again ventured into dangerous waters.

Cindy stood up abruptly and gave him a scathing glare. "The 'old man' can do everything a normal, healthy, masculine stud can do, and then some. I'm going back to my room."

"Hey, I'm sorry," Dexter attempted to apologize. "It must have been that second drink." He threw some money on the table and followed her out.

They remained silent as they rode the elevator up. Dexter's last caustic remark had effectively erased any romantic mood Cindy might have felt during the evening. Behind his charming facade, this man really is a jerk, she thought furiously.

She opened the door to her room and stepped inside. Dexter started to follow but she stopped him with a firm palm to his chest. "Let's get this straight, Dexter Matthews, I'm a happily married woman and I have no intention of having an affair with you. That one drink in the lounge is the only thing you and I will ever share."

He gave her a smug smile and gently kissed her on the cheek. "We'll see." He turned and walked away.

Byron went to the slopes early, and Darlene and Cindy were just meeting for breakfast when Colin entered the dining room. He glanced around, spotted them and came over to plant a light kiss on Cindy's forehead. They found a table and sat down.

"Staying behind was a complete waste of time, darling. Dexter Matthews – you remember him, the young man you met at one of our parties – was scheduled to join Adrian Pahlavi and me to wrap up final details of a project we're working on. He called at the last minute to say he had to leave town to take care of a family emergency."

Darlene gave Cindy a sharp look but said

nothing. Later she cornered Cindy in the ladies' room. "Hey, good buddy, what's going on between you and Dexter Matthews? I saw the two of you together in the lounge last night and I saw him go back to your room with you."

Cindy's face darkened in anger. "That egotistical bastard tricked Colin into staying in Palm Beach and followed me out here. There's nothing going on between us and there never will be. If you had taken the trouble of following us up you would have seen that I did not let him into my room."

Darlene winced. "Sorry. I only know what I saw. Are you going to tell Colin?"

Cindy thought for a long moment. "No, not right now. The business deal between them might be important to Colin. I never stick my nose into his business affairs. I can take care of Dexter Matthews. I'm sure he's left Vail by now. He wouldn't risk having Colin see him here after the trick he pulled."

During the remainder of their stay, Dexter was nowhere to be seen. Probably afraid he'd get that smug smile punched right off his face, Cindy thought.

CHAPTER THREE

Colin did not feel well during their stay in Colorado. He tired easily and had little appetite for food or anything else. Cindy expressed her concern.

"It's nothing for you to worry about,

darling," he assured her, "I must have picked up some kind of a bug." But his listlessness did worry Cindy and she insisted they return home early.

In the salubrious climate of early winter in Florida Colin appeared to become his normal self, quickly plunging back into his rigid working schedule and leaving Cindy to face her own sometimes boring social routine. So it was with a scream of delight she responded to a voice on the telephone a few days after the return from Vail. "Karen Knowles! How wonderful to hear from you. Where are you?"

"Hi, Cindy. I just checked into the Dolphin Motel on A1A. I'll be in town for a few days and hope we can get together. I know Darlene and Fran live near you. Maybe we could finally hold that reunion we agreed to on graduation day."

"Well, check right out. You're staying with me. I know where the Dolphin is. I'm only a ten-minute drive from there. I'm on my way."

When Cindy pulled up in front of the motel in her Mercedes convertible she found Karen waiting outside.

"Wow, what a wagon," Karen exclaimed as she rushed to wrap her arms around Cindy. "I thought my LeBaron ragtop was pretty snazzy stuff. You must be doing pretty well for yourself."

"Well, we are quite secure financially," Cindy replied modestly, "and Colin is very generous to me. You'll like him when you get to know him. Oh, Karen, it's so good to see you. Do you realize that except for my wedding you, I, Darlene and Fran have not gotten together since

21

college?" She sighed. "That seems like so long, long ago. Follow me in your car and I'll lead the way to my place."

As the wrought-iron security gates swung open to the touch of a remote control button, and the cars slowly rolled up the winding drive to the main house, Karen's mouth dropped open and her eyes opened wide in amazement. "A mansion on the ocean in Palm Beach! Wow, kid, you really struck it rich," she called as they came to a stop. She got out and walked over to Cindy. "It must take an army of servants to keep this place up."

Cindy smiled, enjoying her friend's enthusiasm. "We're not exactly in Palm Beach. Only the suburbs. This is the town of Stardust Shores. We really don't need many servants. We have a housekeeper, Hilda Cayce, who also does the cooking. She's very formal but really a dear person. I always call her 'Missus Cayce' and she calls me 'Missus Jamison'. She and our other staff members, Ben and Dicey Brown, were with Colin before he and I married. Dicey takes care of the inside of the house while Ben is the gardener and all-round handyman. They live in the gatehouse we passed just inside the gates. Their teen-age son, Raymond, lives with them.

"When we entertain we have caterers handle everything. Normally, Colin and I live alone, but recently his 'baby sister' Myrna moved in after divorcing her third husband. She's much younger than Colin, actually close to my age. You may find her to be a little outrageous in her speech and manners, but we grin and bear her." She paused to catch her breath. "Here I am rattling on and you must be exhausted from driving. Come on inside. You'll meet them all."

A beaming Dicey Brown met them at the door. "Miz Karen, it sure good to meet you. Miz Cindy always talking 'bout how you and Miz Darlene and Miz Fran was such good friends in college. I got the best guest room in the house ready for you." She picked up a suitcase Karen had removed from her car. "Don't bother 'bout them other bags. Raymond will fetch them. You come right up and get out of them Yankee clothes and put on somethin' fittin'."

"Better do as she says, Karen," Cindy chuckled. "Dicey will try to run your life while you're here, but you really can't go wrong following her advice." She followed Karen and Dicey up the stairs. "Put on some shorts, Karen. I'll change and we can take a stroll on the beach before dinner. Colin will be home in about an hour and then we can eat."

Barefoot, the two walked along the beach, kicking at tiny seashells in the surf and letting gentle swells wash over their feet.

"This is the life," Karen sighed. "No snow and sleet. No honking taxi horns. No pressing crush of humanity. You must be the luckiest person in the world to have what you have."

Cindy nodded. "I'm very content with my life. Colin and I have a good marriage, and as you can see I don't want for any creature comforts. What about you? Are you down for a vacation or do you have other plans in mind?"

Karen stopped and gazed seaward for a long moment. "Cindy, I'm sick of fighting New

York winters and I'm sick of fighting New York. If I can get a decent job here I want to start a new life in Florida."

"Great!" Cindy gave her a warm hug. "You're going to stay with us while you look over the job market. Colin has a lot of influence in financial circles and I'm sure he can get you some good introductions." She paused. "Come on, I'll race you back."

Dicey had a message for Cindy when the two girls entered the house. "Mistuh Colin called. He say he will be a little late and for you to start dinner without him."

Cindy frowned. "That husband of mine works entirely too hard, Karen. But I guess being a workaholic is not the worst vice in the world."

Myrna Jamison Bell was already seated at the table when Cindy and Karen came down for dinner. "Just because my brother chooses to be late so often doesn't mean I have to starve," she pouted. "I swear, Cindy, I don't know what's gotten into him. Maybe he's keeping another woman in town." She looked at Karen. "I suppose you're Karen. Dicey told me you're here. We don't stand on formality in this house so grab a seat and let's eat."

Cindy's eyes flashed. "You don't think any man can be faithful to his wife, do you Myrna?"

"Hell no. They're all a bunch of bastards." She glanced at Karen. "You married?"

Karen shook her head. "I never met the right person."

"You mean 'Mister Right'? Hell, I've been looking for that guy all my life." She speared a piece of steak with her fork, guided it toward her mouth and met it halfway. "All I've found are Mister Wrongs. Three times I married Mister Wrongs, and the Lord knows how many I tried out."

She wolfed down her dinner and wiped her lips on a napkin. "I gotta run. Got a date with Mister Maybe tonight. Don't wait up for me, Cindy. I might not come home at all."

"Well," Karen observed after Myrna left, "there's nothing wrong with her appetite. Her date will probably take her somewhere to eat, and she's already put away a longshoreman's meal."

Cindy laughed. "She has a voracious appetite, and not just for food."

"How does she keep such a trim figure? That stunning gown she's wearing would split at the seams if I tried to get into it."

Cindy shrugged. "Could be genetic. Colin hasn't gained a pound in all the years I've known him."

Colin came home looking tired and drawn. "Sorry to be late again, darling. One of those unavoidable situations." He crossed over to Karen and pressed her right hand between his two. "So glad you came to visit, Karen. Cindy has looked forward to it since your note arrived."

The evening passed in convivial small talk, but about ten o'clock Colin begged off. "I'm going to my room, Cindy. I have to be at the office early tomorrow. I know you two have a lot of talking to do." He kissed Cindy goodnight and left.

After he departed Karen gave Cindy a quizzical look. "Don't you two share the same bed?"

Cindy smiled and shook her head. "No. We have always had our own rooms." She gave a sly wink. "We do commute a lot."

Karen yawned. "It's been a long day for me, too. I'm ready to turn in. How about you?"

"Suits me. Have pleasant dreams. See you in the morning."

As Cindy was getting into bed a light tap sounded on the door. "Cindy, may I come in?" She opened the door. Karen stood there. Cindy motioned her in.

"Cindy, I just want you to know how much it means to me to be here with you." She hesitated. "Back in college I was very much in love with you."

Startled, Cindy laughed nervously. "And I was fond of you, too. You, me, Darlene and Fran-- we were the fearless foursome. Practically inseparable."

"You don't understand, do you, Cindy? I mean I was really in love with you."

Cindy's eyes widened. "You mean...?"

"Yes, I was gay then and I still am."

Cindy shook her head in disbelief. "But I thought you and Byron North had something going during our junior year."

Karen smiled sadly. "Dear sweet Byron. Do you remember on graduation day you, Fran and Darlene were discussing him and I said you really didn't know him? Well, you didn't know the compassionate side of him. Lesbianism was not

26

exactly an accepted lifestyle then, especially at our ultra-conservative old Alma Mata. Byron knew, of course, but he honored his word he would tell no one. I felt it important to be seen around campus with a man. Byron covered for me."

"Oh, you poor thing," Cindy comforted her. "I never realized. He never told me. Not that it makes any difference."

"It still makes a difference to some people. I just lost the best job I ever had because of my sexual orientation. It was with a big insurance company. Oh, they didn't come right out and fire me. That would have been discrimination. But after I took part in a gay rights parade the bigwigs called me in and said it was bad for the company's image. They suggested I resign. They offered me a big severance bonus and a glowing letter of recommendation. I took the money and ran."

"Well, you'll stay right here until you decide where you want to stop running."

CHAPTER FOUR

On the day following Karen's arrival, she and Cindy met Darlene and Fran for lunch at a fashionable waterfront restaurant. Darlene rushed to greet Karen with a broad smile and a hug. "You're really looking great, kid. Life must be treating you right in New York."

Karen grimaced. "If I look good it's in spite of New York. Life in New York is the pits."

Fran, already seated and sipping on a martini, gave a flip wave of her hand. "Hey, life can be hell no matter where you live when you're getting on in years."

"Don't mind Fran," Cindy grinned as they sat down. "She just had a birthday and she's down on the world."

"Oh, come on, Fran," Karen chided. "We're all about the same age and I don't feel like I'm over the hill. Thirty-something is not the end of life."

A waiter arrived to take their orders, bringing a pause to the conversation. They made selections from the menu, and Cindy, Darlene and Karen ordered white wine. Fran tossed down the remainder of her drink and signaled for a refill. She turned to Karen.

"You're the real stranger here, Karen. Where the hell you been keeping yourself since college? Been making a lot of men happy since Byron North dumped you and married Darlene?"

Cindy broke in quickly. "Come on, let's not bring up old romances."

Fran would not be hushed. "Hey, we're big

girls now. We can get a few giggles from our little college escapades." She smirked at Darlene. "How's it feel to be sitting at the same table with three gals who went to bed with your husband?"

A tight smile froze on Darlene's face. "It makes me feel pretty dammed good about myself, Fran. After all, I'm the one he chose to marry so I must have something the rest of you don't."

The waiter returned with their drinks. Fran quickly picked hers up and took a big swallow. Karen sat quietly, her face an impassive mask. Suddenly she blurted out. "I never went to bed with Byron. I never went to bed with any man. You might as well know now because you'll find out eventually. I'm gay."

Darlene's mouth dropped open.

"Didn't Byron tell you?" Karen asked. "He knew."

Darlene shook her head. "Byron has a very strict code of ethics. He probably felt that if you wanted me to know you would have told me. Besides, when we married we agreed that the past is the past and neither of us would ever bring up past involvements."

Fran took Karen's revelation in stride. She tossed down the remainder of the drink and slammed the empty glass down with a table-rattling bang. "Who am I to criticize your lifestyle? Hell, don't knock anything you haven't tried, I always say. But believe me, kid, hit the sack with a good man and you'll forget all about women."

When the waiter brought their lunches Fran reached out and gave him a playful slap on his rump. "Nice buns!" Embarrassed, he hurried away.

Cindy quickly tried to change the subject. "Fran, tell Karen about that intriguing Persian you married. Is he really the mysterious international mover and shaker people say he is?"

Fran's face hardened and her lip curled. "Adrian Pahlavi is not Persian and he's not mysterious. He's Iranian and he's evil." Her voce slurred. "R-e-a-l-ly evil. The things I could tell you would make your hair stand up." She picked up Cindy's half-finished wine and gulped it down. "But you won't get anything out of me." She leered at the group. "I want to live to be a snotty old bitch." She spotted the waiter across the patio. "Hey, Buns, 'nother martini."

"Cancel that," Cindy ordered. "Fran, you've had enough."

Relative silence prevailed as they ate their lunches. Fran's inebriation and Karen's disclosure had put a pall on the meeting. Finally Darlene stood up. "Sorry to be a party-pooper but I promised to pick up some papers for Byron from the courthouse."

"You don't have to rush off," Cindy demurred. "The courthouse won't close for a couple of hours."

"I don't know how long it will take for the clerk to find what I want." Darlene gave Karen a quick hug. "Really nice seeing you, Karen. We'll have to get together again soon." She glowered at Fran. "If you want to live to a ripe old age you had better lay off the booze." She gave Cindy a light touch on a shoulder. "I'll call you later, Cin." She hurried away.

Fran stared hard at Darlene's retreating back for a long moment, then shook her head abruptly as if to clear it. "I've got to split, too. I didn't mean to offend you by anything I said, Karen. Cindy will tell you that I don't think too good when I've had a few drinks." She flashed Cindy an apologetic smile. "Adrian is picking me up so you don't have to worry about me getting home safely."

Karen was thoughtfully silent as she and Cindy got in the car and started for home. When she did speak a touch of sadness tinged her voice. "Fran sure has changed, hasn't she? She was wild and promiscuous in college but always so carefree and full of fun. I don't ever remember seeing her looped."
"Yes, she has changed, and I worry about her a lot. She has her good days and she has her bad days. Today was definitely one of her bad ones. The next time you see her she might be all sugar and spice and won't remember anything she said today."
"What about her husband? She seems to be deathly afraid of him."
"Well, Adrian Pahlavi claims to be a member of the former royal family of Iran. At the time of the shah's overthrow Adrian was studying at Florida State University. He received political asylum and later became an American citizen. Regardless of his family heritage he appears to have strong ties to the present power brokers in Teheran. His name constantly pops up in reports of grey-area international financial dealings and of such things as arms sales to Third World countries and to suspected terrorist groups. Somehow he manages to stay just within the law."
"Is he really the personification of evil Fran

intimates or are they just having domestic problems?"

Cindy's brow furrowed. "I don't know for sure. Adrian has impeccable manners, and when you first meet him you might actually feel a like for him. However, if you study his eyes you get a very uneasy feeling. He's far too oily for my tastes. But let's get home and take a swim in the ocean and put obnoxious people out of our minds."

When they entered the house, Hilda Cayce greeted them. "Mister Jamison called. He's bringing Mister Simmons for dinner. I'm fixing my special pot roast Mister Simmons likes so much."

"Peter Simmons is Colin's secretary and right-hand man, " Cindy explained to Karen. "He took my job after Colin and I married. He's a nice young man but rather shy. Colin frequently brings him home when they have some important unfinished business to take care of, and they'll work in the library for hours."

The two friends quickly changed into bathing suits and raced to the beach.

"Oh, is this ever refreshing," Karen exclaimed, plunging into the surf, "and there's actually room to run and play on the beach. At Coney Island or Jones Beach you would be lucky to find a place to lay out a blanket. And you have this private beach all to yourself."

Cindy smiled. "We don't own the beach below the high water mark. The public is free to use it. But for a half-mile or so in both directions the only access is through private property so we rarely see anyone on the beach except our neighbors."

Later as they stretched out on beach towels
Karen slipped into a pensive mood. "Cindy, I've
been thinking about what Fran said – you know,
about going to bed with a man. I don't think I
could handle it."

"Don't let anything Fran said get to you.
And don't feel you have to do anything you're not
comfortable with just because you feel people
expect it."

Karen gave a deep sigh. "Cindy, did you
ever walk in on your mother and dad in bed when
you were little? I did. My stepfather was on top of
my mother and I thought he was hurting her. I ran
over and started screaming and hitting him on the
back. He became furious. He jumped up and gave
me a hard slap that sent me reeling across the
room. I ran back to my bed and lay there bawling
my eyes out. Mother came in and took me in her
arms and cuddled me, and told me that what I had
seen was something wives had to do with their
husbands. She probably used a wrong choice of
words but to me sounded like some awful
punishment married women had to endure." She
paused. "Mother was always holding me and
caressing me. I never knew my real father. My
stepfather only looked for excuses to slap me
around. Then one night when I was fifteen he
came into my room and attempted to sexually
abuse me. I got away from him and ran away to
stay with an older cousin. Like my mother, she
treated me kindly. It was with her I discovered I'm
gay." She paused. "I have many gay friends who
are close to their fathers, and most of them to their

33

mothers, too. I don't know if my relationship with my parents had anything to do with what I am, or if I was born to be this way."

Poor tormented creature, Cindy thought as she tried to find words to comfort Karen.

Following an afternoon on the beach the two returned to the house and went to their rooms to shower and dress for dinner. As they started down to the dining room Cindy cautioned Karen. "I haven't told Myrna you're gay. I haven't told Colin either."

"I'm not ashamed about what I am. Colin should know; I'm living under his roof and if he has any reservations..."

"He won't have."

"Tell Colin. As for Myrna, I''ll just play it by ear."

They continued down. Colin, who had just come in with his secretary, met them at the foot of the stairs. He gave Cindy a hug and a kiss and turned to Karen. "Karen, I want you to meet Peter Simmons. I told him on the way out that you and Cindy went to college together."

The young man extended a hand. "I'm pleased to meet you, Karen. I hope you're enjoying your visit to Florida."

"Come on, Peter, we'd better get washed up, " Colin broke in. "Missus Cayce gets very upset when we let her delicious food get cold."

Myrna was already seated and toying impatiently with her salad when the others entered the dining room. She motioned to Karen and Peter. "You two sit over here. You never know what kind of sparks might fly."

Cindy quickly picked up her wine glass. "A toast! Here's to friendship. May we always have it."

Myrna sniffed. "What the hell kind of toast is that? Let's drink to good wine, good food and good sex, not necessarily in that order."

"You would, " Cindy groaned. "Incidently, how was your date last night?"

A gagging sound escaped Myrna's throat. "Just another pretty boy who thinks he's God's gift to women. I swear, Peter, after all the creeps I've gone out with I could almost settle for someone like you, except you're so dammed dull. But maybe you're Karen's type and you two can make music together."

Peter's face crimsoned. "I'm sure Karen is a very nice person, but I'm already involved."

After dinner Colin and Peter retired to the library to work. Cindy and Karen watched television until eleven and then went to their rooms.

Near midnight Colin came into Cindy's room and slid into bed beside her. "I've been neglecting you terribly, darling," he murmured.

She playfully teased his lips with a finger. "Don't talk." She snuggled up to him and placed her lips close to his ear. "Colin, Karen told me she's gay."

Cindy could almost feel his smile in the darkness. He chuckled. "I'm just glad as hell you're not gay." Gently he removed her nightgown. She relaxed, closed her eyes, and let her fantasies roam. There were seldom any surprises with

Colin, just an unchanging, predictable routine with
a minimum of foreplay. Suddenly Cindy tensed.
 "What is it, darling?" Colin whispered.
"Am I hurting you?"
 "No. No." She put her arms around him
and drew him closer, responding with short, almost
inaudible gasps to each rhythmic thrust.
Dismayed, she suddenly realized – in her fantasies
the man her arms was not her husband, Colin
Jamison. It was Dexter Matthews.

CHAPTER FIVE

ounds of loud shouting and cursing coming
from the direction of the front gate jolted
Cindy from a fitful sleep. Her clock showed
2 A.M.. Colin snored softly beside her,
undisturbed. She leaped from bed and hastily
called the Brown's cottage on the intercom.
"Dicey, what on earth is happening down there?"

"Oh, Miz Cindy, some of Raymond's no-
count friends come lookin' for him. They all doped
up. Ben done chased them away. You jest go back
to sleep. Everything gonna be all right."

Others in the house had heard the
commotion. Cindy opened her bedroom door to
find Myrna and Karen in the hall. Rubbing sleep
from his eyes, Colin joined them. "Party's over,"
Cindy assured them. "Just a domestic problem
down at the servants' cottage. Go back to bed."

Myrna glanced around. "Where's Peter?
Did he spend the night in your room, Karen?"

Colin frowned sternly. "Don't have such a
dirty mind, Myrna. Peter went home after we
finished working."

As everyone started back to their rooms, Colin called to Karen. "I almost forgot to tell you, Karen. I spoke to a business associate about you. She wants to take a look at your resume. I'll be seeing her tomorrow and can take it to her."

"Wonderful! I'll give you a copy in the morning."

Colin held Cindy back as the other two left the hall. "Darling, we need to say something to Ben and Dicey about the kind of people Raymond is associating with. I've seen some pretty seedy characters hanging around the front gate."

Cindy gave him a light peck on the cheek. "I'll speak to them in the morning. Now, get some sleep."

At breakfast Karen bubbled with enthusiasm as Colin leafed through her resume. "What kind of job have you lined up for me, Colin?"

"ComRisk Insurers have an opening for a claims adjuster. Cindy told me you worked in insurance in New York, and I see here that you did claims work in your previous job. ComRisk is a commercial and industrial insurer. Anita Barnes is in charge of their Palm Beach office. She's the one you'll see if you get a call from them – and from what I see here I'm quite sure you'll receive a call."

"Anita Barnes?" Karen gasped. "That's the name of the person who recruited me from college. She left the company soon after I went to work there. Do you think it could be the same person?"

Colin shrugged. "It's a small world. Could be. Anyway, the starting salary might not be as much as you have been earning, but ComRisk is a growing company so there should be plenty of chance for advancement."

"Get real," Myrna sniffed. "Get a job in an office where a single rich guy is in charge. Play your cards right and you won't ever have to worry about a job. Look at Cindy. She didn't do so bad. And after three husbands I'm in pretty good financial shape."

Colin shot her a chilling glance. "That's enough from you, Myrna."

He finished his breakfast and started to leave for his office. Karen followed him to the door.

She fidgeted nervously. "Colin, I suppose Cindy told you that I'm a lesbian. If I go for an interview with Anita Barnes should I tell her if she asks?"

Colin smiled. "I don't think that would make any difference to Anita. She's quite liberal-minded. Just use your own judgement."

Cindy came over to kiss Colin goodbye. "We'll stay close to the house in case Anita calls. Give her my cellphone number. I've told Karen she can stay here as long as she wants, but I'm sure she is anxious to get a job and get on with her life." She paused. "I'll speak to Dicey about last night."

Later Karen put on a bathing suit and went to lounge by the pool. Cindy was inside the house when a noticeably distraught Dicey Brown came in. "Miz Cindy, that boy of mine 'bout to drive me crazy," Dicey moaned. "He startin' to stay out all hours with a bunch of bums. That not like him at all. 'Til lately he always been a good boy. Now he wearing' gold chains 'round his neck, and a few nights ago I saw him with a big roll of money. I'm 'fraid he gettin' in real big trouble. That money is what them bums was after last night."

"Do you want me to call the police?"

"Oh, no, Miz Cindy. Ben can take care of them rowdies."

"Well, we don't want any trouble."

Near noon Colin called. "Karen has the job if she passes the personal interview. Anita will see her at four. You know where the ComRisk building is, don't you? Are you free to drive her there?"

"Yes, I'll take her. Incidently, I talked to Dicey about the disturbance last night. She promised that Ben will take care of the situation."

A few minutes before four Cindy pulled into the parking lot of the small, modern building housing ComRisk Insurers. She gave Karen a thumbs-up sigh. "Go get 'em, tiger. I'll wait for you on the patio of that little coffee shop across the street."

Karen entered the building and found herself in a large open room with about a dozen desks placed a few feet apart. She approached the receptionist's desk. "I'm Karen Knowles. Ms Barnes is expecting me."

A tall, forty-ish woman with auburn hair and a pleasant smile beckoned from a far corner. "Come on back, Karen. I'm Anita Barnes." She motioned Karen to a chair. "We don't stand on formality here, and as you can see... " she swept the room with a hand, "... we are not at all pretentious. But this is strong, solid company growing fast." She picked up Karen's resume. "This is quite impressive, and Colin Jamison speaks well of you."

"You don't remember me, do you?" Karen asked. "You recruited me from college."

Anita studied Karen's face intently. "Yes, of course. How long ago was that? Eight or nine years?"

"Ten years."

"Time flies, doesn't it? Well, I liked your qualifications then and I like them now. But I have to ask you a few questions for the record. Answer truthfully. Any discrepancies discovered in the future will be grounds for termination. Do you understand?"

"Yes."

"Do you smoke?"

"No, never did,"

"Drink?"

"Only an occasional social drink. Never excessively."

"How about drugs. Pot? Cocaine?"

"No, never."

"I'm going to ask you a rather personal question, Karen."

Uh, oh, here it comes.

Anita smiled disarmingly. "Here at ComRisk a lot of effort goes into training new employees. We must be pretty sure they'll stay with us. Are you involved with anyone back in New York who you might jump up and run back to?"

Karen gave a mental sigh of relief. "Nobody – nothing – could drag me back to the frozen north."

"Good." Anita named a starting salary. "Is that satisfactory?"

"Yes, that will be fine."

Anita extended a hand. "All right, Karen. I'm going to give you a trial at the job."

Taken aback by the quick decision, Karen could only stammer. "Thank you Ms Barnes. I'll work hard to justify your faith in me."

"It's 'Anita', Karen. As I said before, we don't stand on formality here. All we require is that you do your job well and get along with the other members of the staff. As for your private life, just don't do anything that will reflect badly on the company. I won't introduce you to the others right now; you wouldn't remember all their names, anyway. Be here ready to work Monday at nine."

Karen fairly floated from the building and ran to where Cindy waited. "I got the job," she sang. "I got the job."

"Wonderful!" Cindy congratulated her. "Let's celebrate. There's a great stone crab restaurant near here. We'll have an early dinner. Colin is working late, and Myrna can very well eat without us." With a cellphone call she advised the housekeeper of her plans.

When they drove up to the restaurant, Karen's eyes opened wide. "Wow! Look at all those Rolls and Mercedes. And get a load of that red Ferrari. Do you think we can afford to eat here?"

Cindy chuckled at her friend's enthusiasm. "Oh, I think so. We can always wash dishes if we can't pay the tab."

A smartly groomed hostess greeted them as they entered, and guided them to a corner table overlooking the Intracoastal Waterway on one side and the parking lot on the other. She placed menus before them. "If you care for something to drink before you order dinner I'll send the cocktail waitress over."

Both nodded assent.

Karen's eager gaze roamed the room. Suddenly she clutched Cindy's arm. "Look, there's Fran over there."

Cindy looked in the direction Karen pointed. Fran Pahlavi sat at a table with two men and a young woman. "The man sitting opposite Fran is her husband, Adrian," Cindy whispered. "I can't see the face of the other man, but did you ever see a more stunning girl than the one with them?"

The girl sitting across from the unidentified man radiated exotic beauty. Glossy black hair fell almost to her hips. Dark, slightly slanted eyes found a perfect setting in the pale almond of a symmetrical face complemented by porcelain-like skin and pencilled eyebrows.

"She looks Oriental," Karen suggested.

"Probably Eurasian. I wonder who she is. I've never seen her with Fran and Adrian."

The foursome got up and started for the exit. For a brief instant Cindy caught a glimpse of the second man's profile. The face belonged to Dexter Matthews. Her heart pounded. "Quick, Karen, hide behind your menu. I don't want them to see us."

They watched as the four left the restaurant and walked across the parking lot. Dexter and the girl got into the red Ferrari while Fran and Adrian continued on to their own car.

"The man with Fran and Adrian is Dexter Matthews. We went to high school at the same time, " Cindy said. "Lately he's put moves on me, making me very uncomfortable." She told of his approach at the party, meeting again at the polo match, and the incident in Vail.

"He's an arrogant cuss, isn't he?" Karen observed. "But he's really robbing the cradle with his present companion. She can't be more than twenty or twenty-one. I suppose with looks like his he can get any woman he wants."

"Well," Cindy vowed emphatically, "this is one woman he's not going to get."

CHAPTER SIX

Even before they reached home, Cindy sensed something was wrong. Several police cars passed them, and as the gate to the Jamison estate came into view they could see the cars stopped before it and policemen milling about.

Cindy opened the gate with her remote control, slowly pulled inside, and came to a stop. A uniformed officer walked over to them.

"Missus Jamison? I'm Sergeant Ames, Stardust Shores Police Department. I have a warrant to search your servant quarters for illegal drugs."

Cindy's face went ashen.

"I'll be frank with you, ma'am, we've had this place under surveillance for several weeks. Our undercover boys have made a number of buys of crack cocaine here. Since all the transactions were with the son of your servants, I'm assuming you are not involved. Just the same, I'd appreciate it if you'll just sit there in the car until we finish. We'll get through as quickly as we can and try not to make any mess." He motioned his men into the cottage and followed them in, a drug-sniffing dog trotting alongside.

"Wow!" Karen exclaimed. "Just like in the movies." Cindy sat in numbed silence.

Ben and Dicey came out, and with the permission of an escorting officer, rushed over to them. "Oh, Miz Cindy," Dicey wailed, "I knowed them bums Raymond been hanging out with gonna get him in trouble. The cops holdin' him in there while they search his room. What you figure they do if they finds any dope?"

Though churning inside, Cindy tried to comfort the woman. "We'll have to wait and see. Maybe the police won't find anything."

After an agonizing passage of time, seeming to Cindy to be hours, but actually only ten or fifteen minutes, Sgt. Ames came out, an evidence bag in one hand and a grim expression on his face. "We found a small amount of crack cocaine and a sizable amount of cash in the boy's room." He turned to Ben and Dicey. "Your son has been placed under arrest. I'm sorry, but since you're occupants of the house I have to take you in too."

"Ben and Dicey can't be involved in this,"

Cindy objected. "I can vouch for them."

"Sorry, ma'am, I have to follow the law. A judge will decide if they are to be held." He squirmed in discomfort. "Ma'am, since illegal drugs were found on the property I really should search the main house. My warrant doesn't cover the main house, but I think it's best for you in the long run if you permit me to make a search. If the place is clean, there should be no question about your involvement."

Cindy nodded numbly.

The half hour the police were in the house seemed like an eternity. The Browns had already been taken away. Karen tried to cheer Cindy. "Hey, it's no big deal. In New York this happens every day."

"This is not New York," Cindy snapped. "This is the Gold Coast of Florida. Things like this happen in West Palm Beach or down in Miami. Not here." Gawkers standing around nodded agreement.

Sgt. Ames had a faint smile on his face when he returned. "That lady in the kitchen wanted to run me out with a rolling pin when I started poking around in her pantry. And the lady in the bedroom upstairs... wow! She made some pretty suggestive comments."

Oh God, Cindy thought. I forgot about Myrna. "That's my sister-in-law, Myrna Bell. She's always clowning around."

"Yes, ma'am, if you say so. Anyway, we didn't find anything so I won't take it as an attempted bribe." He got in his car and drove off.

47

Cindy turned to Karen. "Do you still want to move to Florida?"

"Sure, more than ever. This place is exciting."

They hurried to the house. Cindy called Darlene. "Hi, Darl, is Byron home? I need a lawyer – fast." She explained what had happened and then could hear Darlene giving a quick summary to Byron before he took the phone.

"What do you want me to do, Cindy?"

"Byron, can you get my household staff out of jail? I'll meet you at the police station. Colin is working late but Karen Knowles will ride down with me."

"I'm on my way."

"Thanks a million, Byron. I don't know what I'd do without you and Darlene. You're the best friends a gal could ever have."

Cindy's car, and the car driven by Byron North, with Darlene at his side, pulled into the parking lot at the same time. Karen jumped out and ran toward Byron. He put his arms around her in greeting. She returned his hug and then stepped back and gave him a long, adoring look. "Byron North, I think you must be the most perfect gentleman who ever lived, keeping my secret all these years."

Byron grinned. "In the legal game it's called lawyer-client confidentiality."

"Well, anyway, I think Darlene really lucked out when she landed you."

"That's what I tried to tell you gals," Darlene rejoined smugly, taking Byron's arm in hers.

"All right," he smiled, "this meeting of the 'Everybody Loves Byron ' club is now adjourned. We have lawyer-type work to do." He led the way inside. They found Ben and Dicey in an interrogation room. Dicey rushed toward them.

"Oh, Miz Cindy, thank the Lord you come. You don't know how 'barrassin' this be. They been askin' all kinds of questions."

"Don't worry, Dicey. Mister North will have you out quickly."

Ben looked at Byron. "Mistuh North, I sure 'preciate you getting us out, but don't get Raymond out 'til tomorrow. A night in jail do that boy a lotta good."

While Byron went to talk with the desk sergeant, Ben fidgeted nervously. "Miz Cindy, I guess you'll be wanting us to move out, and I can't blame you."

Cindy shook her head. "Don't worry. We'll work things out."

"How 'bout Mistuh Colin? I bet he don't take too kindly to all this trouble."

"He'll understand."

Dicey broke in. "Miz Cindy, we try to raise that boy right. It awful hard these days. He see all them punks ridin' 'round in flashy cars with fancy women and I guess he figure the only way to get those things is to deal drugs."

Byron came back into the room. "Ben and Dicey are free to go but will have to show up in the morning for a hearing. Raymond is being held overnight for the hearing. I'll be here to represent them."

Cindy gave Byron a warm embrace. "Thanks for everything, Byron. You're a dear."

49

"Hey, leggo my man," Darlene exclaimed in mock sternness.

Cindy wrapped both arms around her. "You're a dear, too, chum."

Karen rushed over and gathered all three into her arms. "You're all dears. Now let's go home. I've had an exciting day."

Colin greeted them with a desultory wave of his hand when they arrived home. "Myrna and Missus Cayce told me about the police raid. We'll work things out with Ben and Dicey." He turned to Cindy. "Darling, something disturbing happened to me today. I passed out at the office. I was out only a minute or two. Peter called Doctor Charles. The good doctor wanted to admit me to the hospital for observation but I convinced him to let me come in tomorrow for a complete checkup."

Cindy embraced him. "Please, Colin, you must take care of your health. I don't want to lose you."

"You'll be the richest widow in town when I go," Colin quipped.

Cindy's eyes flashed in anger. "Don't joke about things like that, Colin. Don't ever joke about things like that."

CHAPTER SEVEN

F ran's voice on the telephone dripped sarcasm. "Well, Cindy, I see that you have joined the ranks of the rich and notorious. Now Adrian and I are not the only ones in our little social circle to make the front page of the Revealer."

"What do you mean?" Fear clutched at Cindy's heart.

"Haven't you seen this morning's edition of the Inside Revealer?"

"No. I don't read such trash."

"You'd better read this one. It's about the drug raid at your place yesterday."

Hilda Cayce burst into the room waving a paper over her head. "Look at this, Missus Jamison. Just look at this."

"I'll call you back," Cindy told Fran. "Missus Cayce just brought in a copy of the Revealer."

Cindy took the newspaper from the housekeeper's trembling fingers. Her heart sank at the sight of the glaring headlines. POSH OCEANFRONT CRACK HOUSE, and in smaller subheads COP OFFERED SEX AS BRIBE and COOK CHASES POLICE WITH ROLLING PIN.

"This is absurd," she spluttered, "absolutely ridiculous." She quickly scanned the article. Factually, the story was reasonably accurate though filled with innuendos. The Browns were identified as the arrested parties, with Sgt. Ames named as leader of the raiding party. She shook her head. "I can't believe a member of our police department would give a story to this despicable rag."

"Mister Jamison will be furious," Hilda offered. "He'll put them in their place."

"I'll do it myself." Cindy reached for the telephone and called police headquarters. "I want to speak to Sergeant Ames," she demanded. After a brief delay a man spoke.

"Sergeant Ames here. May I help you?"

"This is Cindy Jamison," Cindy's voice seethed. "How dare you to give that sleazy story to that scandal sheet?"

"Hold your horses, Missus Jamison, hold your horses. I saw the Revealer. The boys here at the station have been kidding the hell out of me all morning. I assure you I had nothing to do with their article. I'm sorry if remarks I made as a joke were overheard and misinterpreted by one of the onlookers. It's obvious one of them gave the story to the press. I would never do or say anything to offend you, your cook, or your charming sister-in-law."

Cindy's attitude softened. "I'm sorry I blew up, Sergeant Ames, but something should be done about these so-called newspapers."

"Well, ma'am, you could sue them. People do it every day. But there's almost no chance you could win or even get a retraction. These people are smart. They stay just within the libel law limits."

"Thank you, sergeant. I'm sorry I bothered you."

"Don't mention it, ma'am. I'm here to serve you."

Cindy hung up and turned to Hilda. "It looks like we can't do anything but grin and bear it. Look at it this way – you'll be something of a celebrity in the local housekeepers' league, defending your kitchen and all."

Hilda Cayce gave a horrified gasp. "Oh, no, Missus Jamison. I didn't really threaten the officer. I was rolling out bread when he burst into the kitchen. He startled me and I suppose I raised up the rolling pin involuntarily." She stopped short, embarrassed. "I do hope Ben and Dicey are not in big trouble."

"They'll be all right. Now if you will excuse

me I have to get dressed. I'm taking them down for their court appearance this morning."

Ben and Dicey were apprehensively silent as Cindy drove them to the town hall. To Cindy's surprise she found Colin waiting with Byron North when they arrived. He had left home before she got up. "Hi, dear, I didn't expect to see you here," she called as she got out of her car.

"I'm playing hookey today. I went to the office early to take care of a few matters, and after the hearing here I'm going in for the complete checkup Doctor Charles ordered." He appeared to be in an unpredicted good humor considering the events of the previous day. "Quite a writeup in the tabloid wasn't it, Cindy?"

They entered the small courtroom. Byron motioned Ben and Dicey to the defendants' table where Raymond already sat, his eyes shifting nervously. "I was able to arrange a quick hearing," Byron whispered.

"All stand," a bailiff barked.

The judge strode in and with a downward motion of his palms directed everyone to be seated. He swept the room with a steady gaze, momentarily pausing to scrutinize each face. Then he cleared his throat. "I think we all know each other here. For any of you who don't, I'm Judge Williams. Now this is not a formal trial; it's a preliminary hearing to determine which, if any, of these defendants are to be held for trial on a very serious charge – drug trafficking. We don't have a prosecutor at these hearings so I'm just going to ask each of you some simple questions and I want some straight answers."

54

He peered over his glasses. "Now Colin and Cindy, just because I have been a guest at your house many times and know the defendants doesn't mean your people will get any special treatment. Is that understood?"

"Yes, Your Honor," Byron answered for them.

The judge glanced at some papers. "Ben, Dicey and Raymond Brown, you have been charged with possession with intent to sell controlled substances, and/or being occupants of a house where illegal drugs were found. Mister North, how do your clients plead?"

Byron stepped forward. "You Honor, two of my clients, Ben and Dicey Brown, are completely innocent. While they do live in the raided house they were not a party to nor did they have any firm knowledge of any illegal activities. I respectfully request that all charges against them be dropped."

Judge Williams glanced at Sgt. Ames. "Sergeant, you arrested these people. Tell me the circumstances."

"Your Honor, I obtained a search order..."

"Yes, yes," the judge broke in, "I gave it to you."

"...and I took six officers to the Jamison estate. Missus Jamison was driving up just as we arrived and she opened the gate for us. Mister Brown and his wife were sitting in the living room of the servants' cottage when we entered, and appeared startled at seeing us. The young man ..." he pointed at Raymond, "... was observed fleeing through the kitchen door. Our search turned up approximately four ounces of crack cocaine and fifteen hundred dollars in currency hidden under a mattress in the young man's room. We found no evidence of illegal substances anywhere else in the house."

The judge looked at Ben and Dicey. "Did you folks know anything about those drugs and that money?"

"As the Lord is my witness," Ben raised both hands pleadingly, "Dicey and me don't know nothing. I know Raymond been runnin' 'round with a bad bunch. I chased some of them away jest the other night. But I never 'spected Raymond to be dealing drugs."

"I saw Raymond with a roll of money," Dicey burst out. "I didn't know where he got it."

"Your Honor," Sgt. Ames continued, "we had the place under surveillance for three or four weeks and our undercover boys made several buys there. The parents were never around when the buys were made."

The judge glanced in the direction of Colin and Cindy. "You got anything to say?"

Colin stood up. "Your Honor, Ben and Dicey Brown have been in our employ for many years. I know them to be fine, upstanding, law-abiding citizens. It is unthinkable that they could be involved in this sordid mess. As for Raymond ..."

The judge stopped him with a depreciating gesture. "We're talking about Ben and Dicey now. We'll get to Raymond later." He remained silent for a long moment. "All right, I'm convinced Ben and Dicey Brown were not involved. Charges dismissed. What is your plea for your third client, Mister North?"

"Your Honor, there is strong evidence that

Raymond Brown had knowledge of illegal activities at the Jamison estate. I have no objection to his being bound over for a formal trial at which time his guilt or innocense can be determined. As for the charge of possession with intent to sell we plead 'Not Guilty'. In view of the fact that Raymond Brown has no prior police record, I respectfully request that he be released in the custody of his parents."

Judge Williams peered over his glasses again. "You been in trouble before, son?"

"No, sir."

"Well, because of the seriousness of the charges I can't just let you walk out of here. Bail is set at five thousand dollars. Your attorney will be notified of a trial date in the County Court." He looked at Sgt Ames. "That all right with you, Sergeant?"

"Yes, sir."

"All right, bailiff, bring in your next case."

As the group left the courtroom Byron spotted a man sitting in a back row furiously scribbling notes. "Well, Weiss, what brings you to our little town so early in the morning?" he asked cooly.

"Just gathering evidence, North, just gathering evidence." A wolfish smile spread across the man's florid face. "If you think you're going to get that boy off with a slap on the wrist you're in for a big surprise." He brushed past Byron and the others and headed for the door. Over his shoulder he shot back "Yes, sir, Mister North, you and your high-and-mighty friends are in for a big jolt."

"What was that all about, Byron?" Colin asked.

Byron frowned. "Erwin Weiss is a sleezebag lawyer with political ambitions. Rumor has it he's preparing to run for District Attorney on a law-and-order ticket and will miss no opportunity to get publicity. We'll just have to wait and see what kind of tricks he has up his sleeve for us." He left to post bail for Raymond.

Colin gave Cindy a quick hug. "I'm going for my physical. Doctor Charles said there will be numerous tests that will take several hours. I'll come home when they're through with me."

"Fine, dear, let's pray they don't find any serious problems. I'll take Ben, Dicey and Raymond home."

When Colin returned home that afternoon he immediately summoned Raymond to his den where Cindy also sat dreading what she knew would be an acrimonious confrontation. The boy arrived promptly, shoulders sagging and eyes downcast.

"What the hell is wrong with you, Raymond, putting your parents through this torment?"

"You wouldn't understand," Raymond muttered.

"Wouldn't understand? Wouldn't understand what?"

All the tension Raymond had built up during his arrest and his night in jail suddenly released. "You don't know what it's like being poor. You've got your big house and fancy cars and everything else you want. What chance have I got to get ahead? None."

Colin pursed his lips. "Son, you have everything I had when I was your age, maybe more. You have loving parents ready to put you through college. My parents were working-class people, barely making a comfortable living. I worked my way through college, and I've worked hard a hell for everything I have."

"Yeah," Raymond retorted, "but you're not black."

"Oh, so that's it. You think the only road to a good life for a black man is a life of crime? Well, I'll let you in on a little secret; there's no good life behind bars. And that's where you'll spend the best part of your life if you continue on the course you're taking."

Raymond sat in subdued silence for a long moment before he spoke, then in almost a whisper "So I'm supposed to be goody-goody, ride my bicycle to school, and when I graduate go to work as a handyman for some rich guy like my dad did."

"That's unfair, Raymond," Cindy broke in angrily, "you're taking a very negative view. Haven't you hurt your parents enough without suggesting their lives have been failures?"

Colin hushed her with a slight wave of his hand. He looked sternly at Raymond. "I've given a lot of thought to what has happened. I'm going to do what I can to get you out of the mess you're in. I have some influence in this county and I think I can get you a suspended sentence. Your parents want to send you to junior college. Go. As long as you keep your nose clean and get passing grades I'll let you have the use of a reliable car, and I'll get you a part-time job so you can earn spending

59

money. If you want to go on after two years I'll pay all the costs for you to complete your undergraduate studies at Florida State or the University of Florida. Complete four years in the upper twenty percent of your class and I'll give you a brand-new convertible and pay for postgraduate studies at any college you choose."

"You'd do that for me?"

Colin shook his head. "No, not for you. I'd do it for your parents. They deserve better."

Raymond's face broke into a broad smile. He held out his hand. "You got a deal, Mister Colin." He hesitated. "That is, if those guys I been hanging out with don't kill me for losing their stash and their cash."

"Don't worry about them. I'll see that they don't come within a mile of this place. You just stay away from them."

Later Cindy brought the subject up to Colin. "That was a most generous offer you made Raymond. Do you really intend to do all you said?"

He gave her a kiss on the cheek. "My dear, I always keep my word. And if I'm not around I'm sure you will carry out my wishes."

CHAPTER EIGHT

They just won't let it rest, will they?" Darlene exploded, handing Cindy a copy of the *Inside Revealer* sporting a blazing headline SERVANT TO TAKE RAP FOR WEALTHY SOCIALITES?

"I saw it," Cindy shrugged. "Same sleezy innuendos. They don't come right and say Raymond is taking the rap for us. They just pose the question."

Colin, Cindy and Darlene sat in the courtroom on the day of Raymond's trial. Raymond, neatly groomed, with a fresh haircut and new suit, sat just in front of them at the defendants' table with Byron North. Byron leaned back and whispered over his shoulder to Colin "We could be in for more of a hassle than we anticipated. This is not a jury trial, and we have drawn a liberal-minded judge who I believe will be sympathetic to our plea. What worries me is there are several reporters in the room and I saw a television crew setting up as I came in. Guess who's with them – our old friend Erwin Weiss. I don't know what Weiss is up to; we'll just have to play it by ear. Incidently, the prosecutor, Jim Bishop, is a pretty decent guy."

The stentorian voice of a bailiff announcing the opening of the court session brought a halt to their conversation. Judge Anthony Ziti took his place on the bench and motioned the assembly to be seated. He shuffled some papers and then looked up.

"This is the trial of one Raymond Brown, charged with possession with intent to sell certain controlled substances. The defendant has waived his right to a jury trial and has entered a plea of 'not guilty'. Before this court session began I met with the prosecutor and the defense attorney in my chambers and both acknowledged the credentials of all witnesses scheduled to testify. All witnesses have been sworn in so we can dispense with that formality. Mister Bishops, you may proceed."

Cindy gripped Colin's arm tightly. "How can Raymond plead 'not guilty' when the drugs and cash were found in his room?"

Colin winked. "Leave it to Byron. He knows what he's doing."

Big, jovial Jim Bishop stood up. "Your Honor, this is pretty much of an open-and-shut case. Crack cocaine and a substantial amount of cash were found in the possession of the defendant, and the defendant attempted to flee when confronted by the police. I have just one witness. I call Sergeant Bob Ames of the Stardust Shores Police Department." Sgt. Ames took the stand.

"Sergeant Ames," the prosecutor continued, "on October ninth last did you lead a police raid on the Jamison estate in Stardust Shores?"

"Yes sir, I did."

"Tell the court about it."

"Well, sir, we had the place under sporadic surveillance for several weeks. On two occasions our undercover agents made drug buys there. Using the intelligence gathered I was able to get a search warrant to search the servants' cottage where we suspected illegal drugs might be found. At the aforementioned time we went to the Jamison place."

"Did you meet any opposition?"

"No, sir. Missus Jamison was arriving home as we got there. She opened to gate for us."

"And then what happened?"

"We entered the cottage. The defendant's parents were sitting in the living room."

"Did they attempt to obstruct your search?"

"No, sir. They appeared shocked but cooperated fully."

"Was the defendant in the house?"

"Yes, sir. He was attempting to leave by the back door when we went in. We apprehended him."

The prosecutor paused for a moment and then continued. "When you searched the house, what did you find?"

"Under a mattress in the boy's bedroom we found a small quantity of what the police lab later proved to be crack cocaine. We also found fifteen hundred dollars in small bills."

"How did you know it was the defendant's room?"

Sgt. Ames smiled. "It's a typical boy's room. You know – sports items lying around, posters of rock stars on the walls, a high school pennant, things like that. Besides, his parents confirmed it was his room."

"Did you search any other part of the Jamison estate?"

"After we found the cocaine Missus Jamison gave me permission to search the main house. My warrant covered only the cottage."

"What did you find in the main house?"

"Nothing. The place was clean."

The prosecutor scanned his notes. "That is all I have. Your witness, Mister North."

"Just a moment, Sergeant," Judge Ziti broke in."Just to satisfy my own curiosity. I read in the press that you were offered sexual favors as a bribe. What can you tell me about that?"

A burst of laughter came from the spectators.

The sergeant's face crimsoned. "There was nothing to it, Your Honor. A houseguest of the Jamisons was just clowning around. No bribery was intended."

"Very well," the judge sighed. "You may question the witness, Mister North."

"Thank you, Your Honor." Byron leveled his gaze at the policeman. "Sergeant Ames, you say undercover agents bought drugs at the Jamison place on two separate occasions. Were these purchases made directly from the defendant, Raymond Brown?"

The sergeant squirmed uncomfortably. "Well, actually there was a group of young men involved. In each instance the defendant went into the house and came back with a packet of cocaine which he handed to one of the others who then passed it to the buyer."

"Then Raymond Brown was just a messenger?"

"We assumed he was the seller and the others his agents."

"Did the buyers pay cash for the purchases?"

"Yes, sir."

"Was the cash handed over to the

defendant?"

Sgt. Ames paused before answering. "I asked my men that question. They admitted they did not see the money handed over."

Byron glanced at his notes. "One final question, Sergeant Ames. Were the bills used in the police buys marked?"

"Yes, sir, they were."

"Were any of the marked bills found in the cash seized in the raid?"

"No, sir, they were not."

"I have no more question, Sergeant," Byron dismissed him.

The judge glanced at the prosecutor. "Anything else you want to ask this witness, Mister Bishops?"

"Yes, Your Honor. Sergeant, are you sure the money for the drug buys was not passed to the defendant?"

"As I said before, my men did not see the money passed. I can't say for sure, yes or no."

Jim Bishop shrugged in resignation. "Prosecution rests."

The judge looked over at Byron. "You may call your first witness, Mister North."

"I call Raymond Brown."

Raymond stood up, squared his shoulders, and marched resolutely to the witness stand.

Byron walked over and stood within an arm's length of him. "Raymond, do you live with your parents in a cottage on the Jamison estate in Stardust Shores?"

"Yes, sir."

"In the late afternoon of October ninth last, did police find illegal drugs and a sizable amount

65

of cash in your room?"

"Yes, sir."

"Did these belong to you?"

"No, sir. They were not mine."

Byron feigned surprise. "Oh? If they didn't belong to you, who did they belong to?"

"They belonged to some guys I hang out with."

"Who are these people? Where did you meet them?"

"They go to my school."

"That's the Stardust Shores High School?"

"Yes, sir."

Byron raised his eyebrows. "Oh, they live in your neighborhood?"

"No, sir, they come by bus from West Palm."

"You knew they were dealing drugs. Why did you hang out with them?"

Raymond's voice suddenly rose. "Hey, man, they're my people. I wanted to belong."

Byron leaned over and placed a hand on the boy's arm. "Tell me, Raymond, have you ever been in want in your entire life? I mean, haven't you always been well fed and clothed?"

"My folks take good care of me."

"But that's not true of your friends, is it?"

"They grew up in the ghetto, man."

"And they convinced you that they never got a break in life and the only way they could get ahead is by dealing drugs?"

"That's pretty much it."

Byron stepped back. "Tell me, Raymond, why were the drugs and cash kept in your room?"

"The guys said the cops always hassling

them over in the ghetto but wouldn't think to look in a swell place like Stardust Shores. Sometimes they would bring customers over and make sales outside the gate. Most of the time they would pick up a small amount of the stuff and take it with them. Some times they would leave some money to add to the stash. Whenever they needed money to buy more rocks they would pick up all the money."

"Did they give you a share of the profits?"

"They gave me some gold chain."

"I mean, did you have an agreement that every time a sale was made you would get a definite part of it?"

"No, sir. I got no money. Only the gold chain."

"One last thing. On the night preceding the police raid there was a disturbance at the Jamison estate. A lot of shouting and cursing. What do you know about this?"

"Some guys I didn't know came to the gate and wanted the money. They were all doped up. They scared the hell out of me. My dad chased them away."

Byron stepped back. "Your witness, Mister Bishop."

The prosecutor gave Raymond a stern frown. "Do you expect this court to believe that cock-and-bull story?"

"Yes, sir, because it's true, so help me God."

"I have no further question," Jim Bishop sighed.

Judge Ziti glanced at some papers before him. "I believe you have one more witness, Mister

North. You may call him."

"I call Colin Jamison."

Colin stood up, walked the witness stand, sat down and automatically raised his right hand.

"That won't be necessary," the judge smiled, "you have already been sworn in. You may proceed, Mister North."

"Very well, Your Honor." Then to Colin, "How long have you known the defendant?"

"All his life. His parents were in my employ at the time of his birth."

"During his growing up has he been hard to control, a troublemaker, a worry to his parents?"

"Oh, no," Colin exclaimed, "just the opposite. Until this sordid mess came up I always considered him to be a fine young man."

"And now?"

"I still think that, basically, he is a fine person. I think he got mixed up with a bad crowd and, out of a misdirected sense of loyalty, let them take advantage of him."

Byron pursed his lips. "Mister Jamison, if Raymond Brown gains his freedom as a result of this trial will he be welcome back at your place?"

"Absolutely!"

"Thank you, Mister Jamison. Your witness, Mister Bishop."

Jim Bishop glanced at Byron and then turned to the judge. "May we approach the bench, Your Honor?"

Judge Ziti beckoned with a finger. Byron and Jim approached the bench and an animated exchange of words took place.

The judge raised a hand. "Before we go any further, I declare a brief recess. You may step

down, Mister Jamison. Mister Bishop and Mister
North, come to my chambers."

"All rise!" the bailiff ordered.

Behind has back Byron flashed a "thumbs-
up" sign as he followed the judge.

"How we doing, Mister Colin," Raymond
asked anxiously as Colin passed him.

"Very well, Raymond. I feel we're doing
very well."

Only about five minutes passed before the
judge and the two attorneys emerged. After the
bailiffs officious "All stand" they took their places.

The judge cleared his throat. "Raymond, do
you know what a plea bargain is?"

"Yes, sir."

"Well, we did a little plea bargaining in
there. Your attorney and the prosecutor have
agreed that if you change your plea from 'not guilty'
to a lesser charge of 'aiding and abetting a criminal
activity' you could get off with a lighter sentence.
Do you agree to this change of plea?"

Raymond glanced at Byron, who gave an
affirmative nod.

"Okay, if Mister North thinks it best."

"Very well. The court finds you guilty of
aiding and abetting a criminal activity, and
sentences you to one year in the county jail and
five years probation." He paused to let his words
sink in. "I'm going to suspend the sentence. If you
get into any kind of trouble in the next five years
you will serve the full sentence. Do you think you
can stay out of trouble for five years, son?"

"Judge, I'm going to stay out of trouble the
rest of my life. Thank you, sir, and thank you
Mister Bishop, and thank you Mister North."

A jubilant Cindy hugged Colin as they left the courtroom. "Thank God this horrible mess is over."

In front of the courthouse they encountered Erwin Weiss holding a press conference before television cameras.

"... and if a building in the ghetto used as a crack house can be seized and razed, and automobiles, boats and aircraft used in the transportation of illegal drugs confiscated, why should the waterfront estates of the powerful and affluent be exempt? The drug scourge that is destroying our society must be eliminated, no matter the cost. And no sacred cows can be allowed to escape."

Colin's face turned livid. "Does that son-of-a-bitch think he can take my property? I'll see him in hell first."

Cindy flashed Byron an alarmed look. "Byron, is there any way he can do this?"

Byron stroked his chin reflectively. "Stranger things have happened. I don't think he has a ghost of a chance but he could cause you a lot of embarrassment, Colin. We had better find a way to shut him up--fast."

Days later Colin still fumed over Weiss' implied threat. He, Cindy, Myrna and Karen, who still remained a houseguest though working at ComRisk Insurers, sat on the patio having breakfast when Hilda Cayce came out. "There's a call for you on the house telephone, Mister Jamison. A Mister Matthews. He says it's important or he wouldn't be bothering you at home. Shall I bring you the cordless phone?"

Colin's brow furrowed. "Dexter Matthews? What the devil could he want? Excuse me, ladies, I'll take the call in the library." He hurried away.

Outwardly Cindy remained calm but her heart skipped a few beats. *What could Dexter want? And why should it matter to me anyway?*

A grim smile lighted Colin's face when he returned.

"That's a stroke of good luck. Matthews says he can be a real help in putting our ambitious lawyer friend in his place. I called Byron. He and I will meet with Matthews this morning." He turned to Cindy. "Matthews said to give his regards to 'my charming wife'. By the way, darling, what are your plans for the day?"

"I'm meeting Darlene and we're going shopping for Christmas gifts for the men in our lives."

"If that includes me," Colin laughed, "don't get anything flashy or expensive. Having you is gift enough for me."

"How sickeningly sweet," Myrna rolled her eyes. "When a man gives me a gift I want something that sparkles, and I don't mean Fourth-of-July fireworks. How about you, Karen? Oh, I forgot. You don't go out with men much. You haven't had a date since you got here, have you? Sometimes I wonder if you're one of those gals who prefer women to men."

Karen gave her a scathing glare. "Would it make any difference to you if I were?"

"Hell, no. Just don't come knocking on my bedroom door when you're feeling lonely."

Karen stood up quickly. "I have to get ready to leave for work. But Myrna, you'd better not bring any of your boyfriends around me. I might snatch one away from you."

CHAPTER NINE

Cindy picked Darlene up and they headed for *The Gardens* mall. "Byron told me that Dexter Matthews called this morning," Darlene ventured. "What do you think he has up his sleeve?"

"Who knows what goes on in that sneaky bastard's head," Cindy shrugged, "but I'm sure it doesn't concern me personally. Of course, anything that affects Colin affects me."

They pulled up to the mall and parked. "Hey, Cin," Darlene suggested, "let's get a snack before we start walking our feet off. That little French place in the food court has the best croissants and coffee in town."

"Suits me."

In the cafeteria-style restaurant they picked up their food and headed for a table. "Look," Darlene exclaimed, "there's Fran sitting alone." Their eyes met and Fran beckoned for them to join her. She appeared to be cold sober.

"Hi, kids, what brings you to the mall?"

"Darlene and I are looking for Christmas

gifts for our dear husbands," Cindy answered. "I suppose you're shopping for something for Adrian."

Fran wrinkled her nose. "Strictly a formality." She paused. "Cindy, I saw that piece about you on TV. I'll bet that Weiss character has you and Colin sweating bullets."

Cindy hesitated. "Fran, how well do you know Dexter Matthews? I saw him with you and Adrian at the stone crab place recently. He's offered his help in shutting Weiss up."

"I don't think anyone knows Dexter very well. He doesn't say much about his past. Adrian knew him in college and they now have a business relationship."

"Did he ever make a pass at you?"

Fran raised her eyebrows. "Why Cindy, what a strange thing for you to ask!" She frowned. "No, he never did. But Adrian would probably kill him if he did."

"I didn't mean to get personal." Cindy's face flushed. "I just wondered what kind of man Colin is getting involved with." She paused, hoping there would be no hint of jealousy in her voice. "By the way, who was that stunning girl Dexter was with at the restaurant?"

Fran shrugged. "He introduced her but I'm not much good at remembering names. As near as I can remember she's the daughter of one of his friends who married a Vietnamese woman. She was visiting Palm Beach and Dexter was showing her around."

The three finished their croissants and coffee. "Want to hit the pavement with us, Fran?" Darlene offered.

"Thanks, but I have an appointment with my

hairdresser. You two go ahead."

Colin returned home that evening in good spirits. "We took care of Erwin Weiss, Cindy. He won't be bothering us any more."

"What did you do, buy him off?"

"In a sense," Colin chuckled. "Dexter had learned of a little past indiscretion on the part of our sleezy friend. We were able to convince Weiss that the revelation of this incident could cost him far more votes than he might gain from pressing the issue of the drug raid here."

"Then you blackmailed him."

Colin smiled coldly. "Blackmail is such an ugly word, my dear. I did make a small donation to his campaign fund. Seemed the decent thing to do under the circumstances. But I shall do everything in my power to see he's not elected."

"Sometimes I think I don't really know you, Colin," Cindy slowly shook her head.

He shrugged. "I'm just a simple business man, my darling. By the way, I invited Dexter here for dinner tomorrow night. I hope you haven't made any plans for the evening."

"You invited him here?" Cindy flared. "Colin, can you really trust this man?"

It was Colin's turn to express surprise. "My dear, I hope you haven't taken a dislike to Matthews. He could be useful to me. I learned long ago that in business you have to put a certain amount of trust in everyone. Then if they should ever betray that trust ..." He made a quick pass across his throat with the edge of his hand.

Dexter Matthews arrived promptly for

dinner the next evening, bearing a gift of red roses for the hostess. He handed them to Cindy. "So nice to see you again, Missus Jamison. I hope your husband didn't invite me at an inopportune time. I know I should have asked him to clear the invitation with you. It was thoughtless of me not to."

So, he wanted to make sure I would not refuse to let him come, and tell Colin everything. Well, two can play this game.

"You're very welcome, Mister Matthews. And thank you for the flowers. They're beautiful."

Colin interrupted. "Let's not be so formal. It's 'Dexter' and 'Cindy'. Come on, let's have a drink before dinner." He slapped Dexter on the back. "We really stuck it to old Erwin Weiss yesterday, didn't we?" They entered the game room.

Like everything else in the Jamison mansion, the game room reflected understated elegance. Colin led the way to a leather-covered bar. Cindy and Dexter took seats on stools and Colin began mixing drinks.

Dexter glanced around the room. "That's a handsome pool table you have, Colin. I noticed it the night I was here for the party. Do you play?"

Colin gave a desultory wave of his hand. "I play at it. Cindy is the real champ here. She shoots like a pro."

Cindy blushed, "I'm not really that good."

"I've played a little," Dexter admitted, "but either of you could probably take me."

"Come on, let's play a game of rotation and see who's conning who," Colin suggested. He racked up the balls. "Lady's break."

Cindy picked up her favorite cue stick and

75

let the cue ball fly. Suddenly she gave a little yelp of pain.

"That arm still bothering you, darling?" Colin asked solicitously. Then to Dexter "Cindy pulled a muscle playing tennis last week."

Dexter shook his head solemnly, a Dutch Uncle expression on his face. "You must never ignore muscle damage, Cindy. Hey, I've got just the thing to make that arm like new. I use it on my polo arm and I swear by it. I'm sure I have some in my car. I'll be right back." Before Cindy could demur he rushed from the room.

"Impetuous fellow, isn't he?" Colin laughed.

Dexter returned quickly. "Here, let Doctor Matthews fix you up." He squeezed some lotion from a tube and gently began massaging Cindy's arm and elbow.

"You'll get that stuff all over your jacket, Dexter," Colin warned. "Let me get you a towel." He bounded over to the bar.

Dexter put his lips close to Cindy's ear. "And you said that one drink in Vail is the only thing you and I would ever share."

CHAPTER TEN

T here's good news and there's bad news," Colin quipped when he returned home the following evening. He gave Cindy a warm hug and a peck on the cheek. "Doctor Charles received the results of the tests I took. The good news is the doctors could find nothing wrong with me; the bad news is they are puzzled as to why I have these fainting spells."

"Spells?" Cindy exclaimed in alarm. "I thought there was just that one."

"I had one I didn't tell you about. Didn't want to worry you."

"Colin, you do worry me when you keep things from me," Cindy snapped. "What do the doctors suggest?"

"They want me to go up to Gainesville to the Shands Hospital at the University of Florida for more tests."

"Shands?" Cindy's voice mirrored her concern. "That's a cancer hospital, isn't it?"

"Well, yes and no. It's a research hospital. They have the finest diagnostic facilities in the state. I'm flying up there tomorrow."

"Then I'll go with you."

"No," Colin shook his head. "You don't want to miss your mammagram appointment. We don't want some insidious disease creeping up on you. I'll be there only a few days. You can drive me to the airport, though."

A pervasive silence prevailed at dinner that night as each wrestled with inner thoughts.

"Hey, lighten up you guys," Myrna exclaimed, "you would think we were holding a wake."

"Don't even suggest such a thing," Cindy exploded.

Myrna's attitude softened. "You know I didn't mean anything, Cindy. Colin's going to be okay." She turned to Karen for reinforcement. "Colin's going to be fine, isn't he?"

"Of course he is," Karen assured them. "You have to take the optimistic view. He's going to get the best care possible."

"I'm an optimist," Myrna replied. "Hell, you have to be an optimist to marry three times."

Hilda Cayce brought in the desert. "You have a good trip to Gainesville, Mister Jamison. I want you to know I'll be saying some special prayers for you tonight."

"Why, Missus Cayce," Colin joked, "I didn't know you were a religious person."

"I don't wear my religion on my sleeve, Mister Jamison. But honest prayer never hurt anyone. I'll be praying for you tonight."

After dinner Myrna and Karen went to the game room to shoot pool. Cindy and Colin sat in the library, she trying to read, he studying a travel brochure.

"Look, Cindy, here's a trip that would be fun to take. To Machu Picchu in Peru. It says we can hike the last fifty miles from Cuzco..."

"Stop it. Stop it. Stop it," Cindy screamed. "Aren't you the least bit concerned about what they might find in Gainesville?"

Colin put down the folder and walked over to sit on a hassock by Cindy's side. He pressed her hands between his. "Whatever will be will be, my darling. If there's a major problem I want to know. First, so that I can get the best treatment available and, second, if there is something life-threatening I want to know how much time I have to get my affairs in order."

Tears came to Cindy's eyes. "I don't want to lose you, Colin. Not now. Not ever."

He lifted her from her chair. "Let's go to bed. There's still some life left in the old boy."

As they prepared to leave the next morning Myrna came downstairs unexpectedly early. "I'm going with you," she announced. "We'll take my car."

At the airport Cindy and Myrna accompanied Colin to the gate and kissed him goodbye. Then they wandered over to the large panoramic windows overlooking the field and watched as his plane pulled away from the gate and slowly taxied to the end of the runway. The plane turned, paused as if to gather strength, then roared down the concrete strip and soared into the sky. They watched it become a tiny speck and then disappear.

"There's something sad about seeing a plane take off," Cindy observed. "It must be the same feeling wives of ancient mariners had as they watched sails sink below the horizon."

"Colin is going to be okay," Myrna said with uncharacteristic tenderness. "Come on, let's go home."

They were nearly to the Jamison estate when flashing blue lights approached behind them. "Oh crap, what now," Myrna fumed as she pulled to the side of the road.

A police car stopped behind them and an officer got out and walked up to Myrna's side. "May I see your drivers' license, ma'am?"

"Why, Sergeant Ames," she smiled sweetly as she handed it to him, "how nice to see you again."

The policeman showed no sign of recognition as he glanced at the license. "Missus Bell..."

"That's ex-Missus Bell," Myrna broke in coyly.

"... do you realize you were doing fifty in a thirty-five-mile zone?"

"Oh, come on, officer, nobody holds it down to thirty-five along here. Cars were passing me."

"That's probably true," he agreed, "but I didn't catch them. I did catch you. I'll have to issue you a citation."

Myrna's eyes danced. "Maybe now is the time to offer you that bribe."

A slight smile touched his lips. "I'd still have to issue you a citation, ma'am." He ripped the ticket from his pad and handed it to her. "You may pay the fine by mail or, if you wish to contest it you must appear in court at the time indicated." He looked over at Cindy who had remained silent. "I'm glad things turned out the way they did in court, Missus Jamison. I never did feel that boy is bad."

He started back to his cruiser, then stopped and called over his shoulder, "Missus Bell, I would like very much to take you to dinner sometime."

Myna burst into laughter, then suddenly stopped short. To her own amazement she called back. "Tomorrow at eight. And please don't drive a police car."

Cindy was still up when Myrna returned from her date with Bob Ames. Myrna gushed like a school girl with her first crush. "I had a wonderful time. Bob is forty-five years old. His wife died last year. He has two grown daughters, both married..."

"Whoa," Cindy broke in, "You really found out a lot about him for a first date. Men usually want to spring things like that later."

"We talked, Cindy. Can you believe it? I spent a whole evening with a man and all we did

81

was talk. He didn't lay a finger on me." She let out a little giggle. "Want to hear something cute? He wants to pay my speeding ticket fine. Said he stopped me deliberately because he wanted to get to know me."

"That's harassment!" Cindy exclaimed.

"Yeah," Myrna grinned, "but wasn't that sweet of him? We're going out again tomorrow night." She danced off to her room humming the wedding march from *Lohengrin.*

CHAPTER ELEVEN

Colin returned from Gainesville on Christmas Eve, in good spirits but looking tired and pale. His stay there had been longer than expected. He hugged Cindy tightly when she met him at the airport. "There's not much I can tell you that I didn't tell you on the telephone, darling. They put me through all kinds of tests and finally found a very small tumor deep inside my brain. It's in an inoperable position but the doctors think it can be dissolved with radiation therapy right here in Palm Beach."

"I'm glad you weren't stuck in the hospital for Christmas," Cindy replied as, arm-in-arm, they walked down the airport concourse. "I want you where I can look after you and care for you. I talked with Peter. Everything's going smoothly at the office. I told you about Myrna's dates with Bob Ames. She's acting like a school girl with her first crush. He seems to be a fine person; I hope she doesn't blow it."

"The place look great," Colin enthused as they drove through the gate and up to the house. "We never had the grounds decorated so beautifully before."

"Wait 'til you see them lighted. Everybody pitched in. Ben, Dicey and Raymond did the outside while Myrna, Karen, Missus Cayce and I did the inside. We never had so many willing hands before. In the past Missus Cayce shied away from decorating chores but she insisted on trimming the tree. It's gorgeous. I never knew she was so talented. You think you know someone and suddenly you find you don't. It may be my imagination, Colin, but after all these years she appears to getting less formal."

Cindy drove into the garage, got out of the car and went around to help Colin out. She took his arm as if to lead him into the house but he pulled away gently. "Cindy, I'm not a tottering old invalid.

I can manage very well on my own."

Around the dinner table that evening the conversation turned to the situation in the Arabian Gulf. Colin pursed his lips. "Sanctions are not working. Saddam Hussein will not get out of Kuwait until we drive him out. I predict that when the January fifteenth ultimatum expires a shooting war will start." He paused. "I suppose Dexter Matthews will be in the thick of it."

Cindy looked up quickly. "Dexter is in the Gulf?"

"He will be. He's in command of an army reserve finance unit that has been called to active duty. But I wouldn't worry too much about Dexter Matthews. He's a very resourceful fellow. I'll bet he'll be making business connections left and right. He already has some good information sources in the Gulf region. In fact, he tipped me that Iraq would invade Kuwait. On the strength of his tip I unloaded some investments I had in Iraqi securities. Lucky for me I did; they would be frozen now."

"Do you suppose the information came from Adrian?" Cindy asked. "Fran told me that Dexter and Adrian have a business relationship."

Colin stroked his chin reflectively. "I never thought of that. You could be right. Adrian seems to be involved in all kinds of cloak-and-dagger operations."

"Why do men always want to fight?" Myrna sniffed. "Bob says if a shooting war starts he wants to go. He was in the Military Police in Vietnam. I told him he's too old to go back in and that just made him angry. I swear, I don't think I'll ever understand men."

84

"Well," Karen observed, "ComRisk surely doesn't want to see a war start. We underwrite liability policies for many firms doing business in the Middle East. Of course, there are the usual 'war and civil strife' clauses in the policies but we could still be hit with some heavy claims."

"Come on," Cindy interrupted, "this is the season dedicated to the Prince of Peace. Let's forget about war and go open our presents."

That night Colin held Cindy close. "I never want to leave you, darling." He tapped his head lightly. "I'm going to beat this thing."

She snuggled her head against his shoulder. "Of course you are. We have a lot of years left together." But deep inside she felt a grim chill of foreboding.

New Year's Eve parties at the Jamison estate normally saw the gathering of the cream of Palm Beach society, but this year, in deference to Colin's illness, Cindy invited only a few close friends. Darlene and Byron were the first to arrive. "How is Colin doing, Cindy?" Darlene asked anxiously.

"Pretty well, everything considered. He's started radiation and chemo therapy and that's making him a little edgy and sometimes nauseous. We're lucky the doctors found the tumor early. Come on in. Fran and Adrian are coming. Also Bob Ames and Peter Simmons. Karen is here and, of course, Myrna. I didn't want to tire Colin with a big shindig. We didn't even call in caterers. Dicey and Hilda are taking care of everything"

85

Bob and Peter came in as she spoke. "You boys join Colin in the rec room and fix some drinks and play some pool," Cindy urged, "we girls want privacy for girl talk."

When Dicey opened the door for Fran and Adrian, Cindy stifled a gasp. "My God, Fran, what happened to you?" Carefully applied makeup could not hide an ugly bruise on Fran's face.

"I ran into a door." Fran's voice dripped sarcasm.

"Well, you certainly did job on your face," Cindy winced. She turned to Adrian. "The men are in the rec room."

He shot Fran a warning glance and reluctantly left to join the others. Cindy waited until he left and then placed an arm around Fran's shoulder. "I can pretty well guess what happened to your face but I won't press for details."

Fran gave a wan smile of appreciation. "It's best we leave it at that."

As the final minutes of the old year ticked away, the group gathered in the dining room where champagne glasses sat on the table. Ben Brown suddenly appeared bearing a huge bouquet of red roses.

"Oh, how thoughtful of you, Colin," Cindy exclaimed. They're gorgeous."

Colin frowned. "I didn't order them. Where did you get these, Ben?"

"A man brought them to the front gate. He say to give them to the lady."

Cindy spotted a small white envelope among the blossoms. She picked it up. "It's not addressed," she murmured. "Probably delivered here by mistake." The card she removed from the envelope almost slipped through her nervous fingers. "It's blank!" Quickly palming the card she handed the flowers back to Ben. "See if you can catch the delivery man. There's evidently been a mistake."

"He long gone, Miz Cindy."

"Well, have Dicey put them in some water. I'm sure he'll be back as soon as he discovers his error."

Outwardly Cindy remained icy cool, but her heart raced madly. Indelibly etched on her brain were the words on the crumpled card in her hand– *"We'll see"*.

CHAPTER TWELVE

As the days of the new year flew past, Colin's condition took a roller coaster ride, sometimes up, sometimes down. But to Cindy's alarm, the down days became more frequent. Refusing to be admitted to a hospital, he took radiation and chemotherapy treatments as an outpatient. What hair remained, after his head was shaved in the area of X-ray penetration, gradually fell out. "If I'm going to die, I want it to be right here," he told Cindy. "Hospitals are so dehumanizing."

She drove him to his therapy sessions and waited patiently until the procedures ended. But as she sat in the waiting room her mind was far from being at ease. In sudden attacks of panic, she wondered what her life would be like if Colin died. My life is so secure, so comfortable, she told herself. What kind of life would I have without Colin? And with a rush of guilt for even letting such thoughts enter her mind, she wondered if there would be a place for Dexter Matthews in her future.

Often in the afternoons Peter Simmons came from the office, and he and Colin would discuss business matters. Occasionally Byron North joined them. This afforded Cindy an opportunity to get away from the house for brief respites, sometimes taking long drives alone but more often going to a mall with Darlene.

One afternoon Fran was with Darlene when Darlene came to pick Cindy up. "I think I owe you an explanation of what happened New Year's Eve," she said as Cindy got in the car. "If one of my friends got beat up I would want to know the details."

Cindy protested. "You don't have to tell anything you don't want to. If this has anything to do with Adrian it might be best if you keep it to yourself."

"It has everything to do with Adrian. He put that bruise on my face."

"How did it happen?" Darlene asked gently.

"I picked up the phone in the library at the same time Adrian picked it up in his den. Dexter Matthews was calling from Saudi Arabia. He asked about Colin, Cindy, and then lashed out at Adrian for not doing enough for some employees. I heard Dexter say 'You wouldn't let me pull McHugh and his men out of Kuwait before the invasion, and now they're prisoners in Iraq. If any of them is killed or wounded by our bombs it will be on your head'. I started to hang up but I dropped the receiver. Adrian heard it fall and came charging into the room, raging mad. 'Women have no business snooping into men's affairs' he screamed at me. Then he struck me. Adrian still lives by the male chauvinist code of his ancestors."

"Why don't you get away from him for awhile?" Cindy suggested. "Go some place where you can think out your future with him."

Fran shook her head. "He would find me and kill me." She paused. "One of these days he's going to push me too far and I'm going to kill him"

"You don't really mean that," Cindy reproached her. "But tell me, what is his relationship with Dexter?"

"They have joint businesses. I've met the man Dexter was talking about, Kevin McHugh. He's an engineer with one of Adrian's companies.

Sometimes I feel Dexter would like to get out of his relationship with Adrian but is afraid. I think Adrian has something on Dexter."

That evening Colin took a turn for the worse. Frantically Cindy called in Doctor Charles. After the doctor examined Colin he took Cindy aside. "I must be very blunt, Cindy, Colin is a very ill man. Despite all we have been able to do for him the cancer is spreading."

"Does Colin know this?"

The doctor paused for a long moment before answering. "He has known for several weeks. Cindy, if he has not told you I may be betraying a confidence but I think you should know. The prognosis is not at all good. Determining how long a patient will live is not an exact science. Colin may live for days, even weeks. You must face the harsh probability that Colin will not survive this illness. I've given him a mild sedative to make him rest easier. I'll be at home all evening if you should need me, and I'll stop by in the morning on my way to the office."

"Is he in any pain?"

"No. The brain doesn't feel any pain from a tumor inside it. You can rest assured he's not suffering any physical pain."

After the doctor left Cindy went and sat on the edge of Colin's bed. He smiled weakly. "I'm not going to make it, Cindy."

"Oh, Colin, of course..."

He stopped her. "I've always been a realist, darling, and I'm not going to kid myself now. I don't have much time left. My only regret is leaving you."

"Please, Colin..." Cindy sobbed.

"You're going to be all right, my darling. You remember the living trust we set up a few years back? We put the house and some other assets into it at that time. Now everything we own is in the trust and you are the trustee. I have left a simple will to protect against anyone claiming to be a distant relative from claiming any part of my estate, which actually will have no assets left in it.. Byron will explain everything to you. Peter will stay on at the office as long as you need him." He paused, gasping a little. "I gave him a generous bonus. Byron will take care of all legal matters."

"Please, Colin, we can discuss these things later. Right now you need your rest."

"We have to talk now," he whispered. "I gave Byron a list of things I want you to do. Some money for Ben and Dicey and Missus Cayce. I have set up a trust fund to take care of my promise to Raymond. Myrna and I discussed this eventuality a long time ago and agreed that she needs nothing from me. She's wealthy in her own right."

Colin's voice grew weaker. Cindy held his hand and leaned closed. A faint smile flitted across his face. "I once promised that some day you would be a very rich young woman. Colin Jamison keeps his promises." He paused, gasping to catch his breath. "All kinds of people will try to take advantage of you, Cindy. Be careful of any relationships you enter into, business or personal. Darling, I love you." He closed his eyes. His breath came in soft wheezes, then stopped. The hand Cindy held went limp. Quickly she felt for a pulse. There was none.

For a long time she sat holding his limp hand and blinking back tears. Then she stood up, resolutely squared her shoulders, and marched down the stairs to the den where Myrna and Karen sat.

"He's gone," she announced simply.

CHAPTER THIRTEEN

In the aftermath of Colin's death a strange transformation took place in the Jamison household, as if the passing of the old guard heralded the beginning of a new era. Hilda Cayce became a mother hen, taking Cindy in her arms and calling her by her first name. Hesitantly at first, Cindy began calling Missus Cayce 'Hilda'.

"Don't you concern yourself in the least in getting the house ready for friends who will be stopping by after the services. Dicey and I will take care of everything." And taking care of everything they did, efficiently calling in the caterers, ordering flowers, and handling a myriad of other details.

Colin had left explicit instructions with Byron. "A short viewing at the funeral chapel, and then a simple graveside service. I don't want to put Cindy through any more trauma than absolutely necessary. Get it over with as quickly as possible."

On the evening before the burial Cindy, a serenely beautiful Madonna in black, never lost composure as she accepted words of condolence from their many friends and Colin's business associates. Darlene and Byron stood by her side throughout. But after all the mourners had departed she collapsed in a limp heap. Darlene and Byron took her home. Myrna gave her a sedative and gently tucked her into bed.

Sometime in the small hours of the morning

Cindy awoke with a scream. Myrna and Karen rushed into her room. "What's the matter, Cindy?" Myrna gasped. "Are you all right?"

Cindy sat bolt upright, clutching a pillow tightly and sobbing uncontrollably. "I had a nightmare." She released the pillow and buried her face in her hands. "It was horrible."

"You're all right now," Myrna soothed her. "Now try to get back to sleep."

As if in a trance, Cindy moaned. "Bombs were falling all around. One fell in our yard and made a big crater. Some men came and lowered Colin's coffin into it."

"You've been watching too much TV about the Gulf war," Karen tried to comfort her. "No bombs are falling here. Try to get some sleep."

The morning of Colin's funeral dawned clear and bright. Spring in south Florida differs little from winter, summer or fall. So subtle are the changes of season they often pass unnoticed. But to Cindy there seemed to be an ethereal beauty to this cool morning as she stood, eyes closed, the ever-faithful Darlene and Byron beside her, hearing the traditional reading of the Twenty-third Psalm. *The Lord is my shepherd, I shall not want...* Colin was like a shepherd, Cindy thought, almost a father figure. And because of him she would never want. *He leadeth me beside still waters...* The ocean waters behind their estate were seldom still, but a calm tranquility defined her life with Colin, a placid pool of contentment.

As Colin had wished, the service was short, but to Cindy it seemed to go on forever. At last she stood alone, head bowed, after the others returned to their cars. She was unaware Dexter Matthews had joined her until she felt a light touch on her elbow and heard his voice.

"I came as soon as I heard, Cindy. I'm sorry about Colin. He and I were getting to be good friends."

She shot him a scornful glare. "You were trying to build a friendship with Colin while making passes at his wife. How noble!"

"I made a mistake. I mean coming on to you like I did. I know it now."

"What are you doing here anyway?" she demanded. "I thought you were in Saudi Arabia."

"I was able to get an emergency leave. The shooting war is over but there's still a big mess to clean up over there. Finance units like mine will be the last to leave." He took Cindy's elbow. "I'll drive you home."

She pulled away. "Darlene and Byron are waiting in the limo."

"We have to talk, Cindy."

"Not now, Dexter." She turned and ran, leaving him standing beside Colin's grave.

After the assembly had departed, and cemetery workers had lowered the coffin into the grave and covered it with dirt, a slight, silent figure in black walked slowly over and placed a single white rose on the grave. "Goodbye, Uncle Colin," a soft voice whispered. A sob escaped the girl's lips "Goodbye–Father."

From a short distance away a photographer, a gleeful smile on his face and a telephoto lens on his camera, rapidly snapped away. The next morning one of his pictures would appear on the front page of the *Inside Revealer* under the headline WHO WAS MYSTERY WOMAN AT FINANCIER'S FUNERAL?

The insistent ringing of her telephone dragged Cindy from the deep sleep of exhaustion. She rubbed her eyes and then opened them to the late morning sunlight streaming through her window. Still not fully awake, she reached for the intruding instrument. "Hello."

"Cindy," Karen Knowles' excited voice spoke. "I saw a copy of the Inside Revealer on a newsstand on my way to the office. There's a picture of a woman at Colin's grave. Cindy, it's the same girl we saw with Fran, Adrian and Dexter at the restaurant!"

"Oh my God." Cindy was wide awake now. "What does the story say?"

"I just glanced at it. They call her a 'mystery woman' who arrived late, and suggest Colin might have been having an affair with her."

"That's typical of what that rag prints," Cindy groaned. "Thank's for calling." She hung up.

"Damn that paper," Cindy cursed aloud. She dressed quickly and went downstairs. She did not mention Karen's call when Hilda brought breakfast, but had taken only a few bites before being interrupted by a repeated ringing of the front gate bell. On the intercom she heard Ben open the gate, and then the sound of a car roaring through the opening. A few minutes later Dexter burst into the room.

"We have to talk, Cindy. I have to go back

to the Gulf but I can't leave until we talk."

Be careful of any relationships you enter into... Cindy remembered Colin's dying words. "I don't know of anything we have to talk about, Dexter."

"Dammit, Cindy," he exploded, "can't you see I'm in love with you?" His voice dropped to a pleading whisper. "I know I made an ass of myself coming on to you at the party, following you to Vail and sending roses New Year's Eve. Please take a ride with me and let me try to explain why I acted the way I did."

He might be able to shed some light on the 'mystery woman', Cindy thought furiously. It can't hurt to hear what he has to say. "All right," she agreed, despite a disapproving frown from Hilda. She gently touched the older woman's arm. "I know it seems callous to be seen with another man so soon after Colin's death but Dexter has to return to Saudi Arabia and insists we talk."

Dexter opened the car door for her and helped her in. God, he's handsome, she thought. And that fragrance he's wearing... her heart skipped a beat... *Polo!* The same one he wore that night in Vail.

"Thank's for hearing me out, Cindy." His voice was that of a repentant schoolboy. "I know of a quiet little place near the beach where we can talk."

They drove down Highway A1A and turned into a rutted lane leading to a grove of palm trees. Dexter stopped the car and took Cindy's hands into his.

"Cindy, back in high school I wanted you

97

more than anything in the world, but you were completely out of reach. You were the beauty queen, the most popular girl in the class. I was a shy, gawky guy from the wrong side of the tracks." He managed a weak smile. "But as the old song goes, that was 'long ago and far away', but I could never forget you."

"You still didn't have to act like a complete cad when we met again."

He shook his head slowly. "I can't tell you everything yet, but I can tell you that I went to the party at your place that night with the full intention of making a pass at the wife of the host." He added quickly, "Not that I meant it to go beyond a mild flirtation. You can't imagine the shock when I discovered you were that person. I really wanted to back off then, but I had to continue the game."

"Game?"

"I can't tell you any more now. Please believe me, I wish I could. I was coerced into acting the way I did."

Cindy looked at him sharply. "Does Adrian Pahlavi have something on you? Fran said she thinks he has."

Dexter looked down at the floorboards. "Cindy, I did something in the past I'm not proud of. When the time is right I want you to know everything."

Her face remained impassive. "You say you love me but I saw you recently at the stone crab restaurant with a beautiful girl. Were you playing the game with her, too?"

He released her hands. "Dammit, Cindy," he flared, "since you came back into my life I've thought of no woman but you. As for the girl you saw me with, I showed her around town that one day because Colin asked me to. She's the daughter of one of his Vietnam buddies. Her name is Koo Lin Douglas. She went home to Virginia the next day."

Cindy paled. *Koo Lin–Colin! Impossible! I'm imagining things!* "She was at Colin's funeral, Dexter. The Inside Revealer calls her a 'mystery woman'. Are you keeping something from me?"

Exasperation edged Dexter's voice. "I swear I've told you all I know about her. We didn't come here to talk about her; I want to talk about us."

"I don't feel very well, Dexter. Please take me home."

Gently he put his arms around her. "I never stopped wanting you. I love you more now than I did so long ago in high school." His lips swept over her face, touching her ears, her nose, her chin, seeking her lips.

"No, Dexter, no!" She struggled half-heartedly to free herself as a wild wave of ecstasy engulfed her. His hands caressed her neck and shoulders, then drifted downward. She felt a finger brush her breasts. *Beware of any relationships...* Abruptly she pulled away. "Take me home, Dexter. Now!"

He started the car and slowly backed out of the palm grove. "Well," he smiled ruefully, "I guess I blew it again."

When they pulled up to Cindy's front door she jumped out and dashed into the house. Myrna met her in the entrance hall. "What the hell happened to you?" she gasped, "your makeup is all smudged. And for God's sake, button your blouse."

Cindy brushed past her and ran up the stairs. In her bedroom she picked up the telephone and called Byron North. "Byron, you have a private investigator on retainer, don't you? I want him to find a girl named Koo Lin Douglas. All I can tell you about her is she's from Virginia. She may still be in the Palm Beach area. Have the PI check the airlines and the hotels."

"Is she the 'mystery woman' in the scandal sheet photos, Cindy?"

"Yes. Please find her. Weird as it might seem, I have the feeling she might be Colin's daughter."

"U-m-m, bad news from a legal standpoint if she is. Really bad news."

"Never mind that. Do everything you can to find her."

Byron's call the next morning was blunt and to the point. "We found the girl, Cindy. She's at the Breakers Hotel, Room Seven twenty-three. The desk clerk says she hasn't been out of the room since that picture appeared in the paper." He paused. "Are you sure you want to meet this girl?"

"Yes, I have to talk to her."

"Then I'll go with you."

"No, Byron, I have to see her alone."

"Well, be careful what you say to her. We don't know that she is in any way related to Colin. She could be an adventuress trying to claim a part of his estate. As your attorney I really should go with you."

"I'll be careful. I promise. But if she is related to Colin I have to know."

Cindy hung up the telephone and hurried

100

from the room. She met Myrna on the stairs. "You look upset, Cindy, is anything wrong?" Myrna asked.

"No, Myrna," irritation edged Cindy's voice, "I'm all right. I have to run into town for a couple of hours to take care of some business." Myrna need not know of my suspicions just yet, she thought.

As she sped down the highway a cyclone of thoughts whirled within Cindy's head. *Is it possible this girl is Colin's daughter? He was in Vietnam during the war there. What can I say to this girl?*

Her head was still reeling when she reached the hotel. She left her car with a parking valet and took an elevator to the seventh floor where she got off and walked slowly to the room Byron had said the girl occupied. For a long moment she stared at the door before tapping lightly on it. "Koo Lin, this is Cindy Jamison. May I talk with you?"

No sound came from the room.

"Please, Koo Lin, if you're in there, you and I must talk."

The door opened a tiny crack and one dark eye peered out. "Oh, you're Colin Jamison's widow. I saw you at the funeral."

"May I come in?"

The door swung wide and the girl stepped aside. "How do you know my name? How did you find me? And why?"

Cindy entered the room. "Dexter Matthews gave me your name. I saw you with him at a restaurant. Later, when I teased him about having such a young girlfriend he told me that Colin asked him to show you around town. When that picture appeared in the paper I jumped to some wild conclusions as to your relationship to my husband."

The girl shuddered. "Oh, that horrid story..." She paused, embarrassed. "But I'm forgetting my manners. Please sit down, Missus Jamison. I'll have Room Service send up some coffee. Would you like something with it?"

"It's 'Cindy', Koo Lin. I could use some breakfast. I didn't take time to eat this morning after a private investigator I hired told me you are here. I was afraid you would leave before I could talk with you. I have so many questions to ask."

Koo Lin smiled weakly. "I've eaten nothing today, either. That story upset me so." She picked up the telephone and ordered breakfast.

The two women sat and appraised each other nervously. Koo Lin was the first to break the awkward silence. "I suppose you want to know who I am and why I was at Colin Jamison's funeral." She paused. "Colin Jamison was my natural father."

"I had no idea he had a daughter."

"No, I don't suppose you did. Until three months ago I didn't know, either. To me he was just a friend of my dad, a man I called 'Uncle Colin'. Walter Douglas raised me as his child, and until my mother told me just before she died, I never suspected he was not my father."

"How traumatic it must have been, losing your mother and, so soon after, the man you had just learned was your father," Cindy sympathized.

"I lost three who were dear to me. My dad died in an automobile accident in which my mother received injuries that led to her death. Before she died she told me all the things she had kept from

102

me all my life."

"Do you want to tell me about it?"

Koo Lin nodded.

The Room Service waiter arrived, wheeled his cart in, accepted his tip and departed. Cindy and Koo Lin spread their plates on a coffee table and began eating.

"I didn't realize I was so hungry," Cindy smiled.

Koo Lin chewed and swallowed a few bites before speaking. "Colin Jamison was an American army officer in Vietnam. He and my mother met and fell in love. She became pregnant. He had a wife back home so he couldn't marry my mother. Walter Douglas was a fellow officer who also was very fond of my mother. He married her and brought her to America where I was born. He knew I was not his, but no girl ever had a better father than he was to me.

"As I grew up, Colin visited us many times. I called him 'Uncle Colin'. To me he was just a good friend of my parents. He brought me nice gifts. He used to tease me about my name sounding like his. He often said he wished he had a little girl like me." She paused. "I really did love him."

"Then your mother finally told you the truth?"

Koo Lin nodded. "In the accident that killed my dad, Mother suffered severe internal injuries. The medics rushed her to the hospital where she lived nearly a week. She seemed to be on the road to recovery but took a turn for the worse and died. During those days at the hospital her mind was clear and she had the strength to talk at great length."

Cindy touched the girl's hand. "If you would rather not talk about it..."

"I want to tell you about it because I know you loved my father. And he told me how much he loved you."

"You talked to Colin about me?"

"Yes. Mother telephoned him from the hospital and told him I knew everything. After Mother died I came down here. Colin and I had dinner together several times. He agonized over whether he should tell you about me, but felt you might not understand and would be deeply hurt that he had kept something so important from you."

So that is why Colin 'worked late' so many times! "Oh, Koo Lin, I would have understood." She hesitated. "That is when you met Dexter Matthews?"

"Yes, my father– it seems so strange calling him 'Father'-- introduced me to Dexter. Said Dexter would be a 'good catch'. I found him to be charming but a little too old for me. He was very nice to me but showed no romantic interest at all."

"Did you ever meet Colin's first wife?" Cindy asked, "the one he went home to after leaving your mother in Vietnam?"

"Yes. She came with him one time when he visited my parents. She seemed to be a sweet person but definitely the clinging-vine type. Completely dependant on him. I can believe how difficult the decision was for him to leave my mother and go back to her. But then, that does say something about his character. I'm pretty sure he never told her the truth about me. It's somewhat ironic that the one he left my mother for was largely responsible for my having a secure financial future."

"What do you mean?"

"As I grew up I always had a good allowance, and there was plenty of money for my education. I want to be a medical doctor. I had been led to believe the money came from a fund set up by my Vietnamese grandfather. Grandfather held a high office in the government before the fall of Saigon. Mother, at the end, told me the money came from a trust set up by my natural father, Colin Jamison, at the time of my birth. He was not a rich man then but his wife came from a very wealthy family. The big estate on the ocean had belonged to her family. He made a lot of money in later years but it was his wife's inheritance that gave him his start.

"Anyway, through the years he added to my trust fund. Cindy, I was astounded to learn after Mother died that there's more than a million dollars in that fund." She lowered her eyes. "I also have a substantial inheritance coming from my parents' estate and I expect a very big settlement from the accident that killed my parents. A truck belonging to a large construction company went through a red light and crashed into their car. You need not worry that I will attempt to get anything from the Jamison estate."

Cindy stood up. "Get your things together. You're going home with me."

"I'd like that very much, Cindy, but I have to get back to school. I've missed too many classes already. After I get my medical degree I want to go to Vietnam and set up a charity clinic for my mother's people. Mother taught me the language as I grew up so I should have no trouble fitting in. My bags are all packed and I have a reservation on a flight leaving at noon. Before that horrid story appeared I had planned to just slip away and have no one here ever know of my existence."

Cindy threw her arms around the girl. "You're a most remarkable person, Koo Lin."

"I had most remarkable parents," Koo Lin tried to hold back tears, "All three of them."

Cindy hugged her tightly before releasing her. "You'll have to visit me whenever you have time off from school. Christmas. Spring break. Summer vacation."

"Oh, I'd love that, Cindy. I want us to be good friends."

Cindy glanced at her watch. "You don't want to miss that flight. Come on, I'll drive you to the airport."

"You won't have to worry about money when you open your clinic," Cindy promised as she left Koo Lin at the boarding gate. "I'll make a substantial contribution and I have wealthy friends whose arms I can twist."

Why must all the men in my life have to be so secretive about their pasts? Cindy pondered as she drove home. First Dexter and now Colin. I knew Colin for ten years and now I find I didn't know him at all. And what dark secret from his past is Dexter keeping from me?

CHAPTER FOURTEEN

A calm normalcy settled on the Jamison household after Colin's death. Raymond Brown's rowdy friends, those not in the County Stockade or Youthful Offenders Boot Camp, no longer came around, influenced no doubt by Ben Brown's threat to "fill their tails with buckshot if they come within shooting distance."

Shortly after Colin's funeral Myrna had come to Cindy. "I know I haven't been the ideal houseguest, Cindy. I suppose you'll want me to leave,"

Karen standing nearby added. "I've taken advantage of your hospitality too long, too."

Cindy had embraced the two. "It's going to be lonely around here with Colin gone. I want both of you to stay as long as you will."

No further word came from Dexter, and with a dull ache in her heart, Cindy wondered if she had been wrong in not giving him some encouragement. From Fran she learned that after a long and acrimonious session with Adrian, Dexter had returned to the Gulf.

Myrna returned from an afternoon date and stormed into the house. "I could kill that Bob Ames. Would you believe it? He wouldn't go to bed with me. Says he wouldn't respect me as much after we are married if we had sex first. He wants to marry me! Can you believe that? I guess he thinks that because I live in an oceanfront mansion in Stardust Shores I'm rich." She paused. "Actually I am rich but I bet he doesn't have two coins to rub against each other."

Dicey Brown, dusting furniture in the room spoke up. "That Sergeant Ames ain't poor, Miz Myrna. Don't you 'member? A couple years back he win the big lottery. He say he like bein' a p'liceman and all that money not gonna change him."

Myrna's knuckles flew to her temples. "Oh, this is terrible. Now he'll think I'd be marrying him for his money." She dashed for the stairs leading to her room. "Why must men be so dammed difficult?"

A few weeks later Karen was preparing to leave her office at the end of a busy day when a red-haired, freckled-face young man with a boyish grin set his attache case on her desk.

"Oh, no." she cried, "not you here again Mister McHugh! I've told you repeatedly there's nothing I can do about your claim against Ad Astra Electronics. You'll have to wait for the outcome of your legal action against them."

"Karen–may I call you 'Karen? And please call me 'Kevin– this thing is driving me nuts. You can't imagine what I went through as a 'guest' of Saddam Hussein. The bigwigs at Ad Astra knew the situation in Kuwait was unstable when they sent me and my crew out there on a job. They could have gotten us out before the invasion and they didn't. I went through hell." He paused. "Somebody has to listen to my story. You seem to have a sympathetic ear. Will you have dinner with me and then go some place where we can talk?"

Karen hesitated and then made a snap decision. "All right, for the price of a good meal you can cry on my shoulder. But I can still do nothing about your claim. Let me make a phone call." She tapped in Cindy's number. "Hi, Cindy. I won't be home until late. I'm having dinner with Kevin McHugh. Yes, the engineer who is suing Dexter's company. Crazy, isn't it? If I'm not home by dawn send out the bloodhounds." She hung up. "Okay, Kevin, let's go."

From her desk in the corner, a puzzled frown on her forehead, Anita Barnes watched them leave.

After midnight Karen returned to the

Jamison estate and quietly crept up the stairs.
Seeing a crack of light under Cindy's bedroom door
she approached it and rapped lightly. "You awake,
Cindy?"

"Yes, come on in."

Karen entered, closed the door and pressed
her back against it. "Cindy, I went to bed with
Kevin McHugh tonight."

Cindy looked up in surprise. "And?"

A nervous laugh escaped Karen's lips. "You
can tell Fran her theory is all wrong. It was a
disaster." She paused. "Anita Barnes has been
suggesting I move in with her. After tonight's
experience I've made up my mind. I'll be leaving
here tomorrow."

Cindy rushed over and took the trembling
girl into her arms. "Are you sure this is what you
want? You know you're welcome to stay here."

"You've been wonderful to me, Cindy.
Colin, too, when he was alive. I don't know how I
can ever repay you but I have to get on with my life.
Anita is a really nice person and I think we can get
along well together." A faint smile flitted across
her face. "As Fran said, you can't be sure until you
try something, can you?"

She started to leave for her room. "Oh, by
the way, Cindy, I learned something that might
interest you. Dexter Matthews is the president of
Ad Astra Electronics, which I already knew, but
Kevin says he's only a figurehead. The real power
there is the man who owns most of the stock in the
company–Adrian Pahlavi."

CHAPTER FIFTEEN

Cindy's return to the office was an emotional step back in time. Peter Simmons jumped up from his desk in the outer office–Cindy's desk before her marriage to Colin–and greeted her warmly. "Welcome home, Cindy. Colin's office is all ready for you. Things have been running so smoothly around here you won't have much to do except to keep watch on Colin's..." he hesitated, embarrassed, "...I mean, your investments."

She put her arms around him and squeezed. "Dear, loyal Peter! I knew the office was in good hands. But, you know, in all the turmoil of the past few weeks I never gave a thought to your pay."

Peter grinned. "Colin paid me a year's salary in advance. That's the way he was. When he felt the end was coming he tied everything up in a neat little package. You won't find any lingering problems to be solved." He took her arm and guided her into the spacious, plush, inner office. "Colin was very good to me. Before he died he gave me a generous amount of stock in the new joint venture with Dexter Matthews and Adrian Pahlavi."

Cindy's eyes narrowed. "Joint venture? What kind of joint venture? No one ever told me."

Peter lowered his head. "I didn't know Colin didn't tell you. When we first set it up he told me he sensed you didn't like Dexter or Adrian and so as not to upset you we should keep it mum."

"Well," Cindy shrugged, "what's done is done. What kind of operation is it?"

A smile lighted Peter's face. "It's an international trading firm. We bought an old cargo ship, the Vamar Prince, and immediately got a juicy contract hauling military supplies to Saudi Arabia. Caveat Investments, that's the name of the company, started showing a good profit right from the start. Now we're applying for an export license to ship high-tech electronic components to Israel. That's where the big money is, trading in that sort of thing. Adrian has the connections to get what is in demand overseas. Getting export licenses is the tough part."

Cindy sat down behind Colin's massive desk–her desk now. Peter went back to his. So, she mused, the enigmatic Dexter Matthews is now my business associate. She called to Peter. "What is our share in Caveat Investments?"

Peter came back into the office. "Colin put up ten percent. Another ten percent is in Dexter's name, and Adrian owns twenty percent. The remaining sixty percent belongs to numerous small investors Dexter brought in." He paused. "I'm one of the small investors. I own about two percent of the company."

"I'll bet there are a lot of wealthy widows in the group Dexter recruited," Cindy scoffed. "You say ten percent is in Dexter's name. Doesn't he own those shares?"

Peter frowned. "You know, Cindy, there's something strange about the relationship between Dexter and Adrian. I know for a fact Adrian put up the money for Dexter's stock and he insisted Dexter be named president. Adrian is running Caveat Investments from his office while Dexter is away. All we get here are progress reports." He turned to leave. "You are right, most of the other investors are women."

Convinced all was well, Cindy left the office early and went home. She picked up the telephone and called Darlene. "Hi, chum, I just got home from the office. We high-pressure business

113

types need to unwind sometimes so I feel like doing something really wild. Let's put on our most daring bikinis and go down to the public beach and ogle the hunks."

"Y-e-a-h," Darlene laughed, "and be ogled. You want to pick me up?"

The two sauntered along the beach, eliciting catcalls from a group of young men playing beach volleyball. "We've still got it, kid," Darlene giggled. "But all those guys look so immature. I'll stick with my good, solid man." She hesitated. "Cindy, do you think you and Dexter will ever get together?"

A long moment passed before Cindy answered. "I don't know. I'll admit I'm attracted to him but there's so little I know about him. We'll see." She let out a little laugh. "That's what he's always saying to me, 'We'll see'. But he says it in such an arrogant, self-assured way."

They finished their walk and returned to Cindy's car. "Let's pick up 'slushies' at the convenience store," Darlene suggested.

"Suits me. There's nothing like a 'slushie' to cool you off. When I was a little girl every time my parents took me for a drive I would insist we stop for one. Funny, I haven't thought about my parents in a long time. They died at relatively young ages. But I remember my mother as being a very sage person. If she were here I wonder how she would advise me about Dexter."

"I think she would say 'follow your heart'. That's what I would say."

With giant cups of half-frozen soft drinks in their hands, they headed up A1A. "Look," Cindy suddenly exclaimed, "there's the lane where Dexter put the move on me." Impulsively she spun the steering wheel and headed toward the ocean. Before they reached the seaside palm grove they spotted a red convertible sitting among the trees.

"That looks like Dexter's car," Cindy's brow furrowed. "It can't be him; he's still in Saudi Arabia. But how many red Ferraris can there be?"

"Uh, oh," Darlene murmured as two figures in close embrace could be seen in the car. "I think we've stumbled into lover's lane. Let's get out of here."

Cindy clenched her teeth. "That looks like Dexter's Ferrari." She drove up beside the parked car. Dexter, in his army uniform, sat slumped down under the steering wheel. All over him, a shapely brunette rained passionate kisses upon his face.

Darlene tugged at Cindy's arm. "Back out, Cindy. Back out"

Cindy stood up quickly. "You two-timing bastard," she screamed, hurling her drink at the writhing couple.

"Oh my God," Dexter bolted upright, pushing the woman away. "Cindy, what are you doing here?"

"Not what you are!" She grabbed Darlene's drink and raced around to Dexter's side of the car. The woman with Dexter stumbled out the passenger side, sputtering and cursing, frantically trying to comb the syrupy ice from her hair and clothing with her fingers. Cindy hurled the contents of the cup into Dexter's lap. "That should cool your ardor," she snarled.

She jumped back into her car, started the

engine, jammed the gears into reverse, and roared out of the palm grove. "Let's go home, Darlene. I've ogled enough hunks for one day."

Hilda Cayce came from the kitchen as Cindy stormed into the house and dashed for the stairs. "Mister Matthews phoned while you were out. He said he had just landed at the airport and would call you later."

"I've already seen Mister Matthews," Cindy replied coldly. "Now if you'll excuse me I'm going to my room." She ran up the stairs and into her bedroom, slammed the door and threw herself onto her bed. She started sobbing softly, partly from anger at Dexter's callous disregard of his vows of love for her, and partly in sorrow that any hope for a relationship between them no longer existed. Her telephone began ringing but she ignored it. The answering machine clicked on.

"Cindy," Dexter's voice pleaded, "what you just saw was not what it looked like. You have to let me explain. Please, Cindy. Please."

She finally dropped off to sleep, his voice ringing in her head.

After the incident at the beach Cindy dreaded going back to the office for fear Dexter would corner her there, but she realized that sooner or later she would have to face him. Her refusal to accept his phone calls only made him more persistent. In desperation she pulled the plug on her private line. This left Hilda to field calls on the house line with a curt "Missus Jamison does not wish to speak to you."

Dexter's Ferrari was not in the parking lot, Cindy noted with a sigh of relief when she did return to her office, but she had barely settled behind her desk when he burst in, slammed the door and placed his back against it.

"Dammit, Cindy," he shouted, "you're going to hear me out even if I have to tie you to your chair to make you listen."

"Well, well, well," she smiled coldly, "now the great lover reveals the true animal behind his smooth facade."

Dexter's shoulders drooped "Please, Cindy, you have every right to be upset by what you saw at the beach, but you have to let me explain what really happened." He moved across the room and sank into a chair beside her desk. "I called you as soon as my plane landed. Missus Cayce told me you were out."

"So when you couldn't reach me you latched on to the first female in sight?" Outwardly Cindy remained icy calm but under her blouse her heart beat furiously.

"Dammit, Cindy, I love you. Eve means nothing to me."

"Is that the name of the bitch you were with? I'm surprised it isn't 'Bambi'." Cindy bit her lip, feeling her cool slipping away.

"Please, Cindy, please keep still while I explain the whole weird mess. Eve is an army nurse I met at the Officers' Club. A group of us were sitting at a table shooting the bull. Eve came over and joined us. In deference to our Muslim hosts, no alcohol is served at the club, but Eve had something cooked up by the boys in the hospital lab. It must have been potent stuff because I woke

117

up the next morning with a pounding head, and Eve in bed with me. I swear to God I don't know what, if anything, happened that night."

Cindy felt her anger subsiding. She laughed harshly. "It's obvious Eve knew what happened and she liked it."

Dexter gave a sigh of defeat. "You don't believe me, do you? I swear to God it's the truth. To make matters worse, she drew the seat next to me on the flight home."

"And I suppose the two of you got real chummy on that long flight. What was it, eight or nine hours of practically rubbing your bodies against each other?"

He ignored her biting insinuation. "When we landed at West Palm Beach I went to a phone to call you and let you know I was back. You weren't home. I picked up my bags from the carousel and walked out to the curb to wait for my car to be brought from the storage garage. I saw Eve standing there looking lost and bewildered. Friends from the beach were to meet her but failed to show up. She showed me their address, a place not far from where I live. So I offered to drive her there. Big mistake!"

Cindy started to interrupt but he hurried on. "As we drove up A1A she said she had seen nothing but sand for so long she would like to see the ocean close up. Can you believe the incredible coincidence? Of all the lanes leading to the beach I had to pull into that particular one." He laughed mirthlessly. "As soon as I stopped the car, she was all over me. That's when you drove up."

Cindy stood up and applauded loudly. "Bravo, Dexter, bravo! You really should write fiction. You're very good at it." She sat down and began furiously shuffling papers on her desk. Then she raised her eyes and spoke calmly. "Look, Dexter, it appears you now have an office in this building–I saw your name on the building directory– and we both have an interest in Caveat Investments so we can't avoid seeing each other. But let's keep our relationship strictly business."

Peter rapped lightly on the door then stuck his head in. "Adrian just called. He wants to see you in his office, Dexter. Says it's urgent"

Maybe I can learn something about the relationship between Dexter and Adrian, Cindy thought. "I'll go with you." He held the door open for her and she silently preceded him down the hallway to the elevator. Something about him brought on a nostalgic yearning, and when the elevator door closed she realized what it was. *Polo! Damn, he's still wearing Polo cologne.* As the elevator began ascending Dexter touched her arm. "Cindy," he implored, "you mean too much to me to have you shut me from your life. Please have dinner with me and let's get a new start."

She heaved a heavy sigh of resignation. "You just don't give up, do you. I thought I made it perfectly clear as to our future relationship."

He said no more as they exited the elevator and walked down the hallway. Together they entered Adrian's outer office. His receptionist quickly motioned them toward the inner sanctum. "Mister Pahlavi is waiting for you. Go right in."

Adrian came toward them and took Cindy's hand. "Sorry I haven't had a chance to see you since Colin's funeral. Pressure of business, you know. I presume you are aware of the joint venture

119

we formed before his death." His tone was cooly matter-of-fact.

"All I know, Adrian, is that I am part-owner of something called 'Caveat Investments'. Interesting name. Latin for 'beware', isn't it?"

His eyes narrowed. "Colin's idea. He had a wry sense of humor. Admittedly, this is a high-risk venture but it has great possibilities for immense profits." He turned to Dexter. "Come over to my desk. I have something for you to sign." He handed Dexter a paper. "This is an application for an export licence for that shipment to Israel."

Dexter took the paper and read it carefully. "I didn't know we had received orders for these items. This is highly-technical stuff."

"You're supposed to know only what I want you to know. You WASP types can do business with the State Department when people of my ethnic background can't. Why do you think I made you president of the company. Sign the paper."

Dexter tensed and clenched his fists. Cindy held her breath. For a moment she thought he might strike Adrian. Instead, he grabbed a pen, hastily scribbled his name on the document, then turned and strode from the room.

Cindy glared at Adrian. "What are you holding over Dexter's head"

His face twisted into a crooked smile. "If I told you it would no longer be a secret, would it?"

She almost screamed "You're just as evil as Fran said you are." But she caught herself, turned and ran from the room. Suddenly she felt a wave of pity for Dexter, the brash lion of a man who had turned into a meek lamb. The story he told about the army nurse could possibly be true, she rationalized, but until he's completely honest with me about his past there can be nothing between us.

CHAPTER SIXTEEN

B ob and Myrna agreed to a simple wedding with just a few close friends present. "My first three weddings were Sam Goldwyn extravaganzas and you know how they turned out," she told Cindy. "We would like to hold it here at your house if you don't mind."

"You know you don't even have to ask," Cindy beamed, "this is your home, too."

"Not for long. Bob is buying the old Montgomery place next door. We'll be neighbors. I'll take Ben and Dicey with me..."

"Over my dead body," Cindy bristled in mock anger, "my household staff stays with me."

"Just kidding. I know you wouldn't part with any of them. Bob did talk to Raymond, and Raymond agreed to work part time taking care of the grounds while he attends junior college."

Cindy couldn't hide her excitement. "What's the date? How many guests will we have? Hilda and Dicey will be in their glory getting the place ready, but Hilda will want to know how many the caterers will have to prepare for."

"Bob wants to have it as soon as possible. Says he doesn't want to give me time to change my mind. We decided on two weeks from Saturday. I know that's pretty short notice, but we can make it.

I want you to be my Matron of Honor. Bob will invite about a dozen of his police buddies, and his two daughters and their husbands. I'll invite Darlene and Byron, of course. And Karen Knowles and her friend, Anita. And Fran and..." She wrinkled her nose "...Adrian. Oh, yes, Peter Simmons. " She paused. "Cindy, is it all right if I invite Dexter Matthews?"

Cindy's heart leaped, but an indifferent shrug masked her true feelings. "I really couldn't care less, Myrna."

"C'mon, Cindy, give the guy a break. He's really nuts about you, you know."

Cindy tossed her head. "Dexter and I have an understanding. I go my way and he goes his."

"Tell the truth. You are attracted to him. You know you are."

"He's so dammed self-assured!" Cindy exploded. She paused, remembering the incident in Adrian's office. "Most of the time, that is." Her tone softened. "Go ahead and invite him. I really don't mind."

Organized confusion reigned as preparations for Myrna's wedding progressed, but Cindy slipped away to the office. Peter greeted her as she entered. "We got the export licence for the shipment to Israel. The Vamar Prince loaded at Norfolk, and is on the way. She's picking up a lot of surplus military equipment from the U.S. base on Ascension Island to deliver to Israel. That's the reason she is taking that route instead of the normal route through the Mediterranean. There's also a load of food and medicine for the Jordanian port of Aqaba. From there she'll go to the Israeli port of

Elat."

Cindy smiled. "You're really excited about this venture, aren't you?"

Peter nodded. "Cindy, I've always been very conservative where money is concerned. I've always worked for a salary and put my savings in safe things like certificates of deposit and government bonds. You can't believe the rush I get from having a part in something like this."

"I'm glad for you. By the way, you will be at Myrna's wedding, won't you? And bring your friend."

His face sobered. "I'll be there, but I'll be alone. My friend and I had a falling out."

"I'm sorry to hear that," Cindy consoled him.

She entered her office and began opening accumulated mail. Suddenly Darlene burst in, leaving the door open.

"I've got a big problem, Cin. I need a new gown for Myrna's wedding. I could always depend on Francois to make something nice on short notice, but this morning I went to his shop and found it closed and him gone. Cindy, I got the most terrible shock. The building manager told me Francois has AIDS and has gone somewhere to die."

From the outer office came a low plaintive moan. Looking out they saw Peter sitting with his face buried in his hands. He jumped up suddenly and ran from the office sobbing "Oh my God. Oh, my God."

"What was that all about?" Darlene asked, puzzled.

"I think we just learned who Peter's

mysterious friend is," Cindy replied softly.

A few days later Peter returned to the office. "Cindy, I found out where Francois went and I'm going to join him. I don't see how it's possible he has AIDS. Francois is very impressionable. He could have misinterpreted signs and jumped to the wrong conclusion. I pray that is the case. In any event we'll face this thing together. You really don't need me here anymore. Except for the Caveat venture your investments are rock-solid and don't require any particular watching."

"I'm sorry about Francois, Peter. Are you going to be all right? Do you need any money?"

He shook his head. "I've put away a little money through the years. And I just sold my Caveat Investments stock for a good price." He paused. "Cindy, if I were you I'd get out of Caveat now, too. Based on the Israeli contract the stock just hit a new high on the over-the-counter market. With Adrian Pahlavi involved you can't be sure what will happen to the company in the future."

Cindy's brow furrowed. "I suppose that might be a good idea. I really don't have the stomach for risky investments. Perhaps I should ask Dexter what he thinks."

"I saw him going into his office as I came in," Peter offered, "let me get him on the phone for you." He tapped in a number, listened for a moment then handed the phone to Cindy. "Dexter answered."

She took the phone and spoke quickly. "Dexter, this is Cindy. Now this is strictly a business call. I need your advice on something.

Peter thinks I should sell my interest in Caveat Investments. Do you think I should?"

There was a long silence at the other end, then Dexter answered in a strained voice. "The investors in Caveat are going to make a lot of money. If you sell now you will already earn a hefty return on the investment Colin made. I think you might be wise to take the immediate profit."

"How about you, Dexter, are you going to sell?"

"I can't get out."

"What is Adrian holding over you?" Cindy demanded.

"Do whatever you want," he snapped, "but if you want my advice get out now." He hung up abruptly.

Cindy turned to Peter. "Sell my Caveat Investments shares for me, please."

At the reception following Myrna and Bob's wedding Fran was first at the bar, and throughout the evening a glass never left her hand. Toward the end of the party she staggered over to where Byron, Dexter and Adrian stood talking business. Her speech was noticeably slurred. She wagged a finger at them. "I bet you guys talkin' 'bout girls. You know somethin'? We girls talk 'bout men. Mos'ly men we'd like to go to bed with."

Adrian glared at her. "You're drunk." He grabbed her arm. "We're going home."

She pulled away. "Don' wanna go home. Party's jus' startin'. Hey, Dexter, why don' you stop chasin' Cindy? Lotsa fish in the sea. If we get rid of ole Adrian you could even have me." She began cackling. "I'm a poet! I made a poem. Fish in the sea, even have me. Fish in the sea..." Adrian delivered a hard slap to her face.

Byron quickly stepped between them. "Lighten up, Adrian, she's just had too much to drink. Let's take her into the library and let her sleep it off."

Adrian's face darkened. He took Fran roughly by an elbow. "No drunken bitch is going to make a fool of me. We're going home." He half-dragged her from the room.

Dexter slowly shook his head. "What a miserable life she must lead, married to that man."

After the newlyweds departed, and Cindy had bid the guests goodbye, she stepped out onto the patio overlooking the ocean. She stood with hands on the railing and let the soft breeze ripple her hair. She thought Dexter had left with the others, but even before he spoke she sensed his presence behind her.

"This is where it all started, Cindy. Let's not let it end here."

She spun around angrily. "What is it between you and Adrian? What is he holding over you?"

He gently took her two hands in his. "I told you there's something in my past I'm not proud of. In due time I want you to know everything. But I can't tell you yet. Please be patient. Please."

"If there's ever to be anything between you and me, Dexter, I have to know. I have to know."

He gave a deep sigh. "If you insist, but you'll have to be very understanding and you must swear never to reveal this to anyone."

Hilda came to the door and called. "There's a telephone call for you, Mister Matthews. He says it's urgent."

"Damn it all," Dexter muttered, "every time I get you alone there's an interruption. Adrian is the only one who knows I'm here. I wonder what he wants. Please stay where you are, Cindy, I'll be right back." He dashed into the house.

He returned a few minutes later, his face ashen. "Something terrible has happened. An explosion ripped the Vamar Prince apart after she left Aqaba and she went down in the Red Sea. I have to get to the office." He spun on his heels and left.

Cindy stood for a long moment in shocked silence, tears welling up in her eyes. *He was so close to telling me. So very, very, close.*

CHAPTER SEVENTEEN

Trembling fingers holding the morning newspaper, Cindy read with horror the electrifying headline ARAB TERRORISTS SUSPECTED IN SINKING OF AMERICAN SHIP. A subhead revealed that strategic electronic components destined for Israel were in the *Vamar Prince* cargo. Cindy quickly scanned the full story.

Diego Garcia, Indian Ocean. At this remote U.S. base, captain Lars Erickson, skipper of the American vessel *Vamar Prince* told authorities today that an underwater

129

explosion sent his ship to the bottom. "We
were six hours out of Aqaba, headed for the
Israeli port of Elat, when after midnight all
hell broke loose. The explosion blew a hole
big enough to drive a truck through just aft of
midship. My first mate reported that the
explosion came from outside and that we
were taking water fast. Then my engineer
sent word the engine room was filling up. I
could see the situation was hopeless so I gave
the order to abandon ship. The Prince went
down like a stone. Thank God everyone got
off safely."

The article went on to say Arab terrorists
are suspected of affixing an explosive device to the
ship's bottom while the vessel was unloading a
shipment of food and medicine at the Jordanian
port of Aqaba. Highly sophisticated electronic
components, and a large amount of surplus military
equipment, all bound for Israel, made up the
remainder of the ship's cargo.

Cindy put down the paper and called
Dexter's office. He answered the phone himself.
"Dexter," she asked anxiously, "did you hear
anything more about the sinking than appeared in
the paper?"
"You don't have to worry, Cindy. The ship
and cargo are fully insured. The Caveat investors
won't lose a cent."
"I no longer have an interest in Caveat
Investors, as you very well know, but I was
concerned for the investments of all the lonely

widows you dragged in."

His voice rose sharply. "I'll have you know, Cindy Jamison, I didn't 'drag' anybody in. Some women did invest at my urging but I didn't go to bed with any of them if that's what you're insinuating."

"I'm sorry if I jumped to the wrong conclusion. But you still have a lot to tell me about your past, don't you?"

"I wanted to tell you last night."

Her heart beat faster. "I'm free tonight."

"I'd love to see you tonight but I have to fly up to Norfolk. The State and Commerce Departments are holding an inquiry into the sinking. I may be up there for several days. I'll call you as soon as I return."

"Please do. I'm going to be busy supervising the moving of Myrna's things to her new home next door. I want the place to be shipshape when she and Bob return from their honeymoon."

During the next few days Dexter called regularly. "Damn red tape," he cursed, "they can't seem to get every involved official into the same room at the same time."

While Dexter was away a small article on page two of the *Palm Beach Post* reported the finding of a small carton of contraband electronic parts in a food shipment bound for Iraq. A United Nations ceasefire monitoring team, in a routine inspection of a truck convoy passing into Iraq from Jordan, spotted the contraband hidden in one truck. While conceding that this could be an isolated case of smuggling, authorities were holding the entire convoy for a detailed search. The next morning the story hit the front page

INTERNATIONAL INTRIGUE
CASES OF INTERCEPTED ELECTRONIC
EQUIPMENT BEAR SAME MARKINGS AS
FOOD SHIPMENT UNLOADED FROM
SUNKEN AMERICAN SHIP

The story revealed that though only a small quantity of contraband was found in the convoy, the State Department has asked permission of the Jordanian government to inspect the dockside warehouse where the *Vamar Prince* unloaded.

Cindy was still reading the story when Dexter called. "I'm back, Cindy, I'll be over as soon as I can shower and change."

"Dexter, did you see the morning paper?"

"No, I was on my way home."

"There's a disturbing story about the Vamar Prince sinking."

"Hold it. I'll be there as soon as I can."

Immediately after he hung up Cindy received a call from Karen, speaking in a whisper. "Cindy, I suppose you have seen the morning paper. I could lose my job if anyone finds out I told you this, but ComRisk suspected something fishy about the Vamar Prince sinking right from the start. We had an underwater survey team out there investigating another claim. We directed them to investigate the Vamar Prince sinking. The ship went down in shallow water and the team spotted it from the air on the first day of their

132

search. They sent divers down. Cindy, there are no electronic components aboard. The crates in the hold are full of scrap metal and other junk. We are not paying off the claim, and our legal department is preparing to file insurance fraud charges against Caveat Investments and its president, Dexter Matthews. If Dexter means anything to you you should warn him. I can't say any more now." She hung up.

Sick at heart, Cindy quickly called Dexter and told him of Karen's call. He exploded.

"Damn Adrian Pahlavi, this is all his doing. I'll kill that bastard! Cindy, I swear to you I know nothing about the sinking or the diversion of the cargo. Adrian went up to Norfolk to supervise the loading. He must have had the markings on the containers changed so the Israel shipment would be unloaded at Aqaba. But he's not going to leave me holding the bag. I'll find that son-of-a-bitch and bash his head in."

"Don't do anything rash, Dexter." Cindy pleaded. She paused. " Dexter, I care what happens to you." She gently replaced the receiver on its cradle, not knowing that while she talked with Dexter a frantic Fran Pahlavi was trying to reach her.

CHAPTER EIGHTEEN

L ike a caged tiger, Fran paced the floor of her library, a cordless phone clutched to her ear. *C'mon, Cindy, answer. Answer! I know you're there.* When Cindy did answer, Fran's words came in a torrent.

"Cindy, Adrian alone is responsible for the Vamar affair. Dexter had nothing to do with it."

"Are you sure?" Cindy gasped. "Can you prove it?"

"You're dammed right I can prove it. Adrian thinks I'm just a dumb alcoholic bimbo he can push around, but he's beaten me up for the last time. I had his phone tapped and his office bugged while he was out of town. I've got everything on tape. He hired some frogmen to attach a bomb to the bottom of the ship when it was still in Norfolk. The captain was in on it and had the remote control to detonate the bomb. I just got home from Byron's office. I gave him the tapes. He'll know what to do with them."

Cindy gasped again. "Where's Adrian? You could be in real danger."

"He's gone to the office. Cindy, I called to say 'goodbye'. As soon as I can throw a few things into a suitcase I'm out of here. I don't know if I'll ever come back."

"Get out fast, Fran. Dexter is on his way over there. He can help you."

Another voice broke in on the line. "Nobody can help you now, you bitch. You're dead."

Cindy quickly called nine one one. "Send police to One Hundred Palm Drive. A man is threatening to kill his wife!" She hung up and dashed for her car.

Fran dropped the telephone. *Oh my God, he was listening all the time, and I thought he had left the house.* Her desperate eyes spied a poker by

135

the fireplace. When Adrian came charging in she grabbed it, and with a shriek of terror swung wildly. He dropped to his knees and half-crawled, half-stumbled toward her, blood pouring from a gash on his head. Fear and anger contorted his face. His fingers reached for Fran's throat as she shrank back. "Get me to a hospital, you bitch, or I'll kill you right here!" he screamed.

Wild-eyed with indecision, Fran hesitated. *If he dies, I'll be charged with murder. If he lives he'll kill me.* She attempted to pull free but he wrapped an arm around her neck and dragged her from the house. Her convertible sat on the driveway. He pushed her in, fell across her, and passed out.

She struggled to get out from under his limp body. Suddenly her eyes narrowed and her jaw firmed. *This is the opportunity I've been waiting for.* With strength born of desperation she shoved him over to the passenger side, started the engine and roared away. In the distance she could hear the wailing sirens of approaching police cars.

Dexter and Cindy arrived at the Pahlavi home at the same moment. A police car sat on the drive, doors open. From across the street a neighbor shouted "The Palavis just left in a big hurry." He pointed. "A patrol car is chasing them."

Cindy jumped from her car and into Dexter's. "Oh, Dexter, I'm afraid something terrible has happened to Fran. She was on the phone with me when Adrian cut in. He must have been listening on an extension. He was raving mad. She didn't know he was in the house.

136

They're heading in the direction of the hospital. Follow them."

Dexter took off at high speed in the direction the neighbor indicated. "Fran told me she has proof you were not involved in the Vamar Prince sinking," Cindy gasped.

Suddenly Dexter slammed on the brakes as traffic ahead dragged to a standstill. A short distance ahead the flashing lights of a police car could be seen. Dexter pulled off into the swale area and leaped out. "Come on, Cindy."

They raced down the line of cars beginning to inch past a police cruiser blocking one lane. "What happened?" Dexter shouted in the direction of spectators beginning to gather at the water's edge.

A man pointed down. "Car went off the bridge approach and landed upside down in the lake. The cop's trying to get the passengers out"

Without hesitation Dexter yanked off his shoes and dove in. Heart beating wildly, Cindy watched bubbles breaking the surface as minutes dragged by. An ambulance dashed up and medical corpsmen leaped out.

Suddenly Dexter popped up, fighting for breath, pulling an inert figure behind him. At the same moment the policeman came up holding another person. Both staggered ashore and dropped their burdens on the bank.

"Quick," Dexter gasped to the medics, "She still has a pulse."

The policeman stood up. "You're too late for this one. He's dead."

Attendants rushed the two victims into the

ambulance and it roared away. Cindy put her arms around Dexter and pressed her head against his water-soaked shoulder. "It's Fran, isn't it?" He nodded. She led him back toward the car. "There's nothing more we can do for her now. Let's go home and get you out of those wet clothes."

A police cruiser stood by the red Ferrari when they got back to it. "This your car, mister?" a policeman asked.

Dexter groaned. "I just pulled a drowning woman from a wrecked car and now I'm getting a parking ticket."

The officer's face remained impassive. "Are you Dexter Matthews?"

Dexter stiffened. "Yes, what of it?"

"I'll have to ask you to come with me, Mister Matthews. There's a warrant out for your arrest. You have the right to remain silent..."

Heartsick, Cindy drove Dexter's car home.

CHAPTER NINETEEN

As soon as she reached home Cindy called Darlene. "Something terrible has happened. Fran is in the hospital. Adrian is dead. There was an accident. Fran's car went in the lake. She was still alive when Dexter pulled her out, but Adrian was dead. Then the police arrested Dexter."

"Slow down, Cindy, you're not making sense. Was Dexter responsible for the accident?"

"Oh, no. He was with me."

"Sit tight. I'll be right over."

"No. Meet me at Memorial Hospital. That's where they took Fran."

"Byron just came in. We'll go together and meet you there."

Darlene met Cindy at the hospital reception desk, a torrent of questions pouring from her lips. Cindy took a deep breath and began rattling off answers. "Karen called me and told me Dexter would be charged with insurance fraud because the cargo that was supposed to be on the Vamar Prince wasn't on it. I called Dexter to warn him. He blew up and said he was going to find Adrian and have it out with him. Then Fran called to tell me she had evidence that would clear Dexter and implicate Adrian. She was getting ready to leave town, and she said she left tapes with you, Byron. Then Adrian came on the line He had been listening in. He said he was going to kill Fran. Then the phone went dead. I called nine one one and told them to send help. Then I rushed over to Fran's. Everything happened so fast my head is still spinning."

"Slow down, Cindy," Byron broke in. "Fran did bring me some tapes but I haven't examined them. Why was Dexter arrested? Was it the fraud charge? If so, the insurance company sure acted fast. What happened when you got to Fran's?"

Cindy began to regain her composure. "When I got to Fran's, Dexter had just arrived. A neighbor told us Fran and Adrian had just driven away. We guessed they were headed for the hospital so we followed. In Dexter's car." She paused. "We suddenly came upon an accident scene. A car was under water and a policeman was down there trying to get the passengers out. Dexter jumped right in and pulled Fran out. She was still alive. The cop pulled Adrian out. Adrian was dead. An ambulance took them away."

"How awful," Darlene exclaimed, "but why was Dexter arrested?"

"A policeman was waiting when we got back to Dexter's car. He said a warrant was out for Dexter's arrest. I'm sure it has something to do with the ship sinking."

"Was Fran driving?" Darlene asked.

Cindy looked at her sharply. "I don't know. Why do you ask?"

"Do you remember what Fran said once? That some day she might kill Adrian? You don't suppose..."

"Hold it!" Cindy quickly raised a hand. "We didn't hear a thing. Maybe he deserved to die for the way he treated her but we don't know that she deliberately drove into the lake. Even if she did kill him she took the chance of dying with him."

After an agonizing wait, the woman behind the desk called to them. "Missus Pahlavi is out of Emergency and has been admitted for further observation. You may go up in a few minutes but don't stay long." She gave them a room number.

"That's an encouraging sign," Byron remarked as they ascended in the elevator. "If she is badly hurt we wouldn't be able to see her so soon."

Fran greeted them with a weak wave of her hand and a wan smile. "Hi, guys, I just took a bath and it's not even Saturday."

Cindy gave her an exasperated look. "This is no time for joking, Fran. You could have been killed."

"Yeah, just like Adrian. That's the only good thing that's happened to me today. Adrian is out of my life."

Byron glanced around the room apprehensively. "Don't say anything more, Fran. You don't know if any charges will be made against you."

A nurse came in. "You'll have to leave now. We don't want to tire the patient, do we?"

Cindy and Darlene kissed Fran lightly on her forehead. "Hang in there, kid. We'll be back in the morning," Cindy promised.

"Wait, Byron," Fran called as they were leaving, "I want to talk to you."

The two women left the room and waited in the hallway. A few moments later Byron came to the door. "Cindy, do you mind taking Darlene home? I may be here for awhile. And after I get through here I'm going to see if I can get Dexter out of jail."

* * *

"I arranged bail for you, Dexter. You're free to leave. Where can I drop you off?"

Dexter managed a smile. "Home if it's not too much trouble, Byron. I have to get out of these damp clothes. Cindy has my car." He stopped short. "Is Cindy all right? Have you heard from her?"

Byron nodded. "Yes, she's fine. I saw her at the hospital visiting Fran. Fran appears to be okay. I heard how you pulled her out of the submerged car."

They left the police station, crossed the parking lot and got into Byron's car. He started the motor and put the car in gear. "There's a good chance you can beat the fraud charge they booked you on, Dexter. Fran came to my office today and gave me some tapes she says implicates Adrian and clears you in the sinking of the Vamar Prince. I didn't have time to hear the tapes yet but Fran said Adrian had an explosive charge attached to the bottom of the ship while it was at Norfolk, and the ship's captain set off the explosion with a remote devise. She said that on one tape Adrian brags that he set you up to take the rap if anything goes wrong. If all she says is true it will help you immensely." He paused. "I don't know why you had anything to do with that guy anyway."

"It's a long story."

Byron shrugged. "You can tell it when we have more time. Right now you want to get home, get out of those clothes, take a hot shower and go to bed. A stiff drink might help, too. Come to my office in the morning and we can begin preparing your defense."

With Cindy at his side, Dexter arrived at Byron's office near noon. "Sorry I'm late, Byron. I overslept, then went to the office to see if there's any further news on the sinking. Then I picked Cindy up. She told me she called Darlene with the sad news about Fran. That poor girl really had a tragic life."

Byron nodded. "Yes. It was an unexpected shock. She looked pretty good last night when we visited her. Darlene called the hospital this morning after learning Fran had died. A doctor told her that Fran died of a ruptured aorta. It must have been weakened by the stressful life she led, and the trauma of the accident was the final straw. She had me stay behind last night to draw up a new will, her previous will left everything she owned to Adrian. I had some standard will forms in my car so all she had to do was fill in the blanks. A doctor and a nurse witnessed her signature. I couldn't reveal this to you last night at the jail because Fran was still alive, Dexter, but you're in for a big shock. Her new will leaves her entire estate to you."

Dexter's eyes widened "Me?"

"Did you know she was in love with you?"

"Where did you get that crazy idea?"

"She didn't say it in so many words but she couldn't conceal her feelings. She told me that if

143

she didn't pull through she wanted to 'make up for Adrian's ruining your life' as she put it."

Dexter shook his head slowly. "She never gave any indication she had any feelings for me." He paused. "Except for that incident at Myrna's reception. But she was drunk."

"Well, people often say things when they've had to much to drink that they wouldn't say when sober. Were you ever alone with her when Adrian wasn't there?"

"No, I can't recall us ever being alone together."

"Then that's your answer. She was deathly afraid of Adrian. But let's get to legal matters. I don't believe she owned much in her own name. You could be holding an empty bag. But get this: when Fran and Adrian married they both made out wills naming each other sole beneficiaries. Fran survived Adrian. When Adrian's will is probated all of his estate should pass to Fran."

Cindy gasped. "Wouldn't it be ironic if you ended up with Adrian's wealth, Dexter?"

Dexter appeared stunned. "What do you mean by 'should' go to Fran's estate?"

"That's why it's important his death be found to be an accident. If she was responsible for his death she would not legally be entitled to any part of his estate."

Byron motioned Cindy and Dexter to seats. "Right now, Dexter, we have to plan your defense on the fraud charges. Adrian's money won't do you a whole lot of good if you're in prison." He picked up a handfull of tapes from his desk. I had a chance to listen to some of these this morning.

They're very damaging to Adrian. Some of the conversations are in foreign tongues and will have to be translated. I'll bet they are even more damaging. I'm having copies made and will send them to the State's Attorney's office and to the ComRisk lawyers. I feel really good about this."

"Then you think you can clear Dexter completely?" Cindy asked anxiously.

"Pretty much so. It depends on how badly ComRisk wants to build a case against him. Just this morning I received some good news in that respect. The missing cargo from the Vamar Prince has been found in Aqaba. Jordanian authorities raided an Iranian ship being loaded at the same dock where the Vamar Prince unloaded what was supposed to be food and medicine. Those electronics were destined for Iran where they are desperately needed to keep Iran's American-built warplanes flying. Because of the embargo they can't get them legally. Adrian must have gotten a fabulous price for them. The contraband found in the convoy headed for Iraq was just a smokescreen to conceal the true destination in case the authorities found that they were not on the sunken ship.

"He was shifty bastard," Dexter sniffed.

"He sure was. What I can't get is why he would think anyone would suspect the stuff didn't go down with the ship."

"He covered all the bases. I guess he figured if the ship was found and the switch discovered he would have plenty of time to get the shipment to Iran before it happened, and to get out of the country. But it appears the captain didn't know the waters very well and set off the explosion a few miles short of really deep water. But how does this all help me, Byron?"

"Well, for one thing it will help get ComRisk off our backs. They insured the cargo and will recover most of it. They insured the ship, too, but if they can prove it was sunk deliberately they won't pay the claim." Byron shrugged. "The Caveat investors are the ones who will take a hit. I understand that ship was about all the company owned. The investors could be wiped out."

A broad smile lighted Dexter's drawn face. "Not necessarily so, Byron. Caveat Investments owned accidental death policies on Adrian and on me. Adrian insisted on it when we set up the company. Maybe he planned an 'accidental' death for me. Caveat Investments will get ten million dollars from Adrian's death. That's more than enough to pay off the original investments."

Byron raised his eyebrows. "That's very interesting. Let's hope the insurance company won't balk at paying the claim."

"How could they?" Cindy broke in.

"In cases like this they investigate every angle. They will try to determine if Adrian died by accident, by natural causes, was murdered, committed suicide, you name it. If they can prove his death was not a pure accident they won't pay."

"Do you think Fran might have killed him?" Dexter asked.

Byron's jaw tightened. "I won't even conjecture on that possibility. You can be sure we won't be the ones to suggest it. I got an autopsy report on Adrian. He drowned, so he was alive when he hit the water. There was a high alcohol level in his blood, and also in Fran's."

A secretary entered the room and handed Byron a paper. He scanned it quickly and a smile lighted his face. "Good news! This is a copy of the police report. They concluded it was an alcohol-related accident. Fran was driving. There were long skid marks showing she tried to stop. And the officer who saw the car go into the lake reported it was traveling at a high rate of speed and weaving in and out of traffic." He put the paper down. "We'll never know for sure if she intended to kill him and then had a last-second change of heart, or whether it actually was a tragic accident."

As Cindy and Dexter left Byron's office they were confronted by a television cameraman and a reporter. Erwin Weiss stood beside them. "Mister Matthews," the reporter called, "what do you know about the Vamar Prince sinking?"

Dexter pushed past them and half-dragged Cindy to his car. "That dammed Weiss," he cursed as they sped away,"he'll do anything for publicity. He's a brazen bastard. I thought I shut him up when he went after Colin. As soon as I get you home, Cindy, I'm going to take care of him for good."

"Don't do anything rash, Dexter. You'll only get yourself into more trouble."

"Don't worry. I won't do him any physical harm. What I'll do to him will hurt him even worse."

Later that day Dexter called. "Cindy, the

Revealer found out about Fran's will. Don't ask how. Maybe someone at the hospital talked to them. There's a reporter and a photographer camped outside my apartment building. I'm going to try to slip out the back way and elude them. I won't take my car; it's too easy to spot. Byron doesn't want my case tried in the media so I'm going to hide out for a few days."

CHAPTER TWENTY

B ob and Myrna sat in the dining room of the Hotel Europa in San Jose, Costa Rica, at a table set with sterling silver serving vessels and flatware. A waiter in formal attire hovered unobtrusively in the background. "Did you ever expect to see such ambiance in a small out-of-the-way country like this?" Myrna whispered.

"The guidebook says there are a number of these small hotels scattered around the country," Bob answered. "They're owned by refugees from Europe who brought their culture with them."

"Well, I can't see how they survive. There must not be more than a half-dozen guests in the whole place. Look around," she swept the room with a hand, "only one couple besides us having dinner."

"The host apologized for that when we checked in. Explained this is the off season." Bob nodded toward the other diners. "They're from England."

"How can you tell that, Mister Know-it-all?" Myrna scoffed.

"Simple deduction, my dear, simple deduction. In police work we learn to observe those around us. Their accents. Their dress. Their mannerisms." He paused, and his voice dropped to a conspiratorial whisper. "Besides, I heard the man ask the desk clerk if the London Times was available."

"What scintillating detective work!" Myrna teased. "And what else did you learn?"

"The clerk told him the only English-language newspaper they get is the International Edition of the Miami Herald. We'll have to pick up a copy before we go to our room."

"Don't you dare!" Myrna exploded in mock anger. "We're on our honeymoon and I don't have the slightest desire to know what's going on back home." She gave him a coy smile. "We have better things to do up there than read newspapers."

"Then we had better finish dinner and get an early start on it. We don't want to oversleep and miss the train to Puntarenas."

When they entered the train compartment the next morning Bob and Myrna found the English couple there. "Hello," the man greeted them. He turned to the woman. "It's the American couple from the hotel, luv. They were in the dining room last evening, remember?" He extended a hand to Bob. "I'm Cecil Combes, and this is my wife, Hillary. How jolly nice we'll be traveling companions."

"We're Bob and Myrna Ames," Bob replied. They shook hands all around.

"Have you been to Puntarenas before?" Bob asked as they took their seats.

"Oh, yes," Hillary gushed. "We went there on our honeymoon. We came back to Costa Rica on a sort of sentimental journey."

"We were married in San Jose," Cecil volunteered. "I was with the British Embassy, and Barclay's Bank sent Hillary out as a manager. I gave the poor girl not a moments peace until she agreed to become Missus Combes."

"Bob arrested me," Myrna giggled. "Well, he didn't exactly arrest me but he stopped my car and gave me a ticket for some silly little infraction because he wanted to get to know me. He's a policeman. We're on our honeymoon."

"How romantic," Hillary sighed. "And how did you happen to pick Costa Rica?"

"We didn't," Bob shrugged in resignation. "We booked a leisurely cruise from Miami, through the Panama Canal, and on to San Francisco. Some people we met on the ship told us how beautiful this country is, and when we reached Panama City this unpredictable sprite I married insisted we jump ship and fly up here. So here we are."

"Well, you certainly didn't object," Myrna sniffed.

"I had no choice."

"Oh, sure you did, my darling." Myrna gave a flippant toss of her head. "I gave you two choices. You could go with me or you could stay on the ship and I would go without you." She nuzzled his ear with her lips and then grinned. "My big, handsome lover man said he could never

be happy unless he was with me, no matter where."
She gave Bob a playful jab in his ribs. "You think
I'm unpredictable, do you? Wait 'til you've lived
with me for a while. You ain't seen nothing yet."

"What is there to see in Puntarenas?" Bob
asked Cecil Combes.

"When we were there before there was not
much more than a beautiful, wide beach of black
volcanic sand." He patted Hillary's hand. "But we
didn't stray far from that quaint little hotel
overlooking the Pacific. I understand that large
international chains have now built some fine
hotels there. But no matter what you find in
Puntarenas, the train ride over is well worth it.
We'll pass over some of the most breathtaking
gorges and ravines you could ever imagine.
Almost bottomless, it seems. The train makes
frequent stops at small villages where natives in
colorful costumes swarm around hawking all kinds
of food." He let out a little laugh. "On previous
trip we felt a little skittish eating the local
delicacies but we did try some fresh pineapple.
Mouth-watering."

"Just to be safe this time we had the hotel
kitchen pack a hamper for us," Hillary broke in,
pointing to the rack above their heads. "There's
plenty for all if you care to share."

"Great," Myrna thanked her. "I'll take a
look at what the locals offer but will probably be
too chicken to eat any of it."

"What part of the States are you from?"
Cecil asked.

"We live in Stardust Shores, Florida. It's a
small town on the ocean in Palm Beach County."

Cecil's eyes opened wide in astonishment. "Palm Beach? What a bizarre coincidence! Do you by chance know this chap who's been charged with fraud?" He pulled out a copy of the *Miami Herald*. From the front page a picture of Dexter Matthews stared back at them.

"Oh my God," Myrna screamed. "Dexter's been arrested."

"Then you do know him," Hillary gasped.

"He was at our wedding."

Cecil shook his head sadly. "I can't believe he's guilty. Jolly good fellow. Fine polo player, too. Hillary and I became very chummy with him and his wife, Wendy. He married an English girl, you know. Lovely lass. Lovely lass."

"We exchanged Christmas cards for a number of years after they left England," Hillary added. "But about three years ago they dropped out of sight. Just stopped writing. No explanation. We were puzzled, and a bit hurt."

During the remainder of the trip the conversation centered on Dexter Matthews and his problems. Myrna realized how little they knew about the man.

CHAPTER TWENTY-ONE

Cindy sat in numbed silence after Myrna hung up. *Dexter's married? So that's what he's keeping from me. And what else? The Revealer found out about the will. What else did they find out about him?*

"He might not be married now," Myrna had cautioned, "but three years ago he had a wife."

I'll have this out with him right now! Cindy gritted her teeth and touched the speed-dial button for Byron's office. "Byron, do you know where Dexter is?"

"No, Cindy. I've been trying to reach him but he's dropped out of sight. I did tell him I want his problems settled in the courts, and not have him

tried by the television and print media. He's
probably hiding out from the press. But we do
have an appointment with the ComRisk attorneys
in my office this morning so I expect he'll come out
of hiding."

"The last time I saw him he was going to
'take care' of Irwin Weiss. In this morning's paper I
saw that Weiss has been arrested. Did Dexter have
anything to do with it?" She suddenly exploded.
"Damn that man!"

"Who?" Byron chuckled, "Dexter or
Weiss?"

"Both of them."

"The police arrested Weiss on morals
charges. Having sex with underage girls. I don't
know that Dexter had anything to do with it."

"I'm so confused, Byron. Let me know if
you hear from him."

On an impulse, after hanging up she called
Darlene. "I have to get away from here and go
some place where I can relax and straighten out my
head. Myrna called from Costa Rica and said
Dexter might be married. Now he's disappeared.
Can you go out to Vail with me for a few days?"

"I'd love to, Cindy, but Byron and I have an
appointment I must keep. Byron is toying with the
idea of getting into politics. We have an
appointment with the party campaign committee to
see how much support he can expect from the
party. They want to evaluate the wives of potential
candidates as well as the candidates themselves.
Byron was thinking of running against Erwin
Weiss for State's Attorney. Now that Weiss'
problems with the law will probably take him out

155

of the race, Byron should have a good chance of winning. I can go with you next week."

"I have to get away now. I'll fly to Vail this morning. Please come out as soon as you can. I'll be at our usual lodge."

"Big storm brewing, Missus Jamison," the driver of the lodge van observed as he tossed Cindy's bag in. "Ain't had this much snow this early as long as I can remember. The weather man says we're in for a real humdinger tonight."

"That's all right, Zeke, I don't intend to go out."

"Well, I got one of the cabins ready just like you asked. But if I was you I'd stay at the main lodge. You could get snowed in up on the hill."

"I appreciate your concern, Zeke, but I just want to be alone. I'll be quite all right."

Light snow began falling as they drove to the resort, and by the time they reached the cabin the snow was swirling around in ominous gusts. Zeke hurriedly opened the door and took Cindy's bags in. Cindy followed. "U-m-m it feels good in here," she murmured.

"I started the gas furnace before I left for the airport, Missus Jamison. And there's plenty of wood inside for the fireplace." He strode over to the huge stone fireplace dominating one end of the cabin's sitting room. "I'll jest light 'er up. There's nothing as cheerful as a wood fire on a snowy night, I always say." He struck a match to some tinder, and a thin flame curled up around the logs.

"I agree, Zeke." She pressed a generous tip into his hand. "I'm sure I'll be quite comfortable"

The man turned to leave. "I put plenty of snacks and drinks in the fridge and pantry in case you get snowed in. Some tee-vee dinners in the freezer, too. You can call me down at the lodge if you need anything."

"You're very kind, Zeke. I'm sure I'll be fine."

Cindy stood by the window and watched the van fade into the increasingly heavy snowfall. God, it's lonely, she thought as she turned away. But that's what I want. Plenty of time to think things out. She picked up the telephone and punched in Darlene's number. An answering machine took the call. She spoke to it. 'Hi, Darl, I made it safely. I'm in the first cabin up the hill from the lodge. It's snowing like crazy. If Byron can get away both of you come out. There should be some terrific skiing when the snow stops falling."

After taking a hot shower she slipped into a fleecy robe and reclined on a lounge in front of the fireplace. *What is it about Dexter Matthews? Why is he so evasive about his past? How can he be so charming at times and a complete ass at others? He's a coward!* Then she remembered his jumping into the lake to save Fran. *That took quick thinking and courage. No, he's not a coward.*

She picked up a Judith Kranz novel and tried to read but the words blurred on the page. In a burst of anger she hurled the book across the room. "Judith Kranz should write the story of my life." She stopped, startled to realize she had talked out loud to herself. She gave a short laugh and shrugged her shoulders. *As Mother used to say, "everything will come out in the wash."*

Cindy leaned back and gazed at the fire. Hypnotic flames, as though programmed by some Machiavellian choreographer, danced over logs now fully ignited and crackling merrily. She became drowsy. Drowsier. Drowsier...

Many hours later Cindy awakened to the sound of heavy pounding on the door and a voice calling "Cindy! Cindy! Let me in. It's freezing out here." The voice was Dexter's. She rushed to the door and lifted the bar. The door flew open, impelled by a blast of Arctic air, and Dexter stumbled in followed by a cascade of gale-driven snow. He put a shoulder to the door and forced it shut against the howling wind. He turned to Cindy and grinned. "This sure isn't anything like Florida."

"What on Earth are you doing here, Dexter?" Cindy demanded. "You were not supposed to leave the state until after the trial."

"There isn't going to be a trial, my darling. All charges have been dropped." He took both her hands into his. "For the first time in years I'm a free man."

She snatched her hands away. "Your hands are like ice! Come over to the fire and get warm before you catch pneumonia."

He went to the fireplace and stood there shivering. She sat down on the lounge and studied his forlorn figure for a moment. "You'd better go into the bedroom and get out of those wet clothes."

Dexter left the room but returned minutes later wrapped in a blanket. He grinned. "I didn't see anything in there to put on but one of your nighties, and I wouldn't be caught dead in one of those. My bags are in a rental car stalled at the bottom of the hill, and I'm sure as hell not going down there tonight."

He sat down beside Cindy and tucked the edges of the blanket under him. "Darlene told me where to find you. Cindy, now that Adrian is dead I can tell you all the things from my past that I have kept from you."

"He was blackmailing you, wasn't he?"

"In a sense. Cindy, back in my college days I did a despicable thing. Adrian knew about it and he threatened to expose me if I didn't join him in his business dealings."

"Tell me about it."

Dexter paused a long moment. "Please hear me out, Cindy. It happened during my senior year. I met a girl at a roadhouse. We both had too much to drink, and when she suggested we go to her place I was ready and willing. She insisted we take her convertible and that I drive. Adrian was making out with a girl in his car in the parking lot and saw us leave.

"As we were driving along the girl started playing around and insisting I pull off the road and stop. I'll admit I was getting excited, too, and was watching for a place to stop, but we were driving along a canal. Suddenly she grabbed the wheel. I lost control of the car and we skidded into the canal. I managed to unfasten my seat belt and get out and get to the surface. Suddenly I realized she was still in the car. I went back down, unbuckled her, and brought her to the canal bank. She was

159

not breathing and had no pulse. I tried to
resuscitate her but finally had to face the fact she
was dead."

"How terrible!" Cindy gasped.

"That's not the worse part. I could see
myself serving a long prison term for
manslaughter. Actually, the girl caused the car to
swerve out of control but how could I prove it? I
panicked. I took her body back down and strapped
it into the drivers' seat."

"You were drunk. You didn't know what
you were doing."

Dexter gave a hollow laugh. "Oh, I was
cold sober then. There is no condoning what I did.
I've had nightmares about it ever since. Anyway, I
walked back to the roadhouse, got my car and
drove home. Cindy, the police concluded it was a
alcohol-related accident and the girl was alone in
the car. I wanted to do something for the girl's
family but when the press picked up the story and
made a big thing of her being a wild kid living on a
big inheritance and having no immediate family it
came as a big relief."

"So Adrian guessed what happened?"

"Yes. A few days later he came to me and
said my 'secret' was safe with him. He emphasized
'secret'. But he made it clear he had a good idea
about what happened." He paused. "Isn't it bizarre
that Adrian died the same way that girl did?"

"Adrian had it coming," Cindy snorted, "but
how did you get involved with him?"

"After that terrible experience I was
determined to make something of myself. I quit
drinking. In college I was in a reserve officer

training program. On graduation I went on active duty with the army and was assigned to a NATO unit in England as a finance officer. I met and married a wonderful English girl, Wendy. She died of cancer three years ago."

Cindy's heart leaped. *So he isn't married!* She murmured some words of condolence.

"There's more you should know, Cindy. I have a son. He's seven years old and is living with Wendy's parents in England. Do you have any idea how devastating to his life it would be if the truth about his father came out?

"When my tour of duty ended I took Wendy and our son to New York. I became associated with a prestigious brokerage house and quickly built up a wonderful clientele. Cindy, I had it all! A great family. A home in the suburbs. A promising career. A good reputation. Then my world suddenly collapsed. Wendy became ill. Despite everything that could be done for her she died. I was in a state of shock. Wendy's illness drained me financially. I was almost penniless.

"It was during this low period in my life that Adrian showed up at my office one day. He was looking for an all-American WASP-type guy to front for him. His reputation already suffered badly from his shady activities. He made me an offer I couldn't refuse, as the saying goes. If I joined him he would keep quiet about the canal accident."

"Just as I thought, he was blackmailing you."

"Cindy, I knew the statute of limitations was running out on a possible manslaughter

161

charge, but if the story came out my professional reputation would be ruined. And I had to think about my son, Wendell–we named him for Wendy. I had already sent him back to England.

"Anyway, I joined Adrian. I felt I could exert enough influence on him to keep him honest. He proceeded to create a persona for me. I was a wealthy, sophisticated, man-about-town playboy, the kind of person who fits in with society's 'beautiful people', and I might add, 'big money people'. He leased the Ferrari for me and got me into the polo club–I had learned to play polo in England. It was an exciting life. I have to confess, for awhile I almost felt I was the person I pretended to be."

"And part of your job," Cindy sneered, "was to seduce wealthy women into investing."

"I swear I didn't seduce any of them. All I did was make over them and charm them into investing. And I did it with a clear conscience. I had no doubt in my mind but that they'd make money. All of the ventures were profitable until Adrian fouled things up. Ad Astra was doing great until Iraq invaded Kuwait. We were building a communications system there, and Adrian thought we could complete it under Iraqui control. We could have gotten McHugh and his crew out but Adrian wouldn't permit it. They ended up prisoners. If they win their suit, Ad Astra investors could lose everything. The company did file for bankruptcy, but there is still the matter of the liability policy with ComRisk. We were building the system for the Kuwaiti government so they might shoulder some of the responsibility. Caveat

Investors was making money, too. Then Adrian
pulled his underhanded trick. His intention from
the first was to get export licences for shipments to
friendly countries and then divert the shipments to
embargoed countries at enormous profits."

"And you didn't suspect him?"

"I didn't think him capable of pulling off
something of the magnitude of the Vamar Prince
fiasco. I knew he was untrustworthy and I thought
he might try ripping off the investors. But I felt I
could keep an eye on him. Then I was called away
to Saudi Arabia." He paused and looked down at
the floor. "As I told you before, Cindy, that night
at the party I already knew you were Colin's wife.
Adrian introduced me to Colin a few days earlier
and Colin invited me to the party. Adrian told me
that Colin had a young wife who could influence
him into investing. You can imagine the shock
when I found out who that wife was. But believe
me, Cindy, everything I said to you on the day after
Colin's funeral is true. I did worship you from afar
when we were kids in high school. When you
came back into my life I realized I still love you. I
went a little crazy and made an ass of myself."

Cindy felt her pulse quickening.
"Subconsciously you're still playing the game,
Dexter."

"This is no game, Cindy. There are still a
lot of things I have to clear up before my life
becomes stable again. The Ad Astra and Caveat
messes, for example. You know about Fran's will.
I could become a very wealthy man. Whatever my
future, Cindy, I want you with me."

"I want to believe you, Dexter. Oh how

much I want to believe you. But speaking of blackmail, didn't you blackmail Irwin Weiss?"

For the first time since entering the cabin Dexter gave a hearty laugh. "Good old Irwin Weiss! I bluffed him into getting off Colin's back. One day at my club I overheard two of his political opponents discussing photographs they said they had showing Weiss in sexual situations with teenage girls. They planned to release them at a strategic moment in the campaign when they would do Weiss the most harm. When Colin was threatened I went to Weiss and told him I knew of his activities and had proof, which I didn't. It scared him off. When I saw Weiss outside Byron's office and knew he was targeting me I convinced the holders of the photographs that the time was right to release them to the media."

"And what did you have on these men to 'convince' them to release the photos?"

Dexter gave an exasperated sigh. "You don't want to believe anything good about me, do you? Cindy, I love you. Please say that when this nightmare is over we can get a fresh start together."

Suddenly the suppressed passion of years surged up within Cindy, and an uncontrollable primeval urge overwhelmed her. She stood up, loosened the belt and let her robe slip from her shoulders. For a long moment she stood there, a golden nude Aphrodite illuminated by the flickering flames in the fireplace, her breasts rising and falling as her breath came in ecstatic gasps. She lifted the edge of the blanket covering Dexter and slid in beside him.

"We'll see," she whispered.

ELIZA WASHINGTON
AND THE TUNE HOISTER

liza Washington was just about the prettiest and smartest little gal in Gadsden County, and old Granny Moss was not about to let her forget it. As the time drew near for Eliza to start lookin' for a man to marry up with, Granny kept remindin' her. "Yew too gud fo' enny uv dem fawm han's. Yew knows yo figguhs an' yo lettuhs bett'n mos' whyt gals. An' de gud Lawd done giv' yew mi'ty gud looks. Don' go throwin' yose'f away on sum no-count 'bacca picka. Git yose'f a toon hystuh."

Now everybody here in Florida's shade-grown tobacco country know that next to the boss man, the most important fellow in the big processin' barns is the tune hoister. What's a tune hoister? Well, stranger, he's the one who makes sure the women sittin' at the long rows of tables stacked high with the broad, thin leaves of tobacco grown under canopies of cheesecloth to make them tender earn their dollar-and-a-half a day pay. You see, after the tobacco is brought from the curin' sheds the women strip away the stems and pack the tender parts into barrels to be aged before bein' sent off to Tampa for makin' cigars. In the tobacco barns the women sing as they work, and their fingers move to the rhythm of the song. The faster the beat, the faster they work. That's where the tune hoister comes in; he leads the singin'. When he raises up a lively tune the barrels fill up fast. But you can bet your boots that a soulful rendition of *Swing Low, Sweet Chariot* is sure to attract a stern frown from the boss man sittin' on the high platform at the end of the barn.

166

Even before her sixteenth birthday Eliza was castin' her eyes around. "Granny Moss," she complained, "there jest ain't hardly one tune heister in the county what ain't hitched. If he ain't, you sho'nuff kin tell why. If'n I don't ketch me a man purty soon I gonna end up a ol' maid."

Granny was obstinate. "Don' yew fret none, honey chile, de gud Lawd gonna look afta yew."

Now Eliza would never do anything to upset the beloved woman who raised her, but unbeknownst to Granny she had already picked out the man she would marry. 'Course, he didn't know it yet.

Samuel Dorsey was a few years older than Eliza. When she was just a young'un she took a shine to him but he never paid no mind to the skinny kid she was then. When he came home from fightin' the kaiser, tall and handsome in his uniform, and showin' off the *Purple Heart* medal he got after a Hun bullet nicked his arm, Eliza knew for sure he was the one for her. Now, Eliza had filled out quite a bit while Samuel was away and he didn't fail to notice it.

So it seemed just natural, as the weeks passed, that at the little A.M.E. church, where Samuel's loud, clear voice rang out above all the others in the hymn singin' , Eliza found him sittin' beside her every Sunday. And at church suppers it was not exactly by accident he found the seat next to her empty; she made sure no one took it before he showed up.

Finally, Eliza confided in Granny Moss. The old woman listened in grim silence, then shook her head doggedly. "Wal, if yew ken't fin' a toon hystuh tew git hitched tew , I figguh we gotta mak' a toon hystuh fo' yew." So, as it always has been, the two women put their heads together and hatched up a plan to change the man of choice into the man they wanted him to be.

Of all the tune hoisters in Gadsden County, Mr. Campbell's man Rufus Jackson was the oldest and the best. With a few sips of dandelion wine under his belt, Rufus could raise up a tune that rattled the rafters. But Rufus liked his wine a mite too much and that caused problems between him and Mr. Campbell. "I swear, Rufus," Mr. Campbell would storm, "if I have to come over to your place one more morning and drag you out and sober you up I'm gonna kick your tail clear to the Georgia line." But he never carried out his threat. You see, in these parts there's something folks in other places just don't understand–loyalty! Rufus worked for Mr. Campbell's father, and for his father before him, and Mr. Campbell felt a certain responsibility for the old man.

Anyway, Granny decided it was time for Rufus to retire. "It gonna be mi'ty lonesum 'round here when yew an' Sam'el gits hitched." she told Eliza, "an' I gonna need me a man tew he'p wif de chores."

Eliza got herself a job at Mr. Campbell's barn and most every evenin' 'bout quittin' time Samuel wandered in. By this time of day Rufus was gettin' a mite tired so Samuel would hoist up a few rousing' tunes for him. Mr. Campbell would look down from his platform and nod approval.

Granny Moss now began carryin' out her

part of the plot. Every Sunday after church she invited Rufus over to her cabin. She didn't do anything she would be ashamed to tell the preacher man; just fed him a good meal of fried chicken, or ham hocks with collard greens and cornbread, and made him cozy in front of the fireplace with a jug of her dandelion wine. Old Rufus started feelin' this wasn't such a bad life. Granny had a cow and some hogs, and a flock of chickens. And a vegetable garden (though Rufus shuttered at the thought of gettin' out there with a hoe). But she sure could make good dandelion wine.

Granny made sure Rufus was up early Monday mornin's–that is until the right time came. Then one mornin' Mr. Campbell looked high and low for Rufus but couldn't find him. It just happened that Eliza had Samuel escort her to work that mornin' and a tune hoister was born.

Eliza Washington married her tune hoister. As for Granny Moss and Rufus Jackson? Well, they just sort of lived out their golden years together.

The ticket agents's voice barely masked his exasperation. "Please be patient, miss. As I told you before, your bags have been located. I can assure you they will arrive on a bus due shortly."

The girl heaved a sigh. "I certainly hope so. I don't have a change of clothes, and all my supplies and drawings are in those bags. I'd be totally lost without them."

Though I had been sitting in the baggage area for nearly an hour, and only the two of us were there, she suddenly seemed to become aware of my presence and walked over to me, the tassels on the shoulders of her buckskin jacket bouncing. "I was beginning to think I would never see my things again." She held out a slim hand with long, tapered fingers ending in manicured nails. "Hi, my name is Penelope but I prefer to be called 'Penney '. Penelope is such a funky name, don't you think? What's your name?"

I put down my magazine, took her hand and gave her an amused smile. "My name's 'Brian' and I prefer to be called 'Brian' because I like my name."

Dropping into the seat next to me she gave a quick tug to the hem of her short denim skirt, but not before I caught a glimpse of pink lace-trimmed panties. She kicked off her shoes and curled her feet beneath her.

"Do you come here often, Brian?" She stopped short and burst into laughter. The faint

hint of an embarrassed blush touched her cheeks.
"I didn't mean that the way it sounded. I mean, it
sounded like a pickup line, didn't it? I really meant
to ask if the bus people lose your things very
often."

"I haven't traveled by bus in years. I'm
waiting to pick up a shipment of books coming by
bus express."

"You sell books?"

"No, I write them. I have a book-signing
tomorrow at a local book store so the publisher is
rushing some extra copies in case the store doesn't
have enough in stock."

Her eyes sparkled. "Wow, a best-selling
author!"

It was my turn to laugh. "My books are not
exactly best-sellers. I consider myself lucky when I
get a chance to promote them at signing sessions."

"What kind of stories do you write, Brian?"

"Oh, a little of everything–adventure,
mystery, romance." I paused. "Sometimes I write
about very pretty young women I meet in bus
station baggage rooms."

"You're teasing me!"

"Not at all. You are very pretty. But before
I can write about you I have to know more about
you. I heard you tell the agent your supplies are in
your bags. What kind of supplies, Penney?"

She pointed a finger at me. "Ah, ha, you
were watching me and listening. I thought so but
could never catch you looking at me. I must have
glanced toward you a hundred times during the past
hour but I never caught you." She tossed her head,
sending her long blonde hair swirling around her

shoulders. "I'm a portrait artist. My paints, brushes and canvasses are in my bags." Suddenly she reached out, cupped my chin in her hand, and turned my head from side to side. "You would make a good subject for a portrait, Brian."

I laughed nervously. "I'm not really the art-buying type."

"I'm not hustling you, Brian. I never sell my paintings. I just dream that some day I can display them in a prestigious gallery. I don't need money. If you're wondering why I'm traveling by bus it's not because it's cheaper. I was out west sketching rugged old cowboys and Native Americans. There wasn't an airport within a hundred miles. I took a bus to the nearest city with an airport, planning to hop a plane home, but at a terminal where I changed busses I boarded the wrong bus. My luggage didn't. When I realized my mistake I found I was on an express bus heading for Florida. I know I could have pushed the panic button and gotten off but I've never been to Florida before so I thought 'What the heck'. So here I am."

"You seem to be a real free spirit, Penney. Much like my daughter, Maggie. She's about your age."

"You're kidding me. You're not old enough to have a daughter my age. I'm almost twenty-one."

"Maggie celebrated her twenty-first birthday last month."

"Oh, God, why do men get so handsome as they get older?" She laughed. "I heard that line in a movie once."

"California Suite."

"What?"

"California Suite. Jane Fonda said something like that to Alan Alda in Neil Simon's 'California Suite'."

"Oh, yes. I remember. They were a divorced couple fighting over their daughter." She remained silent for a long moment. "My parents never fight over me. They just fight–period." Her cool grey eyes gazed steadily at me. "Do you and your wife fight, Brian?"

"My wife died last year. Cancer. That ended a beautiful marriage. Linda and I married right out of high school. Maggie came along soon after. With the help of our parents we made it through college. No, Penney, we never fought."

Compassion showed in Penney's eyes. "Oh, how terrible she died so young. You must miss her a lot."

I quickly changed the subject. "Do you think it's safe for you to travel around the country alone? There are a lot of creeps out there."

"Oh, I can take care of myself. Last summer I even backpacked all over Europe."

"Alone?"

"Well, not with anyone specific. I joined a group of college kids, girls and boys. We hiked and biked during the day and spent the nights in Youth Hostels."

"Even that could be dangerous," I persisted.

"Some of the boys did want to get romantic but after I made it clear I wasn't interested in playing their little games we got along fine. You know, Brian, I think some of them were actually

173

relieved when I turned them down. I suppose their macho male images dictated they at least make a pass at a girl." She paused and a slight frown creased her forehead. "Brian, do you think a girl is sexually repressed in not wanting to go to bed with every man she meets?"

"You appear to be a very sensible young woman, Penney."

At that moment a bus groaned to a stop in front of the terminal. I jumped up. "Let's hope our things are on this one."

Penney put on her shoes and followed me to the counter. Through a window we watched the baggage being unloaded.

"There are my bags!" Penney exclaimed.

"I think I see my box of books."

A few minutes later we had claimed our belongings. For a long moment we stood looking at each other. Suddenly Penney turned to the agent. "Is there a decent hotel or motel near here?"

The man smiled and shook his head. "Unless you have a reservation there's almost no chance you'll find a room anywhere near here, miss. It's Spring break time, you know. Every room on the east coast has been booked for weeks. Probably on the west coast, too."

She stamped a foot. "But I must have a room. I need to bathe and get into some fresh clothes."

I had lingered beside her. "There's an unoccupied guest room at my house, Penney."

She spun around. "I couldn't impose on you, Brian." She turned back to the agent. "Don't you know of even a Bed and Breakfast?"

"I wish I could help you, miss, but everything's filled up."

"You would be perfectly safe at my place, Penney. My housekeeper is there and so is Maggie."

She sighed. "I guess I have no other choice." Her face suddenly turned a bright red. "There I go again, saying things that don't come out the way I mean. I would be most grateful if you would put me up for the night."

We took the bags to the parking lot and put them into the back of my station wagon. Penney still appeared uncertain as to whether or not she should go with me. "Are you sure about this, Brian? You don't really know me. I could be a murderess, or a con person, or worse."

I laughed out loud. "I'll take that chance." I could almost feel the twinkle in my eyes. "I can take care of myself."

As she slid into the front passenger seat she still seemed to be having some misgivings. "Won't Maggie be upset by you bringing me home?"

"No, I'm always bringing home stray animals and wounded birds. I don't think Maggie will be the least bit surprised."

Darkness was falling as we left the parking lot and pulled into traffic. For several blocks Penney sat in thoughtful silence before she spoke again. "You didn't ask how I got to the ranch, Brian."

"The ranch?"

"Where I was sketching the cowboys and Indians."

"Oh, yes. You did say you left there by bus.

CHANCE MEETING

I never gave a thought as to how you got there."

"A man took me there–in a helicopter. We met at the Mormon Church Genealogy Center in Salt Lake City. I was researching my family tree. I suppose he was, too. His, that is. We got to talking. He told me that he collected contemporary art, and he convinced me that his ranch would be a great place to do some sketching and painting. I found later that he did have some very nice contemporary pieces. Anyway, we flew there.

"It was a fabulous place, Brian. The first few days we swam in his pool and did some horseback riding, and I did a lot of sketching. He sometimes stood over me as I worked, and he would touch my arms and rub my back and make suggestive comments. I just laughed them off. Then one night he grabbed me and tried to force me into his bedroom. A knee to a tender spot ended that. I gathered my belongings and took one of his jeeps and drove out to the main highway. I left the jeep and flagged down a bus. You know the rest." She looked over at me, a childlike pleading in her eyes. "You wouldn't try anything like that would you?"

"Cross my heart and scout's honor, Penney." But my heart beat faster at the thought of holding this desirable creature in my arms, and almost-forgotten yearnings surged deep within me as Linda's face suddenly flashed in my mind. I quickly changed the subject. "You do have a last name, don't you Penney?"

She gave me a playful jab. "Of course I do, silly. It's 'Randolph'. I'm from an old Virginian family. My ancestors were active in politics in the

early days of this country. That's why I went to the
Mormon Library–to trace my family tree."

I extended a hand in mock formality. "I'm
pleased to meet you, Miss Randolph. My name is
Brian Spencer. May I have the pleasure of your
company for dinner tonight?"

"Why, Mister Spencer," she went along
with the act, "I don't usually go to dinner with a
man I just met." Her manner sobered. "I really am
hungry, Brian. Do you think your housekeeper has
prepared enough dinner for an unexpected guest?"

"This is Maria's Bingo night. Maggie and I
usually just raid the refrigerator Tuesday nights.
But I do know of a good restaurant just up the road.
Do you like seafood?"

"Are you kidding? I grew up near the
Chesapeake Bay. I'd love to go to the restaurant
with you but only if I pick up the tab. I can afford
it." She hesitated. "Won't Maggie be worried
when you don't come home on time?"

"I'll give her a call." I picked up my cell
phone and punched in my home number. Maggie
answered. I spoke into the mouthpiece. "Hi,
honey, I'm going to be a little late. I'm having
dinner with a friend. By the way, I'm bringing you
a wounded bird."

Her lilting laughter sparkled over the
airways. "All right, Dad. I know you too well to
ask what you're up to. I'll be home."

"That takes care of that." I put down the
phone and pointed to a glowing sign ahead. "That's
where we eat. They have out-of-this-world
shrimp."

I pulled in, found a parking space and

stopped. We got out of the car and I locked the
doors. "Can't have anyone stealing your supplies."

"Or your books."

I took her elbow and escorted her inside. A
hostess seated us and a waitress came to take our
orders.

"What's good, Brian, besides those
shrimp?"

"Everything. I'm having the shrimp. You
might want to try the combination platter. It has
shrimp, fish, clams, oysters and scallops. You'll
get a good idea as to what to order next time." In
the soft subdued light of the room I hoped she
could not see the expression on my face that told
how much I hoped there would be a next time for
the two of us.

"Okay, you order for me, and anything you
want for yourself. But remember, I'm paying. I'll
have a tossed salad and iced tea with mine."

The waitress jotted down our orders.
"Would you like something to drink before
dinner?"

I hesitated and glanced at Penney.

"Oh, why not?" She tossed her shoulders.
"Let's have some white wine and drink a toast to
lost luggage."

For a long moment after the waitress
padded away, Penney and I stared at each other.
She broke the awkward silence with a little laugh.
"Do you come here often, Brian?"

"Linda and I dined here frequently. I
haven't been here since she died."

Her gaze dropped. "There I go reminding
you of your wife. I'm sorry."

"It's all right, Penney. I have only pleasant memories of the time we spent together. But tell me more about yourself."

"There's not much to tell. My father is a 'country gentleman', you know, old money. We have a horse farm on the James River in Virginia and he makes a pretense of running it. Actually, the hired foreman runs it. We have never bred a really winning racehorse but we have a fine line of saddle horses. My father drinks more than he should and when he drinks he and Mother fight. She was a debutante from a fine family when they met. Something of a local beauty queen. Her only interests were partying and taking care of her looks. I came along as an intrusion into their lifestyle."

"You sound bitter."

"Do I? I don't want to be bitter. I feel more–disappointed in them. They sent me off to a boarding school when I was old enough. I wasn't a happy child. Perhaps that's why I took up art. When very young I showed some talent. Alone in my room I would draw. My teachers encouraged me. When I was sixteen I took the GED exam to get out of high school. Got the highest grade ever in that school. But I'm bragging, aren't I?"

"That's something to be proud of. Where did you go from there?"

"New York. Without even calling my parents I left school and went to New York. I enrolled in a good art school and stayed there two years before I got the urge to travel. My grandmother set up a trust fund that provides me with more money than I'll ever need, so I don't have to depend on my parents for a handout."

"Do your parents know where you are now?"

"Brian, I don't really know where I am myself. The bus I arrived on was headed for West Palm Beach so I guess that's where I am."

"Pretty close. We met at the West Palm Beach bus terminal. From there we drove east. I live on the ocean just north of Palm Beach."

The waitress brought our wine. With a mischievous gleam in her eye, Penney lifted her glass. "Here's to good friends. Tonight is kind of special."

"You've been listening to beer commercials."

Her manner sobered. "That did sound pretty corny, didn't it? But really, Brian, I do hope we can be good friends."

Our dinners arrived and we began eating. Penney ate ravenously. "This food is delicious. I was really hungry. Bus stop food is not very appetizing."

I got a sudden idea. "Penney, I have a friend who owns an art gallery in Palm Beach. I'll show him some of your sketches. If he likes them he'll want to see some finished paintings. Do you have some you can get to?"

"Before I left for Utah I had all of my best pieces packed in shipping crates. They're stored at the farm. The foreman will ship them to me."

I gave her a stern look. "Penney, aren't you going to call your parents?"

She shook her head. "They're not home. My father took some horses to a show in upstate

New York. Mother is on a Carribean cruise."

"Don't they travel together?"

"Ha! I don't think they even ever sleep together. But enough of the sordid side of life. Do you think your friend will look at my sketches?"

"He will if I ask him to."

Her eyes sparkled. "Please ask him, Brian. Please. Please. Pretty please."

We finished our meal, left the restaurant and drove home. As we made our way up the winding drive to the front entrance Penney's eyes opened wide.

"This is a mansion, Brian. Writing books must pay really big."

I laughed. "If I had to depend on my writing for a living I'd have a shanty on the wrong side of the Intracoastal Waterway. I made a sizable fortune as a stockbroker. After Linda died I no longer had the heart for business so I retired. Now I spend most of my time writing."

We pulled into the carport, stopped and got out. I took Penney's bags from the car and placed them by the front door. As I fumbled for my keys a light came on and Maggie opened the door. I took Penney's arm.

"Maggie, this is Penney. Penney, meet Maggie."

Maggie gave Penney a warm embrace. "So you're Dad's wounded bird! I won't ask either of you any questions now but don't think I'm not curious. Come on, little bird, let me fix you a cozy nest and draw you a bath." She turned to me. "Take Penney's things to the Rose Room, Dad."

Later as I sat in my study opening the day's mail I heard Penney's voice behind me.

"Goodnight, Brian."

I turned. She stood in the doorway, her slender figure, draped in a filmy robe, silhouetted against the hall lights. She ran over and planted an impulsive kiss on my cheek.

"Thanks, Brian. Thanks—for everything."

CHAPTER TWO

I was not fully awake the next morning when Maggie called through my closed bedroom door. "Penney and I are going bicycling. We have a lot of girl-talking to do. We'll join you for breakfast."

Well, I thought, this will save me the trouble of explaining to Maggie the circumstances that led to my bringing Penney home. By the time they finish their ride Maggie will know more about Penney than I do. I tried to get back to sleep but after a half-hour of tossing and turning I gave up, dressed, and went to the patio to relax and make plans for the day. Book-signing sessions usually are dull and ego-deflating and I did not look forward to today's with much enthusiasm. Sometimes an hour or more will pass before a buyer brings a book to be signed. Meanwhile the author must try to look pleasant and interested in what's going on around him. But a lot of publicity has been given today's session, with the 'local author' angle played up big, so today could be different. Then there was Penney. I had to find time to arrange a meeting with Francois LeDuc for her.

Maria came out and put a cup of coffee and a Danish on the table. "I saw pretty young woman in guest room when I come home last night, Mister Brian," she beamed. "Very good. You too young not to have woman in your life."

"Stop right there, Maria. You're jumping to conclusions. The young lady's name is 'Penney' and she is not 'woman in my life'. She is just someone who needed a place to stay last night."

Maria scuttled away, calling back over her shoulder. "She very pretty, Mister Brian. She very pretty."

Another woman in my life? I hadn't given any serious thought to it since Linda died. Penney? This is crazy, I told myself. I'm old enough to be her father. She would probably laugh at the suggestion she be anything to me. My confused fantasizing ceased abruptly as I saw Maggie and Penney, dressed in identical white shorts and halter tops, wheeling up the drive. I greeted them. "The

Bobsey twins, I presume,"

"Penney got me up early and told me all about how you two met." Maggie kissed me lightly on the forehead. "It's not like you to bring home strange women but I'm glad you brought her." She paused. "We're going backpacking in Europe this summer."

"Not unless it's okay with you, Brian. I don't want to get on your bad side by leading Maggie astray."

They seated themselves as Maria brought breakfast. The housekeeper smiled. "What beautiful family you make."

I felt my ears beginning to turn red so I broke in quickly. "I've often said I wish Maggie had been twins. She's such a pleasure that twins would just double my pleasure."

Penney pointed a finger at me, her eyes sparkling. "Now who's been listening to commercials. Double the flavor, double the fun..."

I flashed Maria a warning glance and turned to Maggie. "What do you girls plan to do today. I'll be at the book-signing."

"We know that, Dad. I'm taking Penney on a tour of the town. The public beach is crowded with college kids on spring break so we'll probably go and ogle the hunks."

"Well, just be careful. I'm not sure it's safe for such beautiful girls as you two. Those college girls can be pretty ferocious and will scratch your eyes out if you attract the attention of their men."

"We can take care of ourselves," they both spoke at the same time, then turned to face each other and burst into laughter.

I looked at Penney. "I'll speak to the art dealer I told you about. His name is Francois LeDuc. At least that's what he calls himself. His real name would probably be more familiar in Brooklyn than in Paris or Palm Beach. But he has built up a good following among the nouveau riche. He specializes in contemporary art." I glanced at my watch. "I'd better get moving. I want to get to the bookstore in time to set up before they open."

"Do you want to take some of my sketches to show to Mister LeDuc?" Penney asked.

"No. I'll make an appointment for you to show him your work yourself. Incidently, I haven't seen any of it yet."

Penney jumped up. "I'll get my sketchbook."

"Not now. No time. I'll look at them this evening. You will be here this evening, won't you?"

Maggie broke in. "Of course she will. My twin sister is not going to get away any time soon."

"Good luck," Penney called as I hurried away.

The signing went far better than I had anticipated, with a milling throng in the store all morning and brisk sales of my books. Lunch time might have passed unnoticed if Maggie and Penney had not come in. "Come on, Dad, you're taking two hungry girls to lunch."

I put my "Author will return at 3 P.M." sign on the table and left, a girl hanging onto each elbow. "What do you have a taste for, Penney?

Chinese? Italian? Greek? Polynesian? You name it, we have it here."

"I liked that place where we ate at last night, but I suppose it's too far away."

"I'm afraid so. It's on the other side of the lake. We don't have the time now. Perhaps the three of us can go there for dinner."

"Count me out, Dad. Richard has asked me to go to dinner and a show with him. I told him I would. You and Penney go. Right now, what do you say we try that new Thai place. Do you like Thai food, Penney?"

Penney laughed. "Never tried it. But I'll try anything once."

We walked the short distance to the restaurant, entered and were seated. A waitress arrived promptly, took our orders and glided away.

"How did your morning go, girls?" I opened the conversation. "Did you go to the beach?"

Maggie wrinkled her nose. "Naw. Penney party-pooped on me. Said she isn't interested in watching gorgeous, over-muscled young Adonis's romping on the beach."

"Wait a minute, Maggie," Penney defended herself, "you're the one who said they're all a bunch of conceited asses."

"Okay, maybe I wasn't too keen on the idea. Anyway, Dad, we took a drive down the beach. I showed Penney where the rich and famous live. The Kennedy place. Donald Trump's palace. Places like that. We strolled down Worth Avenue just like wealthy tourists do."

"We went by Francois LeDuc's gallery," Penney interrupted, "but we didn't go in. It's a very impressive place, Brian. I do hope I can get some of my paintings in there."

"I called Francois. He'll see us tomorrow at ten o'clock."

"I'm so excited. But I'm scared, too. Suppose he doesn't like my work. Do you have any idea how crushing it is to have your work rejected?"

"Do I?" I laughed, "I must have received a hundred rejection slips before I got my first book published."

Our lunch, a collage of spicy food and small talk, passed quickly. When we were ready to leave, Maggie picked up the check. "This one's on me, Dad. Richard is taking me to dinner tonight but you have to pay for Penney's dinner." She paid the cashier and turned to me. "Go back to your books, Dad. We're driving down the road a ways."

"All right, but don't get home too late. Remember, you both have dates tonight." A date with Penney? I thought. That's ridiculous. Naw, this isn't a date.

For the rest of the afternoon I had trouble keeping my mind on selling books. Like the refrain of a song that won't leave your head, the thought wouldn't leave mine–this isn't a date. This isn't a date. This isn't a date...

When I arrived home I found Maggie and Penney in the pool. "Come on in," Penney shouted, "the water's delightful."

I quickly changed into my bathing trunks and joined them.

"Did the signing go well, Dad?" Maggie

called from across the pool as I jumped in.

"Better than expected. All of the books the store had on hand sold out by four. The store continued to take orders with the understanding I would sign them before delivery. Then some of the members of my writers' workshop group came by and I stayed awhile to talk with them."

"You teach creative writing, Brian?"

"Well, not exactly, Penney. We have a good group of enthusiastic budding authors who meet once a week. We read our works and critique each others'. Would you like to sit in on one of our sessions?"

"I'd love to, as long as it's not tomorrow. Don't forget, we have an appointment with Mister LeDuc in the morning."

Maggie swam over to us. "Hey, remember me? I'm here, too. Well, I know how to keep you two from hogging the conversation." She placed her hands on the tops of our heads and ducked us under. I grabbed her ankles and pulled her down. Moments later we all popped to the surface, laughing and blowing.

Penney brushed water from her face and eyes. "Gee, Maggie, you sure are lucky to have a father who's a fun person."

Richard arrived promptly at 6:30 to pick up Maggie. Penney and I were leaving and met him at the door. I introduced them. Richard acknowledged the introduction with a solemn "Pleased to meet you, Miss Randolph" and a formal handshake. Maggie came down the stairs and they left.

"This is such a beautiful evening," I suggested, "let's take Maggie's convertible. Station wagons are such stodgy vehicles."

"There's nothing wrong with station wagons, Brian. I drive one when I'm home. But I do like riding in a convertible with the top down. I plan to rent one tomorrow so I won't have to depend on you and Maggie for transportation while I'm here."

As we crossed the causeway to the mainland I glanced over at Penney. She sat staring straight ahead, apparently deep in thought, her long hair blowing in the breeze. "Penny for your thoughts, Penney."

She jumped as if startled. "I was thinking how beautiful it is here. You know, Brian, I think I'd like to live in Florida."

When the hostess passed the menus Penney waved hers away. ""I think I'll stick with the combination platter. I'm not very adventuresome when it comes to trying new things."

I laughed. "Penney, you're the most adventuresome person I ever met."

She wrinkled her brow into a slight frown. "Brian, are Maggie and Richard in a serious relationship?"

"I think Richard is more serious than Maggie is. He keeps asking her to marry him but she keeps putting him off. You met him. What is your first impression?"

"Well, he seems to be kind of..."

"Stuffy?"

"The word I was looking for is 'dull'. I noticed she never calls him 'Dick' or 'Ricky'. Is he always so formal?"

"Richard is a real solid citizen. MIT graduate. Computer engineer at IBM. But I think Maggie wants more than that."

"He isn't a fun person, is he?"

I shook my head. "Not by the wildest stretch of the imagination could he be called a fun person."

Penney leaned across the table and gazed straight into my eyes. "If I should ever marry, Brian, I would want to marry a fun person."

CHAPTER THREE

Penney's face displayed nervous excitement as we sat in Francois LeDuc's salon, waiting as he engaged in animated conversation with a prospective buyer on the other side of the room. Suddenly she reached into her bag pulled out a sketch pad and began sketching furiously, glancing frequently at Francois. As Francois bade goodbye to his prospect she jumped up, ran over and handed him the paper, then darted back to where I sat. Francois glanced at the sketch, raised his eyebrows, and started towards us.

"Look, Brian, it's me! See the thrill of the chase in my eyes! Look at the anticipation of a big sale on my face! She caught the real me, Brian." He undressed Penney with his eyes. "So, this is the talented young artist from New York you promised to bring me?"

"Francois LeDuc, meet Penelope Randolph. Penney, meet Palm Beach's most distinguished connoisseur of art." They shook hands. Francois tossed the sketch onto the table.

"This is quite clever and rather amusing, but can you produce real art?"

"She's the best portrait artist I ever met, Francois. I looked at the sketch book she has with her and quite frankly I think her work is outstanding. Of course, I don't have the eye for art that you do. See for yourself."

Penney handed him her sketchbook. He thumbed through it rapidly, paused, then went back to the beginning and carefully studied each page. After going through the entire book he paused again and stroked his beard reflectively. "Do you have these on canvas?"

"Yes, most of them. I did the western characters recently and haven't had time to paint them."

"I would like to see your finished work. Can you bring some in tomorrow?"

"All of my paintings are at my home in Virginia, but I can have them here in a couple of days."

Francois made a shooing motion with his hands. "Go. Go like the wind and start them on their way. You have real talent, Penney. If your work looks as good in oil as it does in pencil I believe you have a future with the Francois LeDuc gallery." As we turned to leave, Francois touched my arm and lowered his voice. "The payment will be on time this month. I promise you."

Penney pretended not to hear the art dealer's parting words, but when we reached the car she faced me angrily. "Does Mister LeDuc owe you money? Is that why he's willing to take a look at my work? Brian, I don't want you or anyone buying favors for me. If I can't make it on my own merit I don't want to make it." She yanked open the door, got in and slammed the door shut. As we left the parking lot she looked straight ahead, her face dark.

We drove several blocks before I looked over at her and burst into laughter. "You really have a short fuse, little lady."

"Don't patronize me!" she snapped. Suddenly tears began flowing. "I'm not angry at you, Brian. It's just that I had such high hopes that Mister LeDuc would accept my work because it's good, not because he has an obligation to accept it."

"Your work IS good. True, Francois does owe me money. I put up the capital to open his gallery. But you should know one thing about him; he is a very shrewd business man. He is not about to risk the reputation of his gallery by showing inferior paintings. If he decides to display any of your portraits it will be because of their quality, not because of any influence from me." I reached over and lifted her chin. "Besides, since I have a financial interest in his success I wouldn't let him display them if I didn't think they show real talent."

In the afternoon Maggie joined Penney and me in the pool. "How did it go with Francois LeDuc, Penney?"

"Great. He wants to see all of my oils. I called home and asked our foreman, Cliff, to send them by air express."

Maggie turned to me. "Well, Dad, I had it out with Richard last night. I told him I always want to be his friend but that I can't marry him. Oh, I let him down easy. I told him he needs a wife with a brain comparable to his, and that a bubblehead like me would bore him to tears."

"You a bubblehead? Perish the thought, Maggie. You're a very smart, level-headed person."

Her face broke into a broad grin. "Yeah, I know that. But what harm is it to let him think he's the winner in this situation?"

I shook my head. "Women! You're such devious creatures."

Eyes gleaming, the two girls pounced on

me and pushed me under the water. Penney faced me when I came up. "Brian, why did you tell Francois I'm from New York? You know I'm from Virginia."

"Well, New York sounds more sophisticated, and Francois is very status-conscious. You did study in New York."

"So-o-o, you men can be devious, too!"

They pounced on me again, but this time I was ready. Wrestling and squirming, the three of us went to the bottom of the pool.

Penney's shipment of paintings arrived at the gallery and she went down to unpack them, driving the car she had rented. I had just begun work on a new novel and so I sat most of the day at my keyboard trying to get the story off the ground.

In the late afternoon Penney returned, walking on air, and came to my study. "Oh, Brian, I'm so happy. Francois–he asked me to call him 'Francois'–liked my paintings. He's going to clear out one of his anterooms and have a one-artist showing." She danced around the room. "He's taking me to dinner tonight to celebrate. What shall I wear, Brian? Should I dress formal, or casual, or what?"

"He'll probably take you to a very fancy restaurant. Do you have an evening gown with you? If, not, one of Maggie's should fit you."

"I asked him to take me to our place. Do you know what he said? He said that first we have to ride around town in his convertible with the top down so that his friends could see us and die of jealousy. Wasn't that sweet of him?" She paused.

"I have a new white jump suit trimmed in gold. It's semi-formal. Do you think it would be appropriate?"

"You would wow him in a jump suit. Actually, you would look pretty in anything."

I watched her run up the stairs, a lump forming in my throat. The feeling inside me was not that of a father watching his daughter prepare for a date. It was different feeling. It frightened me.

When Penney came down from her room that evening I had just entered the front hall. "You're gorgeous, Penney. Francois' friends will go out of their minds when they see him with you."

There was no smile on her face when she came over to me. "Brian, what kind of man is Francois? Personally, that is."

"Well, he does have the reputation of being quite a ladies' man."

"You don't have to use euphemisms with me, Brian. He's a womanizer, isn't he?"

I fidgeted.

"You don't have to answer. I can tell by your expression that he is. If he makes a pass at me and I rebuff him will that be the end of my show? What should I do?"

I put an arm around her shoulders. "That's something you'll have to decide for yourself. But as I told you before, he's a very shrewd business man, and if he thinks he can make money on your paintings he won't let a little rebuff interfere. He'll back off."

"And try again later?"

"Yes, he would try again later."

She looked down at the floor. "Brian, I'm not a virgin."

I put a finger to her lips. "You don't have to tell me about your personal life."

She ignored my protest. "When I was sixteen the most popular boy in the school asked me out. He was eighteen. I was elated. He drove to a notorious lovers' lane and started fooling around. I don't know if it was curiosity, hormones, or what, but I didn't resist him. He hurt me, Brian, and I screamed, but he wouldn't stop. When it was over he took me back to the dormitory. The next day he acted like he didn't know me, and a few days later I left for New York."

"You were the victim of date rape, Penney."

"Well, I don't know. I didn't resist him at first."

"Penney, don't let one traumatic incident sour you on love. A physical relationship between two people who truly care for each other can be a beautiful thing."

We heard Francois drive up. She gave me a quick peck on the cheek. "Thanks, Brian." She left.

As I heard them drive away Linda's lovely face flashed into my mind. Yes, I thought, it could be a very beautiful thing.

I was sitting at my keyboard when I heard Penney return. "How did it go?" I called. She came into my study.

"Very nicely. We had dinner and then took a long drive down the beach. He was a perfect gentleman. At dinner I got real adventuresome and ordered the stone crab."

"Did you like it?"

"It tasted good but it was a little hard to get to the meat. But I suppose the degree to which food is enjoyed depends on who it is shared with." She looked past my shoulder. "What are you writing?"

I quickly exited the file and shut down the computer. "I'm starting a new novel. So far I'm just developing the characters and outlining the plot. After I've finished a few chapters I'll let you critique them." I wasn't ready to tell her that the story was about a man and a girl who met at a bus station and I didn't know yet how it would end. "A telephone message came for you while you were out. Your mother's cruise ship docks in Miami tomorrow afternoon and she wants you to meet her. Said it's important."

Penney's face darkened. "What could she want? And how did she get this telephone number?"

"I imagine she wants to see her only daughter. You gave the number to the foreman at the farm. I suppose she got it from him." I looked at her sternly. "Penney, you must end this feud with your parents."

She remained glum. "I guess I'll have to go down and meet her."

"I'll drive you."

"Oh, would you? I don't know my way around down there and I'm sure I'd get lost."

I had the vague feeling she wanted someone with her when she greeted her mother.

After Penney went to her room I picked up the telephone and tapped in a number. "Hi, Francois, I hope I didn't get you out of bed."

"No. I was just getting ready to shower."

"So, how did your evening go?"

"Great. Penney is a delightful person. I enjoyed her company so much that I asked her to go to a show at the dinner theater Saturday night. But you didn't call to inquire about my pleasure, did you? What's up, Brian?"

"I don't know just how to put this so I'll give it to you straight. Penney is not the kind of girl you usually go out with. I would consider it a personal favor if you keep your relationship with her strictly on a business basis."

"Now hold on, Brian, I didn't know there was anything going on between you and Penney. You know I'd never move in on your girlfriend."

"Penney is not my girlfriend. She is just someone I'm very fond of and don't want to see get hurt."

"Think no more about it, Brian. Hey, I just remembered I have to go out of town this weekend. I'll have to withdraw my invitation to Penney." He paused. "We're both men of the world, Brian. I understand."

"I'm not sure you do, Francois, but thanks and good night."

As I hung up the phone I felt just a little bit guilty.

CHAPTER FOUR

The cruise ship had already docked and passengers were streaming down the gangplank when we entered the Port of Miami parking lot. "It won't take very long for your mother to clear customs," I told Penney, "these days most of the paper work is done while the ship is still at sea."

We had hardly settled down in the cavernous waiting room before I saw a tall, shapely woman, followed by a Redcap pushing a dolly loaded with luggage, exiting the Customs and Immigration section. A stylish hat topped her upsweep hairdo. She spotted Penney and gave a little wave.

"There's Mother now," Penney whispered.

"Then go meet her halfway."

Penney walked slowly toward her mother. I followed, a step behind. Penney had told me her mother was forty years old, but the woman approaching us looked much younger. As we got closer I could see that expertly applied makeup enhanced the illusion of youth.

The mother and daughter met with a brief hug and an exchange of quick pecks on the cheeks. Penney stepped back. "Mother, meet Brian Spencer. I'm visiting his daughter in Palm Beach.

coming suddenly exploded. "For God's sake don't be so dammed formal. It's 'Brian' and 'Patricia'."

Patricia Randolph shrugged her shoulders. "Very well, Penelope, if that's the way you want it. Now Brian, I'd be much obliged if you will find me a taxi and direct the driver to a decent hotel. I'm sure this good man standing here with my luggage will be most happy to get rid of it. Penelope, I want you to come with me. I have some things I want to discuss with you."

"You won't need a taxi or hotel, Patricia," I broke in. "I want you to come to my home and have a long visit with Penney."

"Oh, I couldn't impose on you Mister Spencer – Brian."

"Brian and Maggie live in a mansion on the ocean near Palm Beach, Mother."

"Oh?" Patricia Randolph looked me over from head to foot. "Well, if an unexpected guest won't upset your household too much. I was raised to believe that hosts and hostesses should have ample warning before receiving visitors."

"There's no formality in Brian's home, Mother. It's a very pleasant place to stay."

I led the porter to my station wagon and helped him stow the luggage. Patricia handed him a generous tip. I opened the door to the rear seat and motioned Penney and her mother in. Penney hesitated but I gave her a sharp look and she slid in beside her mother.

As we pulled out of the parking lot Patricia asked "How far is it to your place, Brian?"

"About an hour's drive on the Interstate if

traffic is not too heavy. Plenty of time for you two to catch up on what's happened in your lives since you last saw each other."

Patricia sniffed. "There isn't much we can talk about. I swear, I don't know what's gotten into this child, traipsing around the world alone doing this silly art thing. It just doesn't seem proper. She should be thinking about marrying a man from a good family and settling down. We sent her to the best schools where she could meet the right kind of people. When she was a small child we always had a competent nanny for her."

I suppressed an urge to tell her what I thought of this kind of "upbringing". "Your daughter is a very talented artist, Patricia. Have you seen any of her work?"

"Not really. When I'm at home she just pops in and pops out."

"She's having a one-artist showing at a Palm Beach gallery. Before you leave you'll have to see it. You'll be very proud of her."

We rode along in silence for awhile. Suddenly Patricia blurted out. "I might as well come right out and tell you why it is so important I talk with you, Penelope. Your father and I are getting a divorce."

"Oh no, Mother!"

"Don't look so shocked. You know we haven't gotten along well in years. Don't worry; it will be a friendly divorce. He wants out as much as I do. Though most of our money came from my family I'm letting him keep his beloved horse farm, with the legal stipulation you get it when he dies.

I've put away a nice nest egg from the money my family left me, so I'll be able to live quite well on my own."

"I don't know what to say, Mother."

Patricia's voice softened. "Don't say anything, Penelope. Just wish for greater happiness for me and for your father in the future."

I had called ahead on my cellphone so Maria had dinner on the table and a room ready for Patricia. Patricia took one suitcase to her room after asking Maria to store the others in a closet. "I won't be here long enough to need opening them."

After dinner Patricia went to freshen up. I slipped out to sit on the patio, while Penney and Maggie dashed off to Maggie's room to, I suspect, talk about the sudden upheaval in the Randolph family.

A little later Patricia came to where I sat enjoying the cool breeze and the prevailing twilight. "Is it all right if I take a walk on the beach, Brian?"

"Certainly. This is a delightful time to walk the beach."

Shortly after she left Penney came out. "Where's Mother?"

"She went for a walk on the beach."

"Which way did she go? I'll catch up to her."

I stopped her. "Not this time, Penney. I think she want's to be alone."

My most inspired writing usually comes in

the late evening, but that night as I sat at my keyboard the words refused to flow. Rushing around in my head were thoughts of the day's happenings. Why had Penney told her mother she was visiting Maggie? Was it because of what her mother would think if she knew that Penney had come home with a stranger met at a bus station?

I heard the soft sound of slippers against marble and looked out into the hall. Patricia was coming down the stairs. The dressing gown she wore made little effort to conceal the fullness of her breasts and the roundness of her thighs. She came to the door of my study.

"May I come in, Brian?"

"Of course. Come right in." I stood up.

She came over and for a long moment stared me in the eyes. "May I ask you a personal question, Brian? Are you and Penelope having an affair?"

"Certainly not! I'm very fond of her and I'm interested in furthering her career. But we are definitely not having an affair."

"Well, I've noticed how she looks at you and I was just wondering. I couldn't blame you if you were involved; she is very pretty. I suppose she did inherit some of my genes." She came closer and pressed her bosom against my chest. "She's just a child, Brian. What you need is a real woman in your life."

I eased back. "Really, Patricia, I'm flattered by what I think you're offering but I'm quite content with my life as it is and have no wish to complicate it."

CHANCE MEETING

She continued to press against me. "Brian, for more than twenty years I've been married to a man who has little interest in lovemaking and even less ability to perform it. Before I get too old and ugly to attract a man I want a real romance in my life."

"You're a very beautiful woman, Patricia. There are many handsome and virile men who would give their right arms to have you. Probably even some among your single male friends."

"The eligible men in our social circle are so stuffy."

I put an arm around her. "Perhaps if you let your hair down and showed some genuine interest in them they would thaw out real fast."

She pulled away. "Well, if there's no chance of a relationship with you, Brian, I guess that's my cue to move on."

"Not at all, Patricia. You're welcome to stay as long as you want. No one need know of our little conversation tonight."

"No," she shook her head, "I have to get on with my life. I'll be leaving in the morning." As she turned to go she looked back over her shoulder. "When Penelope gets through with her little show send her home, please." She went to her room.

A few minutes later Penney came storming into my study. "What did you say to my mother? She says she's leaving in the morning."

"I said nothing to offend your mother, Penney."

Her eyes blazed. "She made a pass at you, didn't she? Don't flatter yourself in thinking you're

204

the first one. I'll bet she's made passes at many men."

"You don't know that." I faced her and placed my hands on both her shoulders. "Penney, your mother is a very lonely person. She needs you more than you know."

"Oh, no, she doesn't need me. Having a twenty-one-year-old daughter around only reminds her of her own age. No, Brian, she doesn't need me." She turned and ran up the stairs.

I arose early the next morning to find Patricia already up, standing in the hall, her bags stacked around her.

"Good morning, Brian, You need not have gotten up to see me off. Maria fixed me coffee and Danish. I'm waiting for a limo to take me to the airport."

"You don't have to leave, Patricia."

"I must."

"Aren't you going to wake Penney up and say goodbye?"

"No, it's best that I just slip away. I want to get to the airport early to have the best chance for a standby seat. Because so many college kids are leaving I couldn't get a reservation."

"Well, if I can't persuade you to stay awhile, cancel the limo. I'll drive you to the airport."

Penney came down the stairs at that moment. "Don't bother, Brian, I'll take her." We loaded Patricia's luggage into Penney's rented convertible and they left.

CHANCE MEETING

After lunch I got into my car and headed down the drive. I met Penney coming in. As we came abreast of each other she waved for me to stop.

"Mother got a flight out, but we had a long wait. I stayed with her until she boarded. We talked, Brian, more than we have talked with each other in years." She paused. "I think we're going to get along much better in the future."

"That's wonderful. I'm very happy that you two have reconciled."

"Brian, we have a couple of good polo ponies at the farm. I'm going to ask my father to bring them down for the next Palm Beach Polo Club show."

"That would be nice. Now I have to go into town on some business. You just make yourself at home."

As she started to drive on she called back "Mother told me what you said about letting her hair down."

When I returned home late in the day I found Penney down at the beach, sitting before her easel in the shade of a grove of palm trees. I looked at what she was painting. The face of a beautiful woman smiled at me from the canvas, the face of Patricia Randolph, long silky hair cascading around her shoulders.

CHAPTER FIVE

During the days following Patricia Randolph's visit Penney busied herself completing the portrait of her mother and bringing her western sketches to life on canvas. Maggie left to attend her high school class reunion. I continued to work on my new novel.

Maria came to me one morning. "Mister Brian, my sister in Hialeah going to hospital for operation. No big thing but she want me to come stay with her for few days after she come home. All right with you if I go?"

"Certainly, Maria. It will be just Penney and me here. I'm sure we can fix breakfast and lunch. We'll go out for dinner."

"Thank you, Mister Brian. I cook big ham

207

and turkey yesterday and put in fridge. Pitcher of ice tea, too. You can make sandwiches for lunch. Plenty milk and cereal for breakfast. Coffee and Danish, too."

After Maria left I began having mixed feelings about being alone in the house with Penney. I had to face the reality that I had feelings for her that were not at all fatherly. Would I say or do something stupid and make a fool of myself? Furiously I hammered away at my keyboard as if the action would somehow excise the demons from my head.

Penney came to the door. "The portrait of Mother is dry enough for it to be put on display. I'm taking it to the gallery. I'll be back for lunch."

Near noon I set two places at a table under an umbrella on the patio and went back to the kitchen to make sandwiches. I had hardly done more than spread mayonnaise on bread when Penney rushed in, breathing hard, her face ashen, her body trembling. "He followed me here, Brian."

"Calm dow, Penney. Who followed you here?"

"Antonio Antonelli, the man who took me to the ranch."

"Two-tony Antonelli?"

Her eyes widened. "How did you know that is what they called him?"

"He's a reputed mobster, Penney." I guided her to the patio table and sat her down. "I swear, young lady, you need a guardian. You get mixed up with the damdest people."

Despite her terror her eyes flashed defiance. "People like you, Brian? I know I made a mistake going to the ranch and now I'm wondering if I made a mistake coming here." She began sobbing. "What am I going to do, Brian? What am I going to do?"

"Are you sure you saw him?"

She nodded. "Yes. I was taking the portrait of Mother in the back door when I saw him looking at my paintings. I'm quite sure he didn't see me. I got back in my car and came home fast as I could."

"You know, Penney, it could be a bizarre coincidence. You said he's a patron of the arts. He could just happen to be in the area and was checking out the local galleries. Why would he want to follow you here?"

She looked down at the floor. "There's something I didn't tell you."

I eyed her sternly. "Penney, I have a feeling there are a lot of things you haven't told me."

She pressed her head against my shoulder, sobbing. "I didn't want to get you involved. The reason I left the ranch so suddenly was not because of the attempted rape; I might have witnessed a murder there."

I sighed. "All right, tell me everything."

She sat down and began to regain her composure. "The ranch has an airplane landing strip running close to the house. Small planes came and went several times while I was there. They landed, unloaded some boxes into vans, and took off. The vans would drive away."

"A typical drug transfer operation."

"I was beginning to think that, too, but I didn't know how I would get out of there. That last night I was looking out the window of my room when I saw a plane come in near dusk. A man got out and Antonio went to meet him. They appeared to be having an argument. Antonio pulled a gun and shot the man. The pilot jumped out of the plane and he and Antonio put the man in the plane and the plane took off. Antonio came back into the house."

"You must have been terrified."

"I was never so scared in my life. I packed all of my things and put on the clothes I was wearing when we met at the bus station. I was getting out of there that night even if I had to walk out. About an hour after the shooting I heard Antonio coming down the hall. I jumped into bed, covered up and pretended to be asleep. He came into my room. I smelled whiskey and knew he had been drinking. I heard him say 'you've put me off long enough, you little bitch', then he yanked the covers off me. When he saw me awake and fully dressed he went berserk. That's when he tried to rape me. I put a knee to a vital spot and he fell and struck his head on the metal bed frame. He went out like a light. I dragged my things outside, loaded them on a Jeep and drove out to the highway where I flagged down a bus."

"What made you decide to come to Florida?"

"That's a weird story, Brian. Maybe fate

intended for me to come here. Anyway, the bus took me to Salt Lake City. I thought Antonio might have someone watching the airport so I decided to go home by bus. I bought a ticket to Richmond and was told the bus would leave in about three hours. I went to the restroom. When I came out I saw one of the men from the ranch. I was scared out of my wits and started to duck back into the restroom. Then I saw him going into the men's room. A bus was loading at the terminal. I ran to the ticket counter and asked the agent to put me on that bus, no matter where it was going. I told him my luggage was checked through to Richmond and asked him to try to get it on this bus. We pulled out immediately after I got aboard. The driver told me the bus was on an express run to West Palm Beach, and with changes of drivers would go all the way."

"You could have changed buses at any stop and gone home."

She looked up at me. "Yes, I know that. But I was frightened and confused, and something told me to stay on that bus. Do you believe in predestination, Brian? I do. I think I was meant to come here to meet you." She gave a nervous laugh. "I have to confess something else. When I approached you in that waiting room I already knew of the hotel situation. An agent who went off duty earlier told me. I needed a friend badly, Brian, and you looked kind of..."

"Safe?"

"You looked like someone I could trust. Besides, you were reading Arts and Literature

Review. I really didn't expect to go home with you. I just thought you might help me find a place to stay that night."

I put my arms around her. "I'm very glad you stayed on that bus. Right now we have a serious situation to face–Two-tony Antonelli. One of the members of my writers' workshop group, Tom Blake, is an agent with the Justice Department's Organized Crime Bureau. Today is his day off and he lives near here. I'll give him a call. I'm sure he would like to hear your story."

When Tom answered the telephone I greeted him with "Hi, Tom, did you know Two-tony Antonelli is in town?"

He let out an expletive. "How do you know this, Brian?"

"I have a young lady here who saw him on Worth Avenue. She thinks he is after her because she saw him shoot a man."

"Hold her there! I'll be right over."

Tom arrived a few minutes later and I introduced them. He took her hand in his two big paws. "Penney, we have been trying for years to pin something on this guy. Brian said you saw him shoot a man."

"Yes." She proceeded to tell him the story she told me.

He stroked his beard reflectively. "I think I know who got shot. The body of one of our undercover boys turned up in an alley in a small town in Texas. He had infiltrated a drug ring we suspected Antonelli was involved in. The Texas town is a long way from Utah, but if we can find

the ranch we should find some blood where our
man fell. DNA evidence will show whether he was
the man you saw shot."

Penney reached into her handbag and pulled
out a slip of paper. "This might help. When I got
on the bus at the ranch the driver wrote out a
receipt for my fare." She handed it to Tom.

He read out loud "Rocking Double-A to
Salt Lake City, twenty-eight dollars. Penney, this
is terrific."

"You might find some blood on the plane,
too."

Tom smiled. "Fat chance. There are
thousands of small planes flying around in the
West. The odds against finding the one involved in
this case are astronomical."

"I know the number painted on the tail.
That same plane came in earlier and parked right
behind where I was sketching a cowboy sitting on a
fence. As a lark, I included the plane in my sketch,
complete in every detail."

Tom grabbed her and gave her a bear hug.
"Penney, you're fantastic. With your testimony we
can send Antonelli to prison for life." He frowned.
"First we have to pick him up. You're in real
danger until we do. How did he know you're
here?"

Penney thought for a moment. "Before I
left the ranch I wrote a letter home. I didn't mail it.
He must have found it and got my Virginia
address. Someone there must have told him my
paintings were shipped to Palm Beach. The
paintings were shipped to Francois LeDuc's gallery

so Antonio doesn't have this address, but he might have this telephone number because I gave it to the foreman."

"He'll find you," Tom replied grimly. "Penney, this guy is dangerous. Don't leave the house and stay out of sight. I'll have a police guard posted here until we pick him up."

That evening Penney and I watched a movie on television. When it ended she stretched and yawned. "I'm going to take a shower and go to bed. It's been a tiring day."

I gave her a light kiss on the forehead. "Try not to worry about Antonelli. The police will find him. Get a good night's sleep."

After she went upstairs I took my .32 automatic from my desk, loaded it and put it in my pocket. I checked all the windows and doors, turned off all downstairs lights, and slipped out on the patio. If he comes for Penney, I thought, he will have to get past me.

A few minutes later a shot rang out from the direction of the beach. Then two more quick shots. A harsh curse ripped the night air, followed by a babble of excited voices.

Tom called out "Hey, Brian, you awake? We got him." He walked toward the house and spotted me. "He came ashore in a Zodiac. When we challenged him he took a shot at one of my men. We returned the fire and plugged him in an arm and a leg. You and Penney can sleep easy tonight."

Penney came running from the house

screaming, one hand clutching her bathrobe closed at the waist. "Brian, are you all right? I heard shots." She threw herself into my arms, trembling like a frightened fawn.

"It's all over, Penney." I stroked her hair. "The police got him. It's all over."

We stood holding each other while medics took away the wounded mobster. When all had left I guided her back into the house. She clung to me, still trembling. "Make love to me, Brian,"she whispered, "the kind of love two people who care very much for each other share."

"Will you marry me, Penney?"

"Yes! Yes! Yes! Do you believe in love at first sight? I believe I began falling in love with you the first day I was here. Do you remember that night at the restaurant when I said I would want to marry a fun person? I felt then that I had met the fun person I would marry. Yes, Brian, I'll marry you."

I released her and her robe slipped from her shoulders. Gently I picked her up and carried her to my room.

THE OPERATORS

I'm sitting in the Broward County jail thinking that I wouldn't be here if I hadn't run into Mick Mitchell at the flea market. Benny Lieberman, my lawyer, who at this very moment is negotiating with the sheriff's people to spring me, has assured me I got nothing to worry about.

"You got nothing to worry about," he says. "You just happened to be at the wrong place at the wrong time."

216

THE OPERATORS

With the way my luck is running I'm having trouble being as confident as he is. But if the details of that little problem I had out on the coast haven't reached here... Well, maybe.

A couple months ago I breeze into Lauderdale in my 300ZX, having departed L.A. very suddenly after a guy in the SEC office who owes me a favor tips me that the Feds are getting ready to ask some embarrassing questions about the very lucrative little penny stocks business I'm running. Since a big flea market is a good place to find out what games are being played in these parts I go out to this Texas-size lot on the edge of town. I'm wandering about getting the smell of things when I hear my name called. "Hey, Vince, over here."

I look in the direction of the voice and I see the Mick, dressed in a three-hundred-dollar suit with a necktie and the works. Now Mick is not noted for real high-class scams so I'm a little surprised to see him in this fancy booth with a backdrop picturing some old guys romping on a beach with a bunch of busty babes. The banner over the booth says "Put vim and vitality back in your life with Vigorade". Having no reason not to talk to Mick, him and me having worked together at various times, I walk over and shake his hand.

Mick has a cooler full of the stuff he's hawking and he pours some in a paper cup and hands it to me. "Taste this and tell me what you think."

I sip a little and roll it around on my tongue. It tastes pretty good so I toss the rest of it down.

217

The stuff, I discover, not only tastes good but packs real wallop.

"Sweetest little deal I ever had," Mick confides to me between customers who plunk down five-dollar bills for pints of the stuff.

"I thought the snake oil bit went out with Hadacol," I says to him.

"That's the beauty of it," he smiles. "I don't make any medicinal claims for it. Look," he hands me a glossy full-color brochure showing older guys with young chicks sailing, and playing tennis and golf, and things like that. "All this really says is it makes you feel good. And it does."

"What's in it?" I'm more than a little suspicious.

He leans close to my ear. "It's really the same stuff football players pour over the head of the coach after they win a big game. See," he picks up a bottle, "all the ingredients are listed right here on the label." He gives me a knowing wink. "That is, all except the special additive made for me by a guy up in the Smokey Mountains. Hey, I got guys pushing the stuff in Miami, West Palm, all over the state. It's going great."

Mick suddenly looks past my shoulder and his mouth sort of drops open, and I hear this voice behind me say "Hi, Mick, long time no see." I turn around and see this dame standing there with a smirk on her face, and I look back at Mick who is more than a little flustered.

"Hi, Velma," he stammers. "Musta been a couple years."

"Three years and four months to be exact,

darling," she purrs sweetly, "since you stranded me in that fleabag motel in Memphis."

While Mick is introducing me to Velma I'm looking her over and I can see that this gal has a lot of mileage on her but must have been a real looker in her day. Then Mick starts apologizing to Velma and at the same time telling me what happened in Memphis.

"Velma and me were pulling the bible scam, working the obituaries and delivering C.O.D. personalized bibles 'ordered' by the recently deceased." He turns to Velma. "That day I ran out the local bunco squad boys stopped me and started asking questions. I jumped in my car and took off. They chased me to the county line then turned back. I kept right on going. I guess I should have gone back for you but I have a strong dislike for Southern jails, and anyway, you had the week's take so I figured you would be okay." He pauses. "How did you know I was here?"

"I ran into Tiny Watson in New Orleans. He put me on to a great gimmick that's working here in Florida and he mentioned he had seen you here. Now, Mick, I just had a long bus ride and I'm tired and I'm dirty. You can make it up to me for Memphis by putting me up for a few days until I can get settled."

Mick gets real uncomfortable. "Gee, I'd like to Velma but my place is at present being shared with a very significant other." His face brightens and he turns to me. "How about you, Vince. Can Velma stay with you for a little while?"

THE OPERATORS

I'm a guy with a tender heart and I can see that this doll is about to drop from exhaustion so I tell her to come along with me. We pick up her bags at the bus station, stop at the Chinese joint for some takeouts, and drive to the townhouse I'm renting.

Velma showers and puts on her pajamas and comes out looking a lot better. While we wade into the chow mein and egg rolls she starts telling me about the deal she has latched on to.

"This British syndicate," she explains, "has built this big resort and gambling casino on a small island in the Bahamas, and the place is dying. To get people out there they are willing to give away a lot of rooms. They can't come right out and advertise free vacations because that would drain off the paying customers."

"So what's the con?" I'm skeptical but curious.

"They will give me as many one-week vacation packages as I want in exchange for running a publicity bureau for them here in Fort Lauderdale. Mostly just manning a booth at a flea market and passing out brochures. Of course, the free vacation package has a stinger in it. It gives two people a room and use of the resort facilities for a week. But it includes air transportation for only one and the deal is good only if two people go. The other person has to pay for the flight. The only way there is on a charter flight operated by the resort, and the fare is not cheap. You have to stay a week before your return reservation is good. That's where they've got you. The only place to eat is at the hotel dining room where the prices are high enough to make a rock star blink. Then they have the slots, roulette wheels and crap tables going for them. They cover themselves by saying the time the trip can be taken is subject to availability of rooms."

"So where do you come in?"

She gets real enthusiastic. "All we have to do is set up the booth and pass out the brochures. We put up a sign saying 'Win a free vacation.' The brochures are in sealed envelopes. People are invited to pick one out of a basket. Half of them have a coupon good for the freebie. All the marks have to do to redeem the coupons is to send us a fifty-dollar processing fee. We validate the coupon and return it to them. From that point we're out of the picture. All arrangements for the trip have to be made with the resort operators." She pauses. "It's psychology, Vince. If the marks think they won something they won't be as suspicious of the deal."

When Velma starts putting "us" and "we" in the conversation I get a strong feeling about what's coming next, but she just leans back, clasps her hands behind her head and stretches a little, pushing out her finer points. Then she gives a sigh and says it's been a long day and she'd like to turn in.

That night I find that though this kid has been around the block a few times she still has a lot to offer, even to a very discriminating guy like yours truly.

The next morning I wake up and I reach

221

over for Velma and my hand comes up empty. I jump out of bed and look for my wallet which I left on the dresser and am relieved to see it is still there and my money is in it. Then I catch the smell of coffee and bacon and eggs coming from the kitchen, which is strange because I don't keep any coffee, bacon and eggs in my kitchen, the corner doughnut dump being sufficient for my breakfast needs.

I go into the kitchen and there is Velma, dressed in a cute jump suit with a bath towel around her middle for an apron. She gives me a big smile and a cheerful "Good Morning."

"I took a twenty from your wallet and bought a few groceries," she tells me, "I hope you don't mind. The change is on the table."

As we're eating breakfast she comes right to the point. "Vince, I need a partner to put up the seed money for the vacation promotion. We'll need a stand at the flea market and an office. And there will be booth decorations, sign painting and other expenses. Will you come in with me?"

I think to myself, what the hell, I got nothing going at this time and this thing might have some possibilities. So I talk it over with Benny Lieberman, who is a very knowledgeable lawyer, and he says it's perfectly legit as long as the 'winners' eventually get their free vacations. Then Velma and I drive out to the flea market to arrange for a booth. While she wanders around looking over the stuff on sale I stop by Mick's stand. He assures me that Velma is a very honest doll and that the scam looks good to him. He also mentions that next to the warehouse where he mixes up his tonic there is a already-furnished office that can be rented at a reasonable fee.

Velma and I set up the game and it works better than I expected. Every mail brings a stack of fifty-dollar checks. Things are going very well except I'm getting this bad feeling about what's going on between Mick and Velma. After his live-in walks out on him Mick has been making a play for Velma, but she just gives him a drop-dead look whenever he comes over to our booth. Which is very all right with me; this babe really cooks up some tasty meals.

A few weeks pass and suddenly the roof falls in. The local fish wrapper prints an expose-type story telling how the deal works and suggesting that a free Bahamas vacation might not be such a bargain. In addition, it warns that the Better Business Bureau is getting a lot of complaints from people who say they're getting the runaround when they try to make reservations for their trips.

I talk the situation over with Velma and we decide it's time to fold. We go down to the office to clean out the desk and filing cabinet. Velma goes back to the car and I step into Mick's warehouse to say "So long."

The guy who supplies Mick's secret ingredient has just pulled up with a load, and as soon as Mick hands over the payment all hell breaks loose and the joint is swarming with Fed and state alcohol control boys. Jeeze, can you believe it? A sweet little operation like Mick's going down the drain because a stupid hillbilly moonshiner lets himself get trailed all the way from Tennessee. Or was that really what happened? I get this weird feeling as I see Velma flash Mick a smug smile as the cops push him into the patrol car. I get hauled down to the police station along with Mick and the bootlegger.

So I'm sitting and waiting for Benny to convince the cops I got no part in Mick's operation and just happened to drop in at the time, which is the truth. I'm thinking I'm getting too old for this kind of hassle and when I get out of this I should go into something solid. Like selling used cars, maybe. I'm hoping Velma will be at the townhouse when I get home. Hey, getting married is not the worse thing that can happen to a guy.

THE PICTURE IN THE WALLET

D an Hendry placed an eight by ten color photograph on his desk and looked up at me. "She's a 'Jane Doe' we picked up in the boonies a few days ago, Jim. What do you know about her?"

We go back a long way, Dan and I. Growing up in the same Miami neighborhood, we fished the canals and sailed the bay together. In high school he captained the football team and I edited the school paper. After graduation Dan became a Metro policeman. I drifted around the country working on one grubby newspaper after another while trying to make my mark as a freelance writer until that fateful day my six lucky numbers coming up on the Florida lottery gave me financial independence. Now I can write what I want to, when I want to, without having to give a damn if I receive enough rejection slips to paper the walls of my den. The byline "Jim Hamilton" has not exactly become renown.

The girl in Dan's picture bore only a slight resemblance to the one in the small picture I held. Her face was contorted and there was an ugly bruise on her throat. She was, quite obviously, dead. But the two had one thing in common; both wore the same jeweled ear clips. There was no doubt but that the two pictures were of the same girl–Angie Adams. What a tragic end for the uninhibited sprite I was beginning to know so well but had never met.

My search for Angie Adams began when I opened a new wallet, a beautiful soft brown Florentine leather wallet received as a gift. The wallet came, as the box in which it nested proclaimed, from Ramon's, a gift boutique in the Tropic Gardens Mall. Ramon's, I knew from experience, is one of those "linen shops" that use pretentious surroundings and illusionary discounts to extort exorbitant prices from the naive and the unwary. Mentally I berated the gift donor for her gullibility; she probably paid far too much for it.

Photo pockets in new wallets usually hold the halftone likeness of some past or present movie queen, but no Sophia Loren or Gina Lolabrigida looked at me from this product of Italy. Instead, to my amused surprise, smiling through the acetate window was the fresh face of a blonde, blue-eyed girl in her late teens. Actually, the expression on the pretty face was more of a grin than a smile, the devilish grin of one who had just pulled a prank on someone and was relishing the discomfort of the victim.

I removed the picture and flipped it over. On the back, along with a photography studio's imprint and an order identification was a neatly penned invitation "For a good time call 555-1959." Ha! I thought, an entrepreneur with imagination. I have often seen similar messages scribbled on the walls of public telephone booths and men's restrooms. But on the back of a wallet photo? For me this was an intriguing first.

Smelling a story behind the cryptic message, I picked up my telephone and tapped in the number shown. The telephone at the other end rang three times before a sultry female voice whispered "Can't talk now, lover, but at the sound of heavy breathing just leave a message and I'll get back to ya." Without waiting for erotic sound effects I hung up.

I tried the number repeatedly during that day and the next, always getting the same recorded response. As my exasperation mounted so did my curiosity. I checked a cross-reference telephone directory; the number was unlisted. There's a story here, I told myself.

Fortunately, I had two leads as to the identity of the mysterious nymph. The wallet in which I found the picture was imported but the telephone number was a local one. It was a good bet that the picture was placed in the wallet at the store where the wallet was purchased. The studio name and order number were more promising. Without doubt the studio would have the girl's name and her address at the time the picture was taken. I headed for the studio first.

The pungent odor of photographic chemicals assailed my nostrils as I entered the dingy waiting room where examples of the photographer's creations covered the walls. I glanced around to see if I could spot the girl in my picture but she wasn't on display.

"Anyone here?" I called.

The man who came from behind a curtain to greet me, small, prim, fiftyish and bespectacled and wearing a lab coat, fitted the scene as if placed there by Charles Dickens. When I introduced myself and showed him the picture he gave a quick gasp. "I'll never forget that one," he exclaimed, "not if I live to be a hundred. Wild as they come."

The picture was made for a high school yearbook, he explained. "I always photograph the young ladies bare shouldered. They remove their blouses in the dressing room and put a drape around their, er, bosoms. Well, sir, this one came out and sat down in front of the camera and quick as a wink..." he made a quick pass across his chest,"...she whipped off the drape and there she sat, stark naked from the waist up, grinning like a Cheshire cat. I snapped the picture, head and shoulders only, of course. Then she picked up her

blouse and brassiere, flipped them across one
shoulder, and strolled out into the waiting room
full of her classmates–boys and girls."

"Do you know here I can find her?" I asked.
"I want to interview her for a story."

He gave me a doubting look. "I really
shouldn't give you any information, but for this
one..." he shook his head. He glanced at the order
number and disappeared behind the curtain. In a
moment he returned holding a file card.

"Her name is Angie Adams. At the time
the picture was made she lived over in Palmdale.
But she came in later and ordered a dozen
Friendship pictures..." he nodded toward the
picture in my hand "...and had them mailed to an
address in the northeast section."

I made a note of the two addresses, thanked
him for his help, and left. Stories turn up in the
strangest places and I felt sure that behind this one
was more than the titillating antics of a highschool
sex queen.

The northeast address was in a
neighborhood of small single-floor courtyard
apartment buildings between Biscayne Boulevard
and the bay. During Miami's glory era of the
twenties, thirties, forties and fifties, the apartments
were occupied during the so-called "Hialeah
season", the prime winter months coinciding with
the racing dates at Hialeah Park, by affluent
refugees from freezing weather in the north and
midwest. For the hot summer months they were
shuttered. Now on the leading edge of creeping

urban blight the area was becoming a Mecca for street walkers, drug pushers and smalltime hoodlums.

As did its neighbors, the building where Angie lived needed paint. A peeling sign on the door of the first apartment identified it as the residence of the manager. I hurried down a trash-littered covered walkway to the end apartment and knocked on the door. There was no answer. I knocked again, louder. The door to the manager's apartment opened and a woman with hair like a worn floor mop stuck her head out.

"If you're looking for Angie, she ain't home," she called.

I walked back toward her. "Do you know when she'll be back?" She shook her head. "Do you know where she went?" I persisted. Her eyes narrowed.

"You a cop?"

"No, I'm a friend of hers." I lied.

The woman's face twisted into a crooked grin. "Yeah, she's got lots of friends, if you get my drift. But I just mind my own business" She started to close the door but I stopped it with my foot. Reaching into my pocket I pulled out a twenty-dollar bill and let it hang loosely in my fingers. She eyed it for a moment and then took it from me.

"Do you know where Angie went?" I repeated my question. Again she shook her head.

"The last time I saw her she didn't say anything about going anywhere."

"When was that?"

PICTURE IN THE WALLET

"New Year's Eve. I remember because I
went to ask her if she would go to the parade with
me. I love the Orange Bowl parades but I don't like
going out on the street alone after dark. She said
she couldn't go because she had some things to do
and besides she had company coming. I figured it
was one of her 'Johns'. She seemed kinda jittery,
like she wanted to get rid of me. Anyway, later a
big cruddy guy went in. I saw him go past my
door. He didn't stay very long, and when he left he
was carrying two large suitcases, the same two I
saw Angie lugging in earlier."

"You don't miss much that goes on around
here, do you?"

She smiled that crooked smile again. "In
this neighborhood you learn to keep your eyes open
and your mouth closed." She gave a little laugh.
"But here I am blabbing to you."

"Did Angie have any other visitors that
night?"

"Well, the guy who pays her rent–some
Cuban or South American guy, I never got his
name–went in. He didn't stay long, either but he
came to my office about an hour later and paid her
rent. I thought it kinda odd because her rent wasn't
due until the fifteenth, but he said Angie was going
away for a few weeks and wanted her rent paid in
advance." She shrugged her shoulders. "In this
neighborhood you don't ask too many questions."

I ignored her implication. "Did she leave
with this guy?"

"Well, I don't really know because that's
when the fire started."

"Fire?"

"Yeah. Somebody set the trash can behind the building on fire and I went to put it out with my garden hose." Her face suddenly took on a concerned look. "Angie never went away before without leaving her poodle with me to look after. You don't suppose something has happened to her, do you?"

"She has a dog?"

The woman nodded. "The next morning I heard Muffy crying so I went into Angie's apartment–I have keys to all the apartments–and brought him over to my place. Angie wasn't there."

"Here," I handed her my card, "have Angie call me when she gets back." Then on second thought, "Let me have your phone number and I'll let you know if I find out anything." She studied my card for a moment and then wrote a number on the twenty-dollar bill I had given her and handed it back to me.

"You know, Angie is not really a bad kid. You look like a decent guy. Find her."

I was beginning to feel a vague uneasiness about the enigmatic Miss Adams. Determined to learn all I could about her I drove out to the other address the photographer had given me.

No one answered when I rang the doorbell of the Palmdale house. In the front yard next door a ponytailed man tinkered with a motorcycle. "I'm looking for Angie Adams," I called to him.

He put down a wrench he was using and ambled over to the low fence separating the two properties. "You won't find her here, pal," he grinned. "She and her stepfather, Hank Boggins, had a big fight a few months back and she moved out. But maybe Hank can tell you where she is. Here he comes now."

A battered pickup truck pulled up on the drive and a burley man with two days' growth of beard got out. I made a quick evaluation: someone I wouldn't want to meet in a dark alley, I decided. A short, dirty tank top imprinted with an obscene slogan exposed a six-pack-a-day belly hanging over a belt holding up faded jeans. Tattooed serpents entwined both bulging biceps. He eyed me with suspicion as I approached him. At the mention of Angie's name he turned his head and spat on the ground.

"That little tramp knows better than to come around here. I kicked her out and I don't know or give a shit where she went." He took a menacing step toward me. "And if you know what's good for you, mister, you'll shag your ass out of here–fast."

I thought better of asking Boggins more about his relationship with Angie. I backed out–fast!

Still puzzled as to how the picture got in the wallet, and feeling the answer might be found at the store where the wallet was purchased, I pointed my car in the direction of the Tropic Gardens Mall.

Ramon's gift shop reeked of pseudo-elegance, from the thick carpet on the floor to the upsweep hairdo of the cooly aloof clerk behind the counter. When I asked for Angie Adams I thought I detected an almost imperceptible start on the part the woman.

"I don't know any Angie Adams," she said hastily, "you must have the wrong store."

"Doesn't she work here?" I fished, showing her Angie's picture.

She stared coldly at the picture and then at me. "She might have been one of the part time workers we had during Christmas. You'll have to ask Mister Ramon. But he's out of the country." She paused. "Now if you'll excuse me I have work to do."

I left the shop but, on impulse, looked back to see the woman disappear through a door at the rear of the shop. The thick carpet muffled my footsteps as I sprinted to the closed door and put my ear against it. I could hear the woman's voice, evidently speaking on the telephone.

"Ramon? Some guy was here looking for Angie." Pause. "He didn't say who he was but he had her picture and he knew she worked here." Another pause. "I don't think he was a cop; he didn't show me a badge. Look, I have to get back up front. Charlene went to lunch and I'm alone in the store. I just thought you would want to know." She paused again and her voice came in a strained whisper. "Ramon, I'm scared."

I made a quick exit before she emerged from the office, then turned and re-entered the shop. "Take my card," I said to the woman. "Have Mister Ramon call me when he returns."

Despite a growing feeling that the girl in

the picture was in some kind of trouble, I could see no harm in letting these people know my identity. Life, I was to learn, is full of such miscalculations.

As I ate breakfast the next morning my telephone rang. Urgency filled the voice on the other end of the line.

"This is Maria Goya. From Ramon's. I have to talk to you. About that girl you were asking for." She hesitated. "I can't talk now but I get off for lunch at noon. Meet me at the north entrance to the mall." Before I could accept or reject her invitation she hung up.

My watch showed a few minutes before twelve when I left my car and started across the parking lot toward the mall entrance. I caught only a fleeting glimpse of a sleek black sports car with dark-tinted windows barreling down upon me before sheer instinct took me on a frantic dive behind a concrete doughnut protecting a lamp post. The car glanced off the barrier and roared away at high speed. I picked myself up. Except for some scrapes and bruises, and the cold realization someone had tried to snuff me, I was okay. I hurried into the mall.

The clerk in Ramon's was not the same iceberg I met on my previous visit. "Maria did not come in this morning," she answered my query.

"It's very important I talk with her. Can you give me her home telephone number?"

"You'll have to speak to Mister Ramon," her eyes shifted nervously, "but..."

"Yeah, I know," I interrupted, "but he's not here."

Outside the shop I dashed to a telephone and called Angie's landlady. "The guy you saw leaving with the suitcases, what was he driving?" "A beat-up pickup truck?" "No, I haven't found Angie but I think I'm getting close. I'll keep in touch with you." I didn't have the heart to voice my suspicion that Angie would not be found alive. Mentally I summed up what I had learned so far. It appeared that the attempted hit-and-run driver and the grubby guy who visited Angie the night she disappeared were two different persons. At least the person who tried to run me over had a more sophisticated choice of wheels. I was beginning to have the uncomfortable feeling that the Goya woman had set me up. But Angie's stepfather drives a pickup. If he was the one who took the bags from Angie's apartment then he lied to me about not knowing where she lives! I figured it was a good time to call in the police.

I found Detective Lt. Dan Hendry in his office and showed him Angie's picture. Without a word he went to a filing cabinet, removed an eight by ten color photograph, placed it on his desk and looked up at me. "She's a 'Jane Doe' we picked up in the boonies a few days ago, Jim. What do you know about her?"

"Her name is–was–Angie Adams." I detailed all I had learned since finding the picture. Dan listened attentively.

PICTURE IN THE WALLET

"We've had an eye on Ramon Velasquez for quite some time." He stroked his chin reflectively. "Besides the gift shop he runs an escort service we are pretty sure is a front for prostitution. But hell, man, we just don't have the manpower to track down every petty racketeer in the county. A few weeks ago Velasquez flew down to Colombia and one of our informants down there reported that he was seen playing footsies with a kingpin in the Medellin cartel. When he returned, customs went through his luggage with a fine-tooth comb but he was clean."

Dan turned his attention back to the photograph on his desk. "We're stumped for a motive for her killing. It doesn't look like a professional hit. She was strangled; the pros use guns or knives. The body was lying about six feet off the pavement in high grass. If it hadn't been spotted by a telephone lineman from atop a pole it might still be there. No footprints or tire tracks near the body. It appears she was killed someplace else and her body dumped there. She was fully clothed and had not been sexually assaulted."

He paused and pointed to her ear clips. "Those are genuine diamonds. Nothing really expensive but something a mugger would not pass up. And she was wearing a ring that must have cost four or five hundred bucks. Robbery was not the motive." He gave a wry smile. "That doesn't leave us very much to work with."

"Dan, the man seen leaving Angie's apartment fits Hank Boggins' description. I'll bet he knows something."

PICTURE IN THE WALLET

Before Dan could answer, a policeman stuck his head in the door. "There's been a shooting out in Palmdale, Lieutenant, on Areca Drive."

"That's the street Boggins lives on!" I exclaimed.

Dan grabbed his hat. "Come on, let's go."

Police cars surrounded the Palmvale house when we screeched to a stop in front of it. Boggins' truck sat on the drive. Beside it sat a sleek black sports car with dark-tinted windows and a crumpled right fender.

"What happened, Mike?" Dan called to a policeman standing in the doorway.

"Two dead guys in here, Lieutenant. A lot of coke, too. It looks like they shot it out in a drug deal gone bad."

The body of a swarthy man lay near the door, a pistol clutched in his hand. Across the room lay another body, a hunting rifle beside it. Dan looked down at the first body. "We won't have to keep an eye on Ramon Velasquez any longer," he smiled laconically.

"The other one is Hank Boggins," I volunteered.

So I had a story–and a lot of unanswered questions. Did Ramon kill Angie? If so, why. And where did Hank Boggins fit in?

Insistent ringing of my telephone jarred me from a fitful sleep the next morning. "Dan Hendry

here, Jim. We picked up the Goya woman for
questioning. She was at the airport getting ready to
leave the country. She's giving us the Sphinx
treatment but she wants to talk to you."

I dressed quickly and hurried down to
Metro Police headquarters.

Through the one-way window of the
interrogation room I could see Ramon's clerk
sitting in stoic silence. "She's a real cool cookie,"
Dan warned. "I hope you can get more out of her
than we have."

The woman looked up as I entered the
room, gave a tight smile and motioned me to a seat
across the table from her. She got right down to
business. "You're a writer. Right? You want a
story you can sell. Right?" She leaned across the
table and spoke in a low, conspiratorial voice. "I'm
the only one alive who knows what happened to
Angie Adams. If you'll do something for me I'll
give you, and the cops, the whole story."

"What could I possibly do for you?"

Her eyes pierced mine. "The cops can't pin
a thing on me in Angie's death except maybe
accessory-after-the-fact." She gave a flippant toss
of her shoulders. "I can cop a plea on that and by
helping the police solve the case get off with a slap
on the wrist unless..." she paused and drummed
nervously on the table with her fingers, "...unless
they try to pin an attempted murder charge on me
for trying to run you down in the parking lot."

"So it was you who tried to kill me?"

Her head made a quick negative jerk.
"Ramon was driving but I was in the car and

pointed you out to him. Now if you will agree not to press charges in the parking lot incident..."

"Incident?" I exploded. "I almost had a date with the angels."

The woman's attitude softened momentarily. "Yeah, I'm sorry about that. You didn't know Ramon Velasquez. He wasn't the kind of guy you messed around with. I did what he told me to do." Just as suddenly she stiffened. "Do you want the story or don't you?"

"All right, we have a deal. Did Ramon kill Angie?"

Maria leaned back and heaved a sigh of relief. "Hank Boggins, the guy who shot it out with Ramon, did it. At least he told Ramon that he had 'taken care' of Angie when he called to try to make a deal to return the coke shipment."

I started to interrupt but she continued quickly. "You see, Angie worked for Ramon's escort service. During the Christmas rush at the gift shop she helped out there. Ramon was working on his first big drug deal and I suppose Angie overheard something. The stuff came in New Year's Eve. Ramon locked it in his office and drove up to Fort Lauderdale to talk to a buyer, leaving Angie alone in the store. When he returned he found both Angie and the coke gone and the store wide open."

"So Ramon went looking for Angie?"

"Yeah. When he found her dead in her apartment he panicked. He knew that when her body was found he would be asked a lot of questions and he didn't want the cops nosing around. He already suspected that Hank Boggins might be involved. He knew Boggins from when Angie lived at home with him. The way I figure it, Angie didn't know what to do with the stuff after she took it so she called her stepfather for advice. He came to her place and probably tried to persuade her to make a deal with Ramon but she wouldn't go for it. I'm only guessing, of course. We'll never know for sure what happened. Maybe they got in a fight and he choked her. Maybe he didn't mean to kill her. All we know is he took the coke and tried to make a deal with Ramon.

"Anyway, after Ramon found Angie dead he wanted to buy a little time. He came and got me and we went to Angie's place. I set fire to a trash can behind the apartments and during the diversion Ramon and I dragged Angie's body out to the car. We drove out into the sticks and dumped it in some tall grass. It took both of us to swing her out away from the road.

"When you showed up at the store Ramon panicked again. He didn't know how much you knew but he didn't want you snooping around. He told me we had to get rid of you. Right after I called you to meet me at the mall, Boggins called Ramon. He said he had the coke and wanted to make a deal.

"After the parking lot incident..." a faint smile flitted across her face "...Ramon dropped me off and went to see Boggins." The woman's shoulders drooped. "You know the rest."

I called Dan Hendry into the room. "She's ready to make a statement, Dan."

PICTURE IN THE WALLET

After leaving police headquarters I walked aimlessly, writing the Angie Adams story in my head. The sound of swells slapping against a seawall snapped me from my reverie. I found myself down by the bay.

Just off shore a sailboat knifed through the light chop on the water, its lee rail almost awash. In the cockpit a boy and girl in swimsuits laughed merrily as they strained on the sheets and tiller, trying to hold the craft on a beat close to the wind. The haunting melody of a cruise ship commercial drifted from a transistor radio beside an elderly man dozing on a park bench. All the world seemed at peace except for the raucous cries of seagulls as they vied with one another and with pelicans for scraps thrown overboard from charter fishing boats.

I took Angie's picture from my pocket, gazed one last time at that impish grin, then slowly tore the picture into tiny bits and cast the pieces into the breeze coming off the bay.

AWAY TOO LONG

The bartender smiled broadly, his teeth gleaming in their ebony setting. "Hey, Jake, where you been? Haven't seen you in a couple months."

"Down in Key West watching the sun set on the water." Sarcasm tinged Jake's voice.

"What'll you have? Scotch or Bourbon?"

"Just gimmee a beer, Sam"

The bartender raised his eyebrows in surprise. "What did they do to you down there?

Ever since you been coming in here you drink nothing but Scotch or Bourbon straight with a water chaser."

"Like I said, Sam, just a beer."

Sam took a frosted mug from the freezer and turned toward the beer tap. He looked back over his shoulder. "Being it's Christmas Eve I got some good eggnog. Real powerful stuff. Half rum and half mix."

Jake's voice rose in exasperation. "Gimmee the dammed beer, Sam."

Sam filled the mug with foaming brew and set it on the bar. "You been coming in here for almost a year and you always order the same things. What's with you tonight?"

"Exactly one year," Jake corrected him. "Last Christmas Eve was the first time I ever came in here."

"Yeah," the bartender grinned, "I remember now. You really were looped that night. I wouldn't serve you anything but black coffee."

A customer at the end of the counter got up, walked to the jukebox and dropped in a coin. The nasal voice of a country singer drifted across the room. *If I came home tonight, would you still be my darlin'...*

"Shut that off!" Jake demanded.

"Can't do that, man. The dude paid his quarter so he's got a right to play what he likes."

Jake started to leap up but Sam restrained him with a firm hand to his shoulder. "Hey, man, I don't like country music myself. Jive and rap is more my speed. But this is a free country. Everybody's got the right to listen to anything he likes." He paused. "Except I don't allow no cop-killer rap on my jukebox."

Jake sank back onto the barstool and took a sip of his beer. "I hit her that night, Sam."

"Hit who, man?"

"My wife. I hit my wife. Only time I ever hit her."

"You were drunk. You didn't know what you were doing."

Jake shook his head. "I got drunk later. But she had it coming. Been riding me for months about not making enough money. She likes expensive things, Sam. Then she made that crack about my manhood."

"Hey, women do that, Jake. I mean, make cracks about your manhood. They know that's where you're vulnerable."

"Didn't give me a right to hit her."

The bartender's voice dropped to a compassionate whisper. "You did make it up to her, didn't you? You did tell her you were sorry?"

"I never went back."

"It's never too late to say you're sorry. It's never too late."

From the jukebox the melancholy voice of the singer twanged out the last verse of his song. *If I came home tonight would you still be my darlin'? Or have I stayed away too long?*

Jake sipped his beer in silence. Suddenly he jumped up, ran to the telephone, dropped in a coin and tapped in a number. A long pause followed. He slowly replaced the receiver on its hook and returned to the bar. "Gimmee a Scotch, Sam. Make it a double."

"What happened, Jake? What did she say?"

Jake stared vacantly at the polished wood of

the bar. "A man answered. I guess I stayed away
too long."

THE SECRET OF
CLARENDEN HOUSE

CO-AUTHORED WITH
DAN GRANT AND RALPH E. ROBINSON

Aged, abandoned, lonely, Clarenden House
quietly deteriorates just off of a weed-
choked gravel road in the northwest corner
of Florida. Behind the shattered windows and
rotting, sagging porch balustrades of the old

homestead lie ghostly memories of intrigue, mystery–and murder. Deep within its bowels, beyond a decaying cellar door, crumbling bricks forming the base of a huge chimney guarded, for a century and a half, a gruesome secret.

The ruins of Clarenden House stand atop a bluff at a bend of the Chatahoochie River, offering a breath-taking view in all directions. Sadly, the once-grand manse now is host only to miscreants who have vandalized the place through the years, the occasional curious history buff, and hunters and fishermen who chance by. A grim chapter from its past might never have been revealed had it not been for an old sea chest that Al and Eva Smith bought at a yard sale hundreds of miles away.

The Smiths had looked forward to the time they could pull up stakes and become modernized gypsies, traveling around the country indulging their passion for buying, refurbishing and reselling anything that could be turned over at a profit. When Al's employers downsized and offered him early retirement he accepted eagerly. They sold their home in the mid-west, bought a motor home to which they hitched a converted snowmobile trailer, and hit the adventure trail.

Al enjoyed working with his hands. He loaded the trailer with his tools, with a small outboard motor for the canoe he lashed on top, with a two-seat scooter bike, and with a tent to serve as a workshop when they parked in campgrounds. Ever the artisan of the family, with fabric and thread, or with words on paper, Eva made sure her portable sewing machine and her laptop computer were not left behind. They planned to supplement their retirement income by selling Al's labors of love and Eva's handmade hook rugs. While Al explored strange places to his heart's content, Eva expected to research local history and folklore of places they visited, and write articles for sale to local newspapers and, hopefully, regional magazines. Yard sales became their buying Meccas and flea markets tested their marketing skills.

At a yard sale in a small town where Louisiana and Mississippi meet at the Gulf of Mexico they spied the chest. Its tooled leather cover, though slightly mildewed, showed little wear, and brass bands around it were not pitted, but the lining was faded and frayed.

"It's beautiful," Eva whispered. "I saw one in a museum once. Ladies in the eighteenth century used them to carry personal items when traveling."

"Sure is nice," Al agreed. "With a little refurbishing it should bring a good price."

The withered man conducting the sale wore bib overalls, a farmer's straw hat and a bored expression.

Feigning a nonchalant indifference, Al edged up to him. "What're you asking for that little trunk?"

The old Cracker brightened and cautiously sized up his potential customer. "Ain't a trunk, friend. That be a gen-u-wine antique sea chest. Belonged to my great-grandma. Been in our attic long as I can remember." He chuckled. "Lots of memories tied to that old chest. When we was kids we played it was a pirates' treasure chest but wasn't nothing in it but this bunch of old letters." He paused, lifted the brim of his hat and scratched his head reflectively. "Don't know I really should sell it."

Two can play this game, Al thought. He turned to leave. "Well, if you don't want to sell it..."

"Now hold on, friend. Didn't say I wouldn't sell it." He sized up the potential buyers. Calculating that Al and Eva were good for more than the ten dollars he had expected to get, he made his bid. "You look like folks who could appreciate that chest so give me thirty dollars and it's yours."

"Fifteen," Al countered.

"And throw in the letters," Eva added quickly.

An extended hand confirmed a deal made.

On the ride back to camp on the scooter bike Eva cradled the chest lovingly in her arms. "I'll bet someone really prized this when it was new. I hope we can restore it. I may want to keep it for myself." Al only smiled. Eva often adopted things they picked up, but in the end her practical side prevailed and the treasures found new owners.

On their return to their campsite Eva set aside the packet of letters and begin preparing lunch while in his makeshift workshop Al surveyed the new purchase. With the leather restored, the

brass fittings cleaned and burnished, and the
interior re-lined, he decided, it could be made into
a thing of real elegance.

Whistling as he worked, he began ripping
out the old lining. His whistle stopped in mid-note
when a faded envelope fell from behind the lining
and fluttered to the ground at his feet. Picking it up
he called excitedly to Eva."Come here, honey, and
see what I've found."

Eva rushed out, still holding a slice of bread
in her fingers. Al showed her the envelope,
addressed in flowing longhand, simply "Adrianne
Devereaux, State Street, New Orleans." He
removed a sheet of folded, brittle, yellowed paper
and began reading:

My darling daughter Adrianne,

*I am desolate and so fearful for my life. This
has been such a distressing journey. As if
the flies and mosquitos were not bad enough,
mud from the incessant rain tests one's will
to go on. To make matters even worse, the
Seminole Indians are giving trouble again,
but they are still far to the south of where we
are. My consumption has weakened me
sorely but I am determined to survive and be
with you for the birth of your baby. I do
hope it's a girl and that you will name her
"Bridget". That is such a pretty name.*

THE SECRET OF CLARENDEN HOUSE

*Each night we have stopped at a way
station, each more primitive than the last,
but where we are tonight, a place called
"Clarenden House", is quite new and is much
grander than the others. We have stopped
early because of the weather. Actually, this
is a farm, but the owners seem to relish the
idea that they're innkeepers. While the
accommodations are better than most of
those we have endured, I don't like or trust
the Clarendens. Our host is a big, burley,
shifty-eyed man while his wife is tall and
gaunt and has a pinched face. The way Mr.
Clarenden looked at me when we arrived
sent cold chills down my spine though I
certainly am no ravishing beauty in my
present state of poor health.*

*You know that your father has always
insisted that we dress well, even in this
forsaken land, and ride in a good carriage so
I fear they will think us wealthy and do the
Lord knows what to us. My good husband
cannot see evil in others and laughs off my
fears, saying my sickness has made me
suspicious of strangers. Never the less, I
face this night with dread.*

*Were it not for my foreboding,
Clarenden House would be a nice place to
stay. It sits on a high bluff above a bend in
the river and one can see for a long distance
both up and down the river. In the parlor is
a huge fireplace, and there is a winding
staircase leading to the second floor. Our*

bedroom is directly above the parlor, and the chimney passes through it, giving off some heat which is most welcome on this damp day.

My darling daughter, I know now that I should have heeded your plea and left grandmother's jewels with you. But because of your own unfortunate situation, which had much to do with my going on this journey despite my poor health, I did not feel they would be safe there. Now I am even more fearful that they will not be safe with me.

The carpenters who built this place appear not to have been very skilled. I have discovered a crevice between the chimney and the wall that they attempted to hide with wallpaper. I will conceal the jewels there and pray that in the morning we will be able to leave here with our persons and possessions intact. The only other guests here are a roving preacher of the Gospel and his wife who are headed west. Since there are few post offices in the direction we are heading these kind people have offered to mail this letter at the first post office they come to. They plan to leave at daybreak.

May God bless and watch over you and my unborn grandchild,

> *With all my love,*

> *Mother.   June 4, 1843*

"Wow," exclaimed Eva, "what a story! I

wonder what happened to them? Let's take a look at the other letters."

The other letters were also to Adrianne from her mother, all predating the one found in the chest. All were accounts of the hardships being endured by the writer and her husband as they traveled east in his job as a timber scout and camp inspector for a lumber company, with frequent references to Adrianne's deteriorating marriage to "that drunken, gambling scoundrel". Through all the letters ran a thread of fear and foreboding. "That poor woman sure was paranoid," Eva observed.

"Let's go back and see the man we bought the chest from," Al suggested. "Maybe he can tell us more about this Adrianne and her mother."

They found the old man reclining in a hammock in the yard of the house where they had first met him. He read the letter slowly and then chuckled. "I guess there was some truth to the stories we was told when we was kids. I remember my daddy saying our ancestors was French plantation owners in Haiti and skedaddled out of there to New Orleans when the slaves revolted and started a war. I thought he was making it up 'cuz we was poor dirt farmers." His face sobered. "My great grandma was named 'Bridget'. Let me get the old family bible."

He went into the house and returned shortly with a large, leather-bound Bible. He opened it to the flyleaf. The first entry of a birth record was for "Bridget Adrianne Devereaux. Born July 10, 1843. Mother died in childbirth."

The old man smiled sadly. "It looks like this Adrianne was my great, great, grandma and it was her ma who wrote that letter. I ain't got the faintest notion what her name was."

"Would you like to have the letters back, since they are part of your family history?" Al offered, drawing a disapproving glance from Eva.

"Nope," the man shook his head, "Got nobody to leave 'em to. When I'm gone they'd jest end up in the trash. The doc says I ain't got much more time." He tapped his chest. "Smoked too much all my life. Big C's got me. You say you folks're hist'ry buffs so you keep 'em." He paused. "Here, take the Bible, too."

Eva bubbled with enthusiasm as, after profusely thanking the old man, they headed back to camp. "Do you think we can find Clarenden House if it's still there? Could the jewels still be hidden in the wall? What do you think happened to Adrianne's mother and father? There were no letters dated after the one we found in the chest, you know."

"Hey, slow down," Al smiled, "the way I figure it Adrianne received the letter just before the birth of her baby and probably hid it from the eyes of her drunken husband. Her mother and father could have returned for the birthing. Of course, after Adrianne died there would be no more letters addressed to her."

"I don't think so," Eva romanticized doggedly. "I think Adriannes's parents were robbed and killed. Please, Al, let's try to find Clarenden House. If it still exists, that is."

Al knew better than to try to reason with Eva when she set her mind to something. They took her laptop computer to the camp office, hooked into a telephone jack and got on line. He typed "Clarenden House " into the web search engine. Eva emitted a squeal of delight when the message appeared. "Clarenden House. Historical site near Postville, Florida. No details listed."

"Let's go there," Eva insisted.

Al studied a map. "Postville is just north of Interstate Ten, east of here. That's the direction we were going after we leave here."

"Then let's leave here tomorrow! There's no real reason we have to stay here longer."

Al and Eva hit the road before sunrise and pulled into Postville just as the one business street of the village began waking up. "The library?" a helpful attendant at a gas station answered their query, "go down one block and turn right. It's just off Main Street. You can't miss it."

True to his directions they found a quaint little building with signs identifying it as Postville Public Library, Postville Chamber of Commerce and Postville Historical Society. The lone occupant, a friendly matron sitting at a reception desk, listened to their story and then read the letter addressed to Adrianne. "Oh, this is wonderful," she exclaimed. "One of our Society members, Sean Conley, has made a study of the history of Clarenden House. I'm sure he would love to see this letter. Let me call him now." She picked up the telephone and tapped in a number. After a brief conversation she looked up. "Sean will be right over."

Sean Conley proved to be a tall, spry,
studious-looking man in his mid-sixties. He could
not conceal his excitement upon reading the letter.
"Come on, I'll drive you out to Clarenden House.
We'll take my Jeep as I doubt your RV could
negotiate the road leading to the old place."
During the ride out Sean revealed some of
the history of Clarenden House. "The place really
has a colorful past. Originally it was called 'Milton
Manor'. Colonel Milton built the place and began
farming the land back in eighteen forty. Postville
had not yet been founded so this was really out in
the wilderness. The colonel was a bachelor so he
hired the Clarendens as housekeeper and farm
hand. A couple years later Colonel Milton
disappeared. The Clarenden's produced a letter
signed by him stating that he was returning to
military service and was leaving them in charge of
the property. They immediately began acting as if
they owned it, giving it their name. A few years
later the Clarendens were set upon by renegade
Seminoles and killed. The letter you have is the
only document I have come across for the era
between the time the Clarendens took over and the
time they were killed. Colonel Milton never
returned and some distant relatives got title to the
place. For many years a succession of absentee
owners leased the place to a succession of tenant
farmers who planted shade-grown tobacco, the
kind that was used for the outer wrapper of cigars.
These farmers kept the place in reasonably good
repair but when the cigar makers began using

synthetic wrappers the demand for shade-grown
tobacco fell to where it was no longer profitable to
plant it. The last tenants died out and Clarenden
House began deteriorating. Eventually the county
took the property for unpaid taxes. For years the
state has promised to put a state park there but can
never find the funds."

Sean turned off the highway, shifted into
four-wheel drive, and proceeded through the
underbrush along what had been a gravel road. "In
the early days this was a main road from Pensacola
and up into Alabama. There were large timber-
cutting operations going on then so the road saw a
lot of traffic. After the timber petered out very few
people used it," he explained. "Now every few
years hunters mow the grass and put down some
gravel. There are several cabins where they camp
scattered throughout the area." He pulled into a
clearing covered with waist-high grass and stopped
the Jeep. "Well, here we are. The county sends
out a crew to cut back the underbrush every now
and then but it grows right back up."

Al and Eva got their first sight of
Clarenden House through the trees. Grabbing a
flashlight, Al leaped out and bolted toward the
house. Eva followed close behind.

"Careful," Sean called a warning, "the
floors might not be too strong."

Gingerly testing the footing, they advanced
across the porch and into the parlor. "It's just like
the letter described it," Eva exclaimed, pointing to
the fireplace and the stairway.

They found the stairs to be surprisingly
solid as they climbed cautiously to the second floor

and entered a bedroom above the parlor fireplace. Al rushed to the chimney and peeled back faded wallpaper on the wall adjoining it. "There's an opening here," he reported excitedly as he thrust a hand in, then in a disappointed tone, "but there's nothing in here."

Al's groping fingers loosened a piece of plaster and after an interminable moment they heard it strike somewhere below. "The basement!" he exulted. "If anything was hidden here it would have fallen into the basement."

They rushed down the stairs, out the front door, and around to a cellar door they had observed as they approached the house. The door fell open after Al gave it a sharp tug. Aided by the flashlight beam they picked their way through decades of accumulated litter to the base of the fireplace chimney. "This thing looks as if it couldn't support its own weight," Al observed. Much of the mortar between the bricks had eroded and some of the bricks moved easily to his touch. Al began slowly removing loose bricks where the chimney base and outer wall met.

At the sound of a low rumble he leaped up, grabbed Eva and stumbled backwards. With a loud crash a section of the wall collapsed in a cloud of dust.

"Whew, that was close!" Al whistled. "We had better get out of here before the whole place comes down on our heads." He pointed the flashlight in the direction of the fallen wall. What appeared to be a small, cell-like room lay beyond. As the dust slowly settled the flashlight beam revealed a ghastly sight. Three skeletal human remains lay there on the floor.

Attracted by the noise, Sean bounded into the basement. Wordlessly, Al pointed to their discovery. Sean smiled grimly. "Well, we can pretty-well guess what happened to Colonel Milton and the two travelers who wrote that letter."

Sean returned to the Jeep to call the sheriff on his cell phone. Arm-in-arm Al and Eva followed. "Oh, Al, " Eva wailed, "there goes our chance of finding a fortune in jewels."

"We couldn't have kept them if we found them," Al comforted her. "This property belongs to the county and you can be sure county officials would claim anything found. But look at the bright side. You have the makings of a great story to write."

Back in Postville they thanked Sean for his hospitality. "Would the Historical Society like to have the letters?" Al offered.

"You bet we would!" Sean's face lightened up. Then he paused. "Surely you don't intend for us to have the envelope the Clarenden House letter is in. It could be quite valuable, especially with the contents intact. I'll just make photocopies of the letter and envelope."

"Why would it be valuable?" Eva asked.

Sean pointed to the stamp on the envelope. "Before the Federal post office issued its first stamps in 1847 a few postmasters had their own stamps printed. The postmaster in Pensacola was one of them, and only a few of his stamps remain in the hands of collectors. At a philatelic auction this 'cover' should bring a very good price indeed."

METAMORPHOSE

O ne thing you bastards better know and
know damn well," Sgt. Duncan barked as
our landing craft headed for the beach,
"THERE ARE NO STRAIGHT LINES IN
NATURE."

Binky Rogers' face had it's usual blank
expression. "What you gettin' at, Sarge?"

The sergeant glared at him. "Just what I
said, Rogers. There are no straight lines in nature.
If you see anything with a straight line in that
jungle we're going into it has to be man-made, and
the Japs made it. And you can bet your ass those
slant-eyed motherlovers are still there."

The battle for Eniwak proved to be a fierce and bloody one, but when we blasted our way into the last coral cave on the atoll and found only dead bodies we savored the sweet taste of victory. But what a terrible price we paid. Nearly a third of the men in our platoon, including Binky Rogers, died in the fighting. Hardly a man came through without a scratch. Both Sgt. Duncan and I left the island on stretchers..

"When the last slant-eyed bastard falls in this motherlovin' war I want to be the guy who pulls the trigger on him," Sarge cursed through pain-clenched teeth. He was not to get his wish; the war ended while we recuperated in an army hospital.

My wounds healed sooner than Sgt. Duncan's, and as I was ready to leave the hospital we exchanged goodbyes and home addresses. I really never expected to see him again. He came from Oregon; I made my home in Florida.

Having a spare bedroom in Florida is akin to maintaining an attractive nuisance; you never know when some long-forgotten acquaintance, or some distant relative will come for a visit. This didn't lessen the shock I received when I answered the call of my door chimes one morning to find a grinning Sgt. Duncan standing there.
"Hi, corporal, aren't you going to invite me in?:"
I grabbed his hand and pulled him inside.

"I'll be dammed, Sarge, you're the last person I ever expected to see again. What re you doing in Florida?"

"Buy me a beer and I'll bring you up to speed."

I took two bottles from the fridge, poured their contents into frosted mugs, and guided him to the patio overlooking the river.

"Nice place you got here," he observed, "you must be doing okay."

"I'm retired. But you didn't answer my question. What brings you to the Treasure Coast?"

"I went to the Miami address you gave me and you had moved, but the people there gave me this address. As luck would have it I was coming up here anyway. You see, after thirty years in the army I retired, too. But I couldn't just sit around on my duff so I got a job. While in the service I spent a lot of time in Japan and I made some connections. Honda is getting ready to build cars in the States and I'm scouting this area for a location for an assembly plant. I work for Honda now."

My look of disbelief amused him. He laughed. "You're surprised that I would be working for a Japanese company, aren't you?" His face suddenly sobered. "You remember when we were going into Eniwak I said that anything with a straight line had to be man-made? Well, these guys really know how to draw straight line."

MISSED OPPORTUNITIES

Joe slammed his beer mug down on the table. "I lucked out when the war ended before I could be sent overseas, and now they're starting it all over again in Korea. And I'm still in the reserves." He and his friends had just completed a round of golf at Miami's municipal course and were unwinding at the 19th hole pub.

"Oh, overseas duty ain't so bad," Tex drawled, "it's a great time to make it with the dames. I was stationed in Australia for three years during the war. Most of the Aussie men were in North Africa fighting Rommel. The women were really hard up for male companionship, if you know what I mean. I got more in them three years than all the rest of my life put together. You just got to recognize your opportunities when they come your way."

Pete punched him playfully on the arm. "Don't give us that crock of crap, Tex. You're a married man and have been for a long time. Don't tell us you're not getting it regularly."

The big Texan gave him a condescending look "It's true I been married a long time, good buddy, but like I said I got more during them three years..."

"I missed one good opportunity when I was in the army," Matt broke in. "I was in Calcutta, India when the war ended. One day I went down to the docks to say 'goodbye' to some friends leaving on a troopship. I noticed a gorgeous Irish girl scanning the ship with her eyes. I figured she was Irish because girls with long flaming-red hair were not exactly a common sight in those parts. I went over to her and struck up a conversation. She told me her name was Meg and that her boyfriend was going home on that ship and she hoped to get one last glimpse of him because she expected never to see him again. She said that her father was an officer in the British army and that she had lived in India most of her life.

"After the ship pulled away from the dock I invited her to go to the Red Cross Burra Club for a hamburger and a Coke. The Burra was about the only place in town where you could get a decent hamburger, what with the Hindu religious taboo and all. She accepted. We went there and spent a couple of real nice hours just talking. I told her I could get a Jeep from the motor pool Sunday and asked if there was there any place she would like to go. Her eyes lighted up and she said she would love to go to Chandernagor.. Chandernagor was one of the last French-ruled enclaves in India. It was a neat, clean little place on the Houghly River. There was a Catholic convent there and she had friends among the nuns. So we made a date.

"When it came time for her to go home we exchanged addresses. I put her in a rickshaw, paid the coolie, and sent her on her way. She lived at the British fort across the parade ground from the Burra.

"The next morning my outfit was suddenly ordered to go up into Burma to close down an airbase there. I gave my bearer a note to take to Meg explaining why I couldn't meet her Sunday. When we finished the job in Burma the army flew us straight home. I didn't go back to Calcutta. I've often thought that if I did it might have led to a beautiful relationship with Meg.
I wrote to her after I returned home but she didn't answer."

"Maybe her old boyfriend wrote first," Pete suggested.

"Yeah, I thought of that."

Joe took a few sips from his beer. "When I was about fifteen..."

"Fifteen?" Tex roared. "Hell, man, when I was fifteen I never missed NO opportunities."

With a scowl, Joe started over. "When I was fifteen, living on the Gulf coast, I went into a bathhouse to get out of my wet bathing suit. The bathhouse was just a small shack with two rooms–one for the boys and one for the girls. As I was going in I noticed a real cute girl going into the girls' side.

"Inside a wooden partition separated the boys' side from the girls' side. Some of the boards had shrunk leaving small cracks between. I took off my bathing suit and then just thinking about that girl being naked in the other room I got really aroused–I don't think I have to draw you a picture. I moved my head back and forth trying to see through the cracks without actually going over and putting my eye to one, but I couldn't see a thing.

"When I went outside the girl was already out and when she saw me she gave me the strangest look. I suddenly wondered if she had been peeping at me."

"Did you go over and talk to her?" Matt asked.

"No, I was too embarrassed. What if she had seen me in that... condition?"

"Women don't get all hot and bothered like men do when they see naked bodies," Tex opined.

A waitress brought a pitcher of beer to refill their mugs. "Hey, Wanda," Matt asked, "do girls react when they see naked boys the way boys react when they see naked girls? Say, when you were fourteen or fifteen and saw a naked boy, how did it make you feel?"

She laughed. "By the time I was fifteen I had seen naked boys many times. I had three younger brothers."

"I mean, in a sexual situation."

Wanda thought for a long moment. "Well, there was one time when I was fifteen that I might have been talked into doing something I shouldn't have. I was at the beach one day and I went into a bathhouse to change. It was just a two-room shack with a partition separating the boys from the girls. As I was going in I saw this real hunk going into the other side. After I stripped off my bathing suit I noticed there were cracks between the boards of the wooden partition. Maybe I was just curious but I went over and peeped through. This guy was standing in the middle of the room, facing me, and weaving back and forth. I had never seen a boy with a full erection before and I suddenly felt tingly all over and began breathing hard. I could feel my breasts–what little I had then–begin to swell. I dressed real quick and ran outside, and when I heard him coming out I started to walk away. Then I stopped and looked back over my shoulder. He took off like the devil was chasing him."

"Aw, come on, Wanda," Joe laughed nervously, "you're just putting us on. You heard us talking. That didn't really happen, did it?"

She leaned over and planted a light kiss on his forehead. "You'll never know for sure, will you Panama Beach boy?" With a saucy smile, hips swaying seductively, she sauntered across the room.

Joe's face crimsoned. "I never said it happened at Panama Beach! Did you guys ever hear me even mention Panama Beach? Oh, Lord, she was there! She was the girl in the bathhouse!" He stole a quick glance in Wanda's direction. "Geeze, she's giving me that same look."

Tex gave him a rough shove toward the waitress. "Like I said, good buddy, you gotta recognize the opportunities when they come your way."

A PHOENIX RISING

268

A PHOENIX RISING

*W*ho in the world would want to buy that *dilapidated, run-down old place?* Laura wondered as she jogged past the once-elegant mansion. But apparently someone had. Emblazoned in bold red letters diagonally across the face of the Realtor's faded sign a single word attested to the fact–SOLD. She stopped and pressed her face between the rusting bars of an ornate gate in the wrought iron fence separating the weed-choked lawn from fashionable Flamingo Drive.

Suddenly from behind her a malevolence-dripping stage whisper hissed "Curiosity killed the cat, you know."

Laura jumped back. "Oh, you startled me! I didn't hear you come up."

A young man stood there grinning. "I was sitting in my car across the street looking over my new acquisition."

"You bought this place?"

"Guilty." He stared at her for a few seconds. "You really know how to crush a guy's ego, Laura Fredericks. You don't remember me, do you?"

She blushed. "Oh, of course, now I remember. You're Paul Evans. We met briefly a few years ago in my father's office. As I recall, he was helping you arrange financing for a building project. But tell me, why did you buy this old place? It looks as if it's waiting for the wrecking ball."

A PHOENIX RISING

"It's not really in as bad shape as it appears from outside. The structure is sound and the interior is beautiful. If I can get a zoning variance I plan to turn it into a congregate living facility for the elderly."

"Oh?"

"You don't approve?"

"The Homeowners' Association here in Hibiscus Park would never allow it. This whole subdivision is zoned for upscale single-family residencies."

He smiled. "I've fought city hall before and won. Come on, let me show you the inside."

"Not now. I'll be late for a dinner engagement."

"Who's the lucky guy?"

She wrinkled her nose. "Why do you assume it's with a man? But you're right. I'm dining with the most charming man in the world." She turned and started to jog away.

"You are curious as to how the inside looks, aren't you?" he called. "How about tomorrow morning?"

She looked back over her shoulder. "All right. Tomorrow at nine."

That evening, after the waitress took their orders and softly padded away, Laura broke the ensuing moment of silence. "I ran into a client of yours today, Dad. Paul Evans."

John Fredericks looked up sharply. "I didn't know you knew Paul."

A PHOENIX RISING

"Well, I don't really know him. When I was home on Spring break during my senior year I dropped by your office and he was there. Today is the first time I've seen him since and I almost didn't recognize him."

"Paul is a bright young man but too much of a bleeding heart for his own good, I'm afraid."

"How's that?"

"He came to me fresh out of college, with a degree in architecture and a half-million dollar inheritance. He wanted me to help find financing for a shopping center he planned to build in Overtown. I cautioned him against building in that area but he was adamant. He felt that poor minorities should have good shopping facilities near their homes. Paul built his shopping center but within a year hoodlums had trashed the place. The development went belly-up and he lost everything he put into it." John shook his head. "During the race riots last year the center burned to the ground. But by that time Paul no longer had a financial interest in the place."

Laura smiled. "He must have recovered some of his fortune. He just bought the old Rippon place on Flamingo Drive."

"What he lacks in business sense," John laughed, "he makes up in luck. A college buddy of his developed a computer software program. Paul put up a few thousand dollars to get the project off the ground. It was a fabulous success; the stock went through the stratosphere. Paul must be worth several millions now. You say he

271

bought the Rippon place? Did he tell you what he plans to do with it?"

"He wants to convert it into a congregate living facility for the elderly."

John chuckled. "Same old Paul. But I'm afraid he's in for a big disappointment. Zoning would never permit it."

"He wanted to show me the inside of the place but I told him I'd be late for a dinner date with the most charming man I know."

Her father's face sobered. "I've meant to talk to you about that, Laura. You haven't looked at a man since Tom was killed. Oh, I know losing your loved one just days before your wedding was a terrible blow, but you have to get on with your life. You're only twenty-five, much too young not to have some romance in your life."

"Look who's talking," Laura chortled, "I haven't seen you circulating since Mother died. And I've noticed that several of the ladies at the club become very attentive when you enter the room."

"That's different. I'm older and set in my ways. Now, Paul Evans is only two or three years older than you..."

Laura tossed her head. "Don't go playing Cupid on me, Dad." She settled back in her chair and a broad smile lighted her face. "By the way, I'm meeting Paul in the morning. He's giving me a guided tour of the interior of the Rippon place."

A PHOENIX RISING

Workers were busily scraping and painting walls of the old mansion as Laura jogged up the next morning. Paul, waiting at the gate, yelled above the loud hissing of a sandblaster removing rust from the wrought iron fence, and the roar of a mower cutting swaths through the overgrown lawn. "Right on time! Come on, let's go inside where it's quieter." He led the way to the front door and grasped the doorknob. "I already had a cleanup crew in so you won't have to dodge bats or fight your way through cobwebs."

When the door swung open Laura gasped. "What a fantastic entrance hall! It looks large enough to be the main sitting room."

Paul laughed. "That's what I'm going to convert it to. I'll put some writing desks around the walls and scatter some lounges and easy chairs in the middle, like a hotel lobby. The residents can entertain visitors or just relax here." He pointed to massive mahogany doors leading from the hall. "The formal living room is over there, and beyond that a large library. They'll make half a dozen bedrooms with private baths."

"Well," Laura teased, "I'd like to see it the way it is now. At the speed you move, the job could be completed while we tour the house." He guided her through the doorway. Laura shook her head. "I never would have dreamed from viewing the outside that this place is so magnificent."

"You ain't seen nothin' yet. Come on, let me show you the dining room and the kitchen." They crossed the entrance hall and entered a room

273

opposite the living room. "I'll remove all of this massive furniture and put in tables for two or four." He led the way into the kitchen. "The appliances are old and obsolete. I'll replace them with modern ones. This kitchen is ample to serve as many guests as will live here, don't you think?"

"Ample? It's large enough to service a restaurant."

"In their younger years the Rippons entertained a lot, I am told." He impulsively grabbed Laura's hand and tugged her back through the hall and to the graceful stairs spiraling upward. Without pausing, he bounded up the steps, still holding her hand; she had no choice but to stumble after him. "There are twelve bedrooms with adjoining baths on the second floor, Laura. The rooms are large enough for two residents to share." He pointed to where the stairs continued upward. "Servants' quarters were on the third floor."

"They had live-in servants?"

"Oh, yes. A housekeeper, a butler, maids. The chauffeur had quarters above the garage."

"Then, in a way, this once was a congregate living facility."

Paul glanced at her sharply, then threw his arms around her. "Laura, you're a genius! I think you just discovered a chink in the zoning board's armor." He released her and became serious. "I know I'm in for a real battle with the board and I'll need a good lawyer. Do you think your dad's available?"

A PHOENIX RISING

"I don't know. He always has a heavy case load. That's his refuge, I think. But I'll ask him."

At dinner that night Laura described her visit to the Rippon mansion. "Do you think you can help Paul with the zoning case, Dad?"

John Fredericks laughed. "If I took the case and won I really would be persona non grata in this neighborhood. The other residents of Hibiscus Park would not take kindly to having Paul's facility here." He thought for a moment. "Have him call me in the morning. I'll see what I can do."

During the days following John Frederick's agreement to represent Paul in his zoning case, Laura and Paul became frequent companions, usually studying plans in the living room of the Rippon place, or sometimes taking day trips to Palm Beach or St. Augustine to tour historic estates.

"He's a architecture freak, Dad," she told her father when she returned home at dinner time one day and found him in the kitchen. "All he thinks about is architecture."

"Maybe he's thinking about the plans for a cute little honeymoon cottage."

"You're playing Cupid again. There's nothing romantic in my relationship with Paul. We're just friends." She lowered her gaze. "He's never made the slightest amorous move on me."

"Ha! So you are interested in him."

She thought for a moment. "I do like him. I like him a lot." She quickly turned to the stove. "What's cooking?"

"Beef stew. Fix yourself a bowl."

Laura ladled some stew into a bowl and sat down across the kitchen table from her father. "You know, Dad, Paul is not as far left as I originally thought him to be. He's more of a compassionate conservative. He really expects to make money on his home for the aged. The residents will be people of means, though he plans to set aside some rooms for needy persons. He expected to make money on that shopping center he invested in, too. He just didn't count on hoodlums destroying it."

John Fredericks leaned back and cupped his hands behind his head. "I learned something interesting about tthe Rippon place today."

"Good news?"

"Very good news. I went through some old zoning records at the County Courthouse. Eli Rippon was a wealthy industrialist who came to Florida during the boom days of the early twenties. He. built his mansion in the middle of a thousand acres of former orange groves and wetlands. A hard frost had killed the citrus trees so he decided to develop an upscale residential community, what is now Hibiscus Park. He kept one acre to build his own home on, and then donated all of the land to the west of it , mostly wetlands, to the Nature Preserve with the stipulation it never be built on. Then he platted all of the land to the north, south and east of his acre into estate-size lots. It appears he wanted to be 'lord of the realm' so he placed severe deed restrictions on the lots. He set minimum size for houses so that all would be pretentious, and he set maximum sizes so that no one could build a house rivaling his. Then he specified that only immediate family members could occupy the residences and there could be no live-in servants."

Laura's eyes sparkled "But he had live-in servants."

"That's the clincher. When he filed the plat with the county he left his estate outside the new subdivision."

"So Paul's property is not subject to Hibiscus Park zoning?"

"Exactly. I've set up a meeting with the County Zoning Board for tomorrow morning and I'll petition for a zoning that will permit Paul to build his congregate living facility. I don't see how they can refuse.

"Oh, Dad, that's wonderful." Laura paused and her brow wrinkled. "But why did the place become so rundown?"

John sighed. "That's a long and complicated story. Eli Rippon was once very wealthy but he made some bad investments and died nearly broke. His only heir was a nephew with the reputation of being a shiftless wastrel. Eli left what remained of his fortune to this nephew with the provision that Eli's faithful butler would have a lifetime interest in the mansion. The property was put on the market, but no one would buy it while the butler retained his interest, and the butler, who had a strong dislike for the nephew, refused to be bought out.

"A few years later the nephew died. The aging butler could not pay for the upkeep of the property, and liens began to pile up for unpaid taxes and garbage fees, and fines for not keeping the lawn mowed. When the butler died early this year the county was preparing to seize the property for taxes. The dead nephew had some heirs but they were in no financial position to pay off the heavy liens against the property. Paul was able to buy their interest for a song, and he also was able to negotiate with the county to greatly reduce the amount of the liens."

"Have you told Paul the news?"

"How could I? He was not at home or his office, and I was not about to call him on his cell phone while he was out on a romantic date with you."

"Oh, quit it, Dad." She paused. "May I give him the news?"

Her father nodded and Laura whirled off to a telephone.

"We did it!" Paul exulted, shaking John's hand. "Thanks to you we won."

"Not so fast, son. We won the battle but the war goes on. The Hibiscus Park Homeowners' Association has filed an appeal with the Zoning Board. I don't think they have a chance to overturn the Board's ruling but politics can do some strange things."

Paul grabbed Laura's hand. "Come on, let's go celebrate."

Something disturbed Laura's sleep, and for a long moment her sleep-fogged brain struggled to decipher what it was. Was it the loud voices coming from the street below? The close-by wailing of sirens? The rosy glow dancing on the walls of her bedroom? Suddenly she bolted upright and glanced at the clock on her night stand. The digital display stood at 3:15. She jumped out of bed and ran to a window. "Dad! Dad!," she screamed, "there's a big fire over on Flamingo Drive."

Her father rushed in, still tying the belt of his bathrobe. "Uh, oh, it looks like the Rippon place. Let's get over there."

They dressed hurriedly and joined neighbors running toward the fire. As they got near, Laura spotted Paul standing at the edge of the gathering crowd, dejectedly watching flames envelop the building.

"Oh Lord, Paul, you're burned."

He shook his head. "Just singed a little. But the house will be a total loss."

John put his arm around Paul's shoulder. "Tell us what happened."

"I worked late in the house, drawing up some plans. I got tired and lay down on a bed in one of the upstairs bedrooms and fell asleep. I guess it was the smell of smoke that awoke me. I opened the door to the hall and a blast of fire almost knocked me down."

"How terrible," Laura gasped. "How did you get out?"

"Fortunately, the painters' scaffolds were still up. I went out through a window."

"Do you have any idea how the fire started?" John asked.

Paul pressed his lips into a hard line before answering. "I talked with the fire chief. He said it has all the earmarks of being the work of professional arsonists. The fire started in many places at the same time. A man living across the street was coming home late and saw two men in a pickup truck driving away just before the place burst into flames."

"Professional arsonists?" Laura's eyes widened. "You mean someone paid to have your place destroyed?"

"That's the way it looks."

Paul remained silent as they watched until only a skeleton of the old mansion remained. The crowd dispersed, and except a small crew left to prevent the fire from spreading, the firefighters returned to their stations.

Suddenly Paul's pent-up emotions erupted. "The people in Hibiscus Park are no better than the hoodlums in Overtown, only they hire others to do their dirty work for them."

"You don't know for sure that the neighbors had anything to do with the fire," Laura tried to console him. "Come on home with us and I'll make breakfast."

He shook his head. "No, I've got to get away somewhere and straighten out my thoughts." He paused. "An architect's convention starts in Vienna this weekend. I was going to pass it up, but now I think I'll go." He gave Laura a quick hug. "I'll be back in a couple of weeks."

Even before she jogged around the corner onto Flamingo Drive Laura could hear the sound of a wrecking ball crashing against resisting masonry and timber, and as she approached the Rippon place she could see fire-blackened walls crumbling in rising clouds of dust. She pressed her face between gate bars to get a better view.

"Curiosity killed the cat," a soft voice behind her whispered..

She spun around. "Paul, you're back."

"Got in late last night. I called your house this morning and your dad said you were out for your morning run. I hoped I'd find you here."

"Paul, I'm totally confused. Things are moving so fast. What's going on here?"

He smiled broadly and hugged her. "While in Vienna I made an important decision, and I made arrangements by telephone to have a demolition crew start clearing this lot. You've heard the expression 'If you can't beat them, join them?' I couldn't beat the people of Hibiscus Park so I'm going to become one of them, or at least a close neighbor. I'm going to build here the most

281

beautiful home ever designed. Kind of like a
Phoenix rising from the ashes. It will be a present
for my bride."

Laura's heart fluttered. "You - - you're
getting married?"

Paul dropped to one knee. "Laura
Fredericks, will you share my dream castle with
me?"

She threw herself into his arms. "If this is
a marriage proposal the answer is 'yes'." She
paused and began giggling. "Are you sure you
want to marry a curious cat?"

THE MISTRESS

Through the pre-dawn hours he sat there gazing rapturously at her slim shape as she stirred restlessly, until the groping fingers of the rising sun gently parted the curtain of mist hanging over the river. He knew that with the morning wakening he would taste of all the joys she was capable of giving, but until then he was content to sit and drink in her ethereal beauty as the pale moonlight bathed her graceful curves. Anticipation enhances the fulfilment, he knew, and this was his time to dream.

She had given pleasure to many men, he was sure, but he could harbor no resentment in the knowledge that he was not the first to have her. Was it not her destiny, in the grand scheme of things, to lift to unparalleled peaks of ecstasy the hearts of all who possessed her? So what if other men, their jaded desires satiated, had cast her aside in favor of new, more glamorous loves. Could she in any way be faulted? No! Never!. Now she was his. Forever.

THE MISTRESS

"By what name did men call her?", the
man who had her last stroked his beard
reflectively,. "Every man who's had her called her
something different. All loving names, mind you.
As for me, I called her 'Gusty'" He gave a sly
wink. "She's as
unpredictable as a gust of wind, and she has a wild
spirit, she does." Then he grew serious. "I had a
lot of fun with her and I loved her dearly. But I'm
just getting too old to give her all the affection she
needs. It's a demanding mistress she is, but you
look like a virile young fellow so you should be
able to handle her."

The sun ascended rapidly into a Florida
sky filled with billowing white clouds, clouds
hinting of ominous winds that could swoop down
with no warning. Already brisk breezes skipped
over the water, sending tiny wavelets slapping
against the dock. *Gusty* (why not?) stirred.

With the breathless expectancy of every
sailor who takes his craft to sea for the first time,
the new owner stepped aboard and cast off the
mooring lines. Lovingly he lowered the swing
keel and raised the gleaming white sails. With
skillful hands caressing the tiller he brought
Gusty's bow around to a course forty-five degrees
to the wind. The jib snapped tautly to starboard
and the mainsail gulped great quantities of air.
Gusty leaped forward, her lee gunwale almost
awash.

"Come on, you capricious winds," the man
shouted in exhilaration, "come on you turbulent

seas! We're ready for you, my ship and I."

THE GIRL NEXT DOOR
UP THE STREET

Y ou see, I'm driving this tour group from
        Orlando to Miami. They're from
        somewhere in the Midwest and they
bought this package that gives them a week at
Walt Disney World, Universal Studies and Sea
World in Orlando, and a weekend cruise to the
Bahamas. All are middle-aged couples except for
a fifty-ish tour director who prances around like
maybe he's gay, and a sultry doll in her late
twenties who could double for that old-time
movie actress Hedy Lamar. This one takes the
seat right behind me.

        We're hardly out of the terminal before she
says to me "My name is Lola. What's yours?"

        "Nick," I reply and then I point to the sign
DO NOT TALK TO DRIVER WHILE BUS IS IN
MOTION.

        She ignores my warning. "I'm bored,

Nick, and I got nobody to talk to."

"If you keep on talking to me, miss," I tell her, "I'll have to stop the bus."

She shuts up but stays in the seat behind me.

When we pull into the Fort Pierce-Port St. Lucie Service Plaza for a potty break, Lola gives me a pat on the butt. "Come on, Nick, I'll buy you coffee and a Danish."

There's no company rule against drivers fraternizing with passengers at rest stops, so I follow her into the restaurant. As soon as we sit down she starts unloading on me.

"I'm taking this trip to get away from a bad relationship that I want to get out of," she says.

I tell her I don't want to hear all the sordid details of her love life, but she keeps on. By the time we're ready to hit the road I know more about Lola than I really want to know.

Arriving in Miami I drive out onto the cruise line pier. The tour director herds his flock aboard the *Bahama Queen* and I turn around and drive to the motel where I always stay. I go to my room and freshen up, then go out for a bite to eat. When I get back to the motel I get a shock. Lola is sitting there in the lobby.

"You're supposed to be on that cruise ship," I scream at her. "Did you miss the boat?"

She shakes her head. "I've been on cruises before. They bore me."

286

THE GIRL NEXT DOOR UP THE STREET

"But the tour director will miss you and think you've fallen overboard or something." I'm exasperated.

Again she shakes her head. "I told old Fancy Dan that I wasn't feeling well and would wait in Miami until they get back. I left the ship before it sailed. The truth is, I wanted to spend the weekend with you."

Now, I'm a married man and my wife, Petal, and I get along real good. But, hell, I'm only human. When a hot babe practically throws it into your face, well...

I have a fantastic weekend. Lola is a flaming nymphomaniac. I'm feeling pretty guilty, but that this will be a one-time fling kinda eases my conscience. Comes Monday, Lola will be on her way back to where she came from. Then I make the really stupid mistake of telling her that I make this run three times a month–three consecutive weekends in Miami and then one at home.

Monday morning Lola rides to the pier with me to pick up the group. As soon as she spots the tour director she rushes over to him and tells him that she is leaving the tour and staying in Miami for a while. She collects her luggage from the bus baggage compartment, hails a cab and disappears.

Two weeks later I bring another group to Miami. When I get to my motel I find Lola waiting for me. There's a big grin on her face. "I got a

THE GIRL NEXT DOOR UP THE STREET

Monday-to-Friday job and all my weekends are free."

She's also got an apartment in a complex off Biscayne Boulevard, where there's a swimming pool, a sauna, and a crowd of young singles who don't ask questions.

My brain tells me that this woman is poison and I should run as fast and as far as I can. But like I said before, I'm only human. At her apartment I have another great weekend..

This goes on for several months but my conscience is giving me hell. If Petal finds out it will kill her–or she will kill me. I really try to break it off with Lola but she throws a tantrum and threatens to blab to my wife. And knowing her as I now do, I'm pretty sure she would find Petal

When I'm home I'm on edge all the time and fly off the handle for no reason at all. Petal is concerned that I'm not my usual self and asks what's wrong. I tell her that the long drives to Miami and all the time away from home is getting to me.

"Can't you transfer to a different route?" she asks innocently.

Now why didn't I think of that? I go to the boss and get assigned the Orlando-Kennedy Space Center run. This is a day-long round trip with no overnight stays.

On my final mission to Miami I tell Lola that I've been transferred and won't be back. She takes it real hard and starts crying. "You're the best man I ever had," she sobs, "and I don't want to lose you", which does wonders for my ego; I have a strong suspicion that Lola has had a lot of men.

Things begin to go really good for Petal and me. She's happy that I'm not away from home so much, and I'm relieved that I don't have butterflies in my stomach all the time. We even begin thinking about starting a family.

Then one day we're coming home from grocery shopping and see a moving van in front of a new house that's just been completed up the street from us. There's a station wagon sitting on the drive and we get a glimpse of someone taking stuff inside from the wagon. Petal gets all excited. "Look, people are moving in. We'll have to come back and welcome them to the neighborhood."

The street we live on makes a wide circle, and the backyard of the new house butts up to our backyard. There are heavily-wooded vacant lots on both sides of our house. "Won't it be wonderful," Petal enthuses. "At last I'll have a next-door neighbor."

We put away the groceries and then walk up the street to greet the new arrivals. As we get close I suddenly get a very eerie feeling. A woman is taking things out of the station wagon. Her back is to us and I can't see her face, but her rear end looks awful familiar. When she turns around I nearly pass out. It's Lola.

THE GIRL NEXT DOOR UP THE STREET

Petal walks up and introduces herself and then turns to me. "This is my husband, Nick."

Lola doesn't bat an eye. She sticks out her hand. "Pleased to meet you, Nick. I hope we can be good neighbors."

The next morning we're having breakfast on our terrace when Lola comes out of her back door. Petal waves to her. "Come have breakfast with us."

Lola comes over and sits down. I'm shaking inside but I pour her a cup of coffee and start to put sugar in it. Lola holds up a hand. "No sugar for me. Do you have any of those little pink packets?" *Damn, that was close. Lola always takes two lumps of sugar. And she hates those substitutes. Man, she is one cool cookie.*

This is the beginning of a real close friendship between Petal and Lola. But I'm sweating bullets whenever they're together.

Then Petal gets word that her mother in Georgia has to have an operation and wants Petal to come up and look after her for a couple weeks while she recuperates.

When we're getting ready to leave for the airport, Lola is in her yard sunbathing in a bikini that leaves nothing to the imagination. "Take care of Nick while I'm gone," Petal calls to her.

Lola jumps up and reaches for a cover-up. "Wait, I'll go to the airport with you."

THE GIRL NEXT DOOR UP THE STREET

At the terminal parking garage Lola giggles "I'm hardly dressed to be seen in public. I'll wait in the car."

I see Petal through Security and then return to where Lola is waiting. When I open the car door she throws her arms around me and squeals "Let the good times roll!"

I can feel an erection coming but I manage to make it home before peeling that bikini off of her. Fantasia! It's Miami all over again. Then, Petal did tell Lola to take care of me.

During the two weeks Petal is gone Lola practically lives at my house. But I make it clear to her that when Petal returns this little affair is over. Finished. Kaput.

When Petal is ready to come home Lola says she won't go to the airport with me. She rolls her eyes. "Petal might get the wrong idea." Then she smiles a wicked smile, like a she-wolf licking her chops. I shudder.

Petal likes to go to afternoon movies, which I really don't care for, so she goes with some girl friends. Lola begins to join them, but some Saturdays when I'm home she starts getting "headaches" and begs out of going. As soon as the girls are out of sight she comes bouncing over to my place. I try to put her off but she gets nasty and threatens to tell Petal everything. I'm starting to sweat bullets again. Sex with Lola isn't that great anymore.

THE GIRL NEXT DOOR UP THE STREET

Then one night when Petal and me are making love, Petal whispers in my ear "I think I'm pregnant."

That does it! Now I know I got to get rid of Lola. But how? I begin to get some real weird thoughts.

Suddenly a light gleams at the end of the tunnel. A dispatcher job opens in Atlanta. It's a desk job with regular hours and a big pay boost. The Orlando-area drivers are given a chance at it.

I talk it over with Petal. She says she would hate to leave Florida but a move to Atlanta would put her closer to look after her mother, who is failing fast. I bid for the job and get it.

As I follow the moving van out of my old neighborhood I heave a deep sigh of relief. That's the last I'll see of Lola.

I hope.

A PIECE OF SPANISH SILVER

The sleek black Cigarette glided up to the boatyard pier. Two men jumped out and quickly fastened bow and stern mooring lines. One man returned to the boat while the other, his massive frame silhouetted against the setting sun, started toward the yard's machine shop. A group of workers in the shop watched idly.

"That looks like Butch Bryson," Mike Clark observed, "Haven't seen him around lately." When the man got near, Mike called out "Where you been keeping yourself, Bryson? Haven't seen you around."

The swarthy man came into the shop, tossed a yachting cap onto a work bench and began wiping his florid face with a large bandana.

"Been running a transportation business between Colombia and Aruba. Things got a little warm down there after that highschool girl disappeared so I figured now was a good time to have my boat brought up to Miami for engines overhaul They've got a lot of hours on them and they've been running rough."

"Sure you didn't have anything to do with that girl's disappearance?" one of the men laughed. "I hear that good-looking young blondes bring top dollar at Medellin bordellos."

The big man spat toward the floor. "I don't mess with that kinda of shit. I don't haul anything that can talk." He looked around the shop. "Where's that sexy redhead, Rita, the hottest thing this side of Key West? I heard she was working here."

The men in the group glanced at each other but didn't answer.

"I knew her back in Jersey," Bryson went on. "Man, she was one good lay. Wherever she is I bet she's keeping a lot of men happy."

Cliff Powers straightened up from where he had been bending over an engine, wiped his hands on an oily rag, and slowly walked over. "You'd lose that bet, Bryson. She's keeping only one man happy. Me. I married her."

Bryson stepped back and thrust out both hands defensively. "Hey, man, I was just kidding around. You got a great gal there."

A car pulled up outside and a young woman jumped out and came running into the

shop. "Cliff, Cliff, look what I..." She stopped
short at the sight of Bryson, and her lips curled in
a contemptuous sneer. "The cat's been out
scavenging again and look what it dragged in."

A crooked smile twisted the man's face. "I
see you still got that sharp tongue that almost got
me in a lotta trouble, Rita."

Her eyes blazed. "You raped me, you
bastard! If you hadn't had your buddies tell all
those lies about me at the trial your ass would be
rotting in prison now. But if you ever come near
me again you're going to feel something sharper
than my tongue."

Cliff Powers stepped between them. "Get
lost, Bryson. We don't want your business."

The man hesitated a moment then turned
and walked away.

Rita's anger slowly subsided. She opened
her hand. "Look what I found. A piece-of-eight."

Cliff took it from her and examined it.
"Where'd you find it?"

"I was searching with my metal detector
just off the beach at Key Biscayne. I found it in
shallow water."

At that moment Butch Bryson came back
in. He spotted the coin in Cliff's hand. "Hey, that
looks like Spanish silver. You guys on to some
sunken treasure?"

Cliff raised a fist. "I told you to get lost."

"I forgot my hat. I'm going. I'm going."
He grabbed his yachtsman cap from the work
bench and beat a hasty retreat.

"Do you think there might be a sunken

treasure ship out there?" Rita asked eagerly.

Cliff smiled. "Highly unlikely. But even if you located a sunken wreck, the treasure would be hard to get to. Silver and gold coins don't just lie there on the ocean floor waiting to be picked up. The remains of old shipwrecks are usually buried under tons of sand, and it's a costly operation uncovering them. It takes sand blowers, dredges and other heavy equipment to get to the cargo. And you need a permit from the State of Florida before you can even start." He glanced at his watch. "It's quitting time, Rita, let's go home."

They got into Rita's car and, Cliff driving, left the yard and headed down the road. Neither spoke until Rita broke the silence. "Bryson said some bad things about me, didn't he?"

"He did express some personal views."

"You didn't believe what he said, did you?" Cliff kept his eyes on the road. "Honey, when we first got together we agreed that the past was the past. I didn't tell you about my past and I didn't ask about yours."

"He did rape me."

"If you say he raped you I believe it, and knowing Bryson as I do erases any doubt."

She remained silent for a few moments before speaking again. "At a party one night he doped my drink and dragged me into a bedroom and forced himself on me. I was fully aware of what was happening but had no control over my muscles. I had him arrested, but at the trial he had a bunch of his friends lie that I had had consenual sex with all of them. His lawyer convinced the jury that I was a tramp trying to build a case for a civil suit. They acquitted him."

Cliff took a sharp breath. "If he touches you again I'll kill the bastard."

After a few moments of silence she looked over at her husband. "Could there be a sunken treasure ship off Key Biscayne?"

He smiled. "Not much chance. A large Spanish fleet was destroyed by a hurricane in 1715, but those ships went down more than a hundred miles up the coast."

"But couldn't there have been a single ship, at another time, " she persisted, "maybe even a pirate ship?"

"Anything is possible. Admiralty records of that period are not always accurate or complete." He paused. "Don't get your hopes up, honey, but if you would like to we can take the dive boat and look around out there."

She smiled and squeezed his arm. "I'd like to."

The next morning as they sped down Government Cut toward the sea, Mike shouted above the roar of the engines "Cliff, there's a Cigarette following us. I bet it's Bryson."

Cliff scowled. "Nothing we can do about it."

When they reached Key Biscayne, Cliff cut the engines to trolling speed. Rita scanned the shoreline. Suddenly she sang out "Stop. It was just off shore at about this point that I found the coin."

Cliff switched off the engines and Mike dropped an anchor. As they were putting on their scuba gear, Bryson's Cigarette anchored a few hundred feet from them. Bryson called across the water "Hey, Powers, I got a permit for this area. Keep moving."

"He's lying," Cliff muttered to Rita, "It takes months to get a permit and he didn't know until yesterday about that coin you found. Ignore him."

Rita and Cliff splashed overboard while Mike stayed on the boat. From the Cigarette Bryson also went into the water, leaving a crewman behind.

As previously agreed, Cliff and Rita separated and each surveyed a different section of the ocean floor. They had been looking for only a short time when Rita spotted something shiny resting in the sand. As she swam over and picked it up she saw, from the corner of her eye, Bryson swimming toward her. She gave him a warning shake of her head and reached for the knife at her belt. He swooped in and grabbed at the small metal fishing lure she had picked up, and as he did the point of her knife bit into his hand. Blood flowed.

Mouthing a curse, the big man turned and started for the surface, trailing blood.

Suddenly a huge gray shape flashed past Rita, following the trail of blood. "Shark!" she screamed, though no one could hear her.

Bryson saw the shark coming and yanked a

When I begin my journey
into the Beyond
erect no monument to my memory
nor in futility place
a profusion of flowers
upon the emptiness
that was I

But if the recall
of some small bit
of my wisdom or wit
brings forth a smile
let that suffice

For unless I have left
some lasting impression
upon your soul
then to you I never lived
and deserve not
to be remembered

EDWARD BRUCE BEW